2036 A.D.
The Return

William L. Sharon

2036 A.D.
The Return

William L. Sharon

ISBN 0-9655952-0-X

PUBLISHED BY:
BRENTWOOD CHRISTIAN PRESS
4000 BEALLWOOD AVENUE
COLUMBUS, GEORGIA 31904

Preface

In preparation of this volume there are sources of help almost innumerable. One does not attempt such a huge, and such an important a subject without having through the years sampled much in one's reading from the dramatic stories of the Old and New Testaments, the histories of the early church and the aposticy, the Roman Catholic Church, Inquisitions, Reformations, and the future history of the world as told to us in the Word of God. History is the teacher of perspective (along with philosophy) and without a perspective one inclines to formalism and myopic dogmatism of opinion.

It would not be amiss to suggest to the reader of this volume to note that there have always been Protestants. And the reader will not fail to note how all along in the path of history, institutionalism and the leaders settle in their foundations only to be provoked and even unsettled by some prophetic Protestant spirit.

The Day of Atonement, both the earthly and the heavenly, are essential to understanding the times we live in as we count down to the second coming of our Lord. This book tells the story of the shattering upheavals, in a unique way, that leads to the return of the Christ in the clouds of glory.

It begins with a brief word picture of the nations that have a direct connection with and control of God's people as given to us in Scripture, including those of today.

It continues with the ceremonies of the Sanctuary of the Old Testament people of God, physical Israel, explaining some of the weaknesses within the early Day of Atonement which prepared the way for the end it suffered. It tells of the two Days of Atonement – the type and the antitype – which are both deeply indebted to our personal God, their creator and protector, and also of the Antichrist who continually endeavors to halt its completion.

The countdown begins with the evening of the heavenly Day of Atonement, spring of 1031 A.D., the beginning of the year 5001 A.S. It leads us through the intense darkness of the midnight hour, the dawning of the light of the morning, and the high point of the day, the momentary act of making the heavenly Temple clean, free from the sins of the children of God.

Finally, a large part of the book is devoted to the United States of America, which is inspired by the unseen hand of Satan and yet contributes her own principles and developments to bring about the greatest rebellion the world has ever seen, one which produces total destruction of the world, the second coming of the Lord.

This book was compiled for my own understanding and personalized with proofs that I needed in order to be able to give a reason for my belief (1 Peter 3:15). The only way that I was able to put this together with my limited skills was with the help of my wife, Jo, for spelling and grammar, the wisdom and technology gained from connection with those of experience – Nathan Pruett, and last, but first, the guidance of the Holy Spirit.

Acknowledgments

Acknowledgment is given by the author for extensive quotes from other books and authors.

The Scriptures, by God.

Daniel and Revelation, by Smith.

The Great Controversy, by White.

God and His Sanctuary, by Maxwell.

Our Great High Priest, by Heppenstall.

God Speaks to Modern Man, by Lickey.

Planet in Rebellion, by Vandeman.

The Rise and Fall of Antichrist, by Vandeman.

The Reformation, by Cowie.

Firsthand America, by Bernhard, Burner, and Fox-Genovese.

The Sabbath Sentinal, by The Bible Sabbath Association.

And others not listed.

Thank you.

Contents

Opening

This old ball of clay is rocked with innumerable physical, agricultural, ecological, political, military and medical disasters. The criminal element runs rampant throughout the spectrum of civilization. The whole of mankind gathers for the final battle, "The Battle Of That Great Day Of God Almighty".

In the book of Amos God tells us that He will do nothing except He reveals it to His people, the Saints. The remarkable symbolism and prophecies of the Word of God reveal undeniable parallels between God's Plan and current events.

The intent of this writing is to make you aware of the wisdom, love, warmth, and long suffering of God and to strengthen your hope and faith in Him and His Word. The hope and faith that prepares a people for the world's ultimate, most miraculous event, the return of the Man of Destiny, Jesus, the Christ.

The people of God must ever witness for truth in traditional and cultural Christianity and in a world of darkening and narrowing horizons.

Jesus is coming again! I've heard this all my life and some have said He has already come, others that if Christians had worked harder and not drug their feet in the telling of the Good News of the Kingdom of God centered in Jesus, the Christ, He would have come a long time ago.

The Christ has not come the second time and there is nothing anyone can do to change the march of time in eternity. God's foreknowledge has set a time when His will is accomplished. Nothing that you and I can do will change or deviate it.

God's people can have power with Him as their will is yielded to Him. As power is received through the infilling of the Holy Spirit, understanding and power is given in the Word.

In the Scriptures God has given much about the past, and He reveals the present and the future including the time of His return.

In the sinful state of His professed people and the world, there is great confusion and misconception of God, Creation, and the scenario of sin and salvation. This scenario is played upon a stage called Planet Earth with a playing time of 7,000 years and characters that play their parts for 70 years, each in their generation. God is judged by humanity's standards and concepts, forgetting just how far down the scale we have slipped from His image and likeness.

At the end of the scenario the curtain will descend upon mankind, the obedient go with the producer, the disobedient are fired. God will come to the disobedient as a thief in the night, but to the obedient He has revealed the time of His arrival.

The reliability of the Word of God in Scripture is confirmed in history and His foreknowledge of future events is sure (Isaiah 46:9, 10). God is the only historian who writes history in advance. It is written as if the events of the future are the history of the past. His power, His divinity is proven in this act.

Introduction

What does the future hold? Where is history going? Will the human race become better during the next several years, or a thousand years, or will mankind destroy itself and bring forever to the end its hopes and dreams – and, yes, its sins and perversities too?

Extraordinary predictions made by the prophets of God, who lived some 1,000 years before and during the time of the Christ, have amazed countless millions since they were written. Daniel is one of these prophets that lived during this time, John the revelator is another.

Just what did Daniel and John write that makes their prophecies so important to us today?

One of Daniel's most astounding prophecies, is his prediction of the exact time of the Messiah's coming and death. Before Daniel's time the children of Israel had long waited for the coming of the Messiah, the divinely appointed leader their prophets had promised would deliver them. Then over 500 years before the Christ, Daniel made a prediction that pointed to the year 31 A.D., the 14th day of Nisan, year 4001 A.S. (after sin), as the time the Messiah would die. In that very year Jesus of Nazareth, the Messiah, was put to death. No other prophecy in the Bible quite matches its daring.

Daniel's prophecies point out important facts concerning God and history and the impossibility of man's being able to control the future. He predicted that though strong kingdoms would arise after his time – even a powerful church-state alliance – none would bring about a lasting peace. All of man's attempts to bring about peace through legislation or conquest must ultimately fail.

Where then is history going? Is there no hope for a lasting peace for this world? Both John and Daniel answer these questions. They clearly declare that after all of man's attempts to bring about peace have failed, God will set up an everlasting kingdom of peace and righteousness. The claims of Daniel and John about what the future holds, strange and astounding as they may seem, are worth the consideration of all who desire peace, all who want to understand the meaning of history. That means all owe it to themselves, and to God, to carefully consider what is written, to weigh and evaluate what is predicted, to compare the prophecies with history, for if what is said is true, the world's probation must soon end. The spring of 2031 A.D. is the end of mankinds 6,000 years of probation and time is running out.

Turn the pages and follow us to the end of the World as we know it and the return of Jesus the Christ as King of kings and Lord of lords.

1

The End of the World

Today we hear many voices telling us this is what is going to happen. Or no, this is what will happen. Then other say, No, it will be this way or that way. But never have we heard so many speaking of "The Rapture," the tribulation, the conversion of the Jews, the revelation of the antichrist, Armageddon, and the glorious return of the Christ. Now, is this the order of events predicted in Holy Scriptures? Let's look at those events again in that order.

1. The Rapture.
2. The conversion of the Jews during the seven year period.
3. The tribulation when the beast, the mark of the beast and the image of the beast will be set up.
4. The revelation of the Antichrist.
5. The preparation for the Battle of Armageddon.
6. Then the glorious return of the Christ.

Is this the order of events that we find predicted in the Holy Scriptures? What are the final events as we look forward and prepared for the end of the world?

One of the reasons for so much confusion in the religious world today is because of the difference in schools of Bible interpretation, the difference in interpretation of Bible prophecy.

We must note three things at this point:

1. The prophecies of the Bible are written with the time schedule of the calender of God's year, the year established in the beginning and that we will use in the new earth. This calender is explained in the following chapters.

2. Bible prophecy is not to be privately interpreted for it interprets itself through the power of the Holy Spirit. "First of all you must understand this, that no prophecy of Scripture is a mat-

ter of one's own interpretation, for no prophecy ever came by the impulse of man; instead, holy men spoke from God as they were inspired by the Holy Spirit." (2 Peter 1:20)

3. Prophecy in the Old Testament is local and physical and in the New Testament universal and spiritual.

A dramatic end to the system of life as we now know it on Planet Earth is predicted in your Bible. Jesus said: "And then shall the end come." Matthew 24:14. Later, He stated: "You go therefore, and teach all nations, baptizing them in the name of the Father, the Son, and into the Holy Ghost: Teaching them to observe all things whatsoever I have commanded you: And, lo, I am with you always, even unto the end of the world." Matthew 28:19, 20. Jesus said the end will come!!!

But in all our study and thinking together on this vital topic, let us never forget the comforting assurance of our blessed Master. No matter how hectic, how unsettled, how tense life may be, or may become in these last days, Jesus said: "Lo, I Am with you. I will be with you right up to the very end of the world."

Your world is going to end! Your world that today is shaken and convulsed by the most fantastic revolutions of all time is going to end. Your world that is experiencing today a complete moral revolution – a shift from an absolute ethic to a situation ethic, from a morality based on God's eternal law to one based on man's personal "likes" – is going to end!

Yes, your world with all of its pleasure-seeking; your world of politics and revolution; your hum-drum, dog-eat-dog, work-a-day world is going to end!

I am no psychic, crystal ball gazer, nor prophet – just a plain, ordinary man who reads his Bible and has a deep concern for people who are not reading It; for people who have tried to read it but couldn't understand It; for people who have been misguided by false teachers, and their private interpretations, and are unprepared for the end of the world.

Turn the pages for a synoptic view of the calender God has for mankind.

Turn the pages for a synoptic view of World History Foretold as we march through time, to an end of all things as we know them, as foretold in Scripture.

Turn the pages for a synoptic view of the kingdoms, the nations that have a direct connection with God's people through time to the end of all things as foretold in Scripture.

Turn the pages for a synoptic view of the Passion Play in the wilderness and in the temple that sets the time when the Christ says, "It Is Finished" as foretold in Scripture.

Turn the pages for a synoptic view of the Antichrist as foretold in Scripture.

Turn the pages for a synoptic view of the Image to the Beast as foretold in Scripture.

Turn the pages for a synoptic view of the Mark of the Beast as foretold in Scripture.

Turn the pages for a synoptic view of the great time of trouble as foretold in Scripture.

Turn the pages for a synoptic view of "The Battle Of That Great Day Of God Almighty" as foretold in Scripture.

Turn the pages for a synoptic view of the place Armageddon as foretold in Scripture.

Yes, turn the pages, for the Lord returns as King of kings, and Lord of lords on 1 Nisan 6006 A.S., spring of 2036 A.D., as foretold in Scripture.

Dear friend, are you ready?

2

7,000 Years from Sin to Salvation

Adam *Sinned 1 A.S.	Seth *born 101 A.S.	Enoch *born 201 A.S.
3969 B.C.	3869 B.C.	3769 B.C.
Kenan *born 301 A.S.	Mahalalel *born 401 A.S.	Jared *born 501 A.S.
3669 B.C.	3569 B.C.	3469 B.C.
Enoc *born 601 A.S.	Methuselah *born 701 A.S.	Lemech born* 801 A.S.
3369 B.C.	3269 B.C.	3169 B.C.
Adam *died Enoc taken* 901 A.S.	Seth died* Noah *born 1001 A.S.	1101 A.S.
3069 B.C.	2969 B.C.	2869 B.C.
1201 A.S.	1301 A.S.	1401 A.S.
2769 B.C.	2669 B.C.	2569 B.C.
Flood Judgement Shem *born 1501 A.S.	Methuselah died* The Flood 1601 A.S.	Tower of Babel* 1701 A.S.
2469 B.C.	2369 B.C.	2269 B.C.

	Abraham *born	Noah *died	Isaac born*
1801 A.S.	1901 A.S.	2001 A.S.	
2169 B.C.	2069 B.C.	1969 B.C.	

Abraham *died	Jacob & Esau *born	Israel in *Egypt
2101 A.S.	2201 A.S.	2301 A.S.
1869 B.C.	1769 B.C.	1669 B.C.

Joseph *died		Moses *born
2401 A.S.	2501 A.S.	2601 A.S.
1569 B.C.	1469 B.C.	1369 B.C.

The Exodus	Conquest of *Canaan	Saul Saul David *born *king *king
2701 A.S.	2801 A.S.	2901 A.S.
1269 B.C.	1169 B.C.	1069 B.C.

Solomon *king	Divided *Kingdom	Israel *Exile
3001 A.S.	3101 A.S.	3201 A.S.
969 B.C.	869 B.C.	769 B.C.

	Babylon *captivity	Persian *Medes	Zion *restored
3301 A.S.	3401 A.S.	3501 A.S.	
669 B.C.	569 B.C.	469 B.C.	

	Greek *rule		Maccabean *rule
3601 A.S.	3701 A.S.	3801 A.S.	
369 B.C.	269 B.C.	169 B.C.	

Roman Jesus *rule born* 3901 A.S.	The *Christ 4001 A.S.	Jerusalem *Destroyed 4101 A.S.
69 B.C.	31 A.D.	131 A.D.
  4201 A.S.	 4301 A.S.	Rome *falls 4401 A.S.
231 A.D.	331 A.D.	431 A.D.
Catholic *Church 4501 A.S.	The Dark Ages 4601 A.S.	The Dark Ages 4701 A.S.
531 A.D.	631 A.D.	731 A.D.
The Dark Ages 4801 A.S.	The Dark Ages 4901 A.S.	The Dark Ages 5001 A.S.
831 A.D.	931 A.D.	1031 A.D.
The Dark Ages 5101 A.S.	Inquisitions *begin 5201 A.S.	The Darkest Age 5301 A.S.
1131 A.D.	1231 A.D.	1331 A.D.
Americas discovered* 541 A.S.	Reformation *begins 5501 A.S.	Colonizing *Americas 5601 A.S.
1431 A.D.	1531 A.D.	1631 A.D.
U.S.A born* 5701 A.S.	Catholic Church *falls 5801 A.S.	You are here* 5901 A.S.
1731 A.D.	1831 A.D.	1931 A.D.

*Probation closes
*The Christ returns   There is no one, no one,

6001 A.S.	6101 A.S.	6201 A.S.
2031 A.D.	2131 A.D.	2231 A.D.

no one alive on Planet Earth but that old dragon,

6301 A.S.	6401 A.S.	6501 A.S.
2331 A.D.	2431 A.D.	2531 A.D.

Satan, the Devil.

6601 A.S.	6701 A.S.	6801 A.S.
2631 A.D.	2731 A.D.	2831 A.D.

| | Holy City and | Satan & sin |
| | saints descend | * Destroyed |
6901 A.S.	7001 A.S.	
2931 A.D.	3031 B.C.	**Eternity** on an earth made new

3

God's Year

God's year, the year of the Hebrews, is needed to understand properly the prophecies of God as given to us in His Word, the Bible. The year of the Hebrews, or physical Israel, consisted of twelve months, "Solomon also had twelve overseers in charge of all Israel, who supplied food for the king and his household, each one supplying food for one month in the year." (1 Kings 4:7). These are lunar months and the lunar year would accordingly contain 354 days, 8 hours, 48 minutes, 32.4 seconds.

The annual festivals were inseparably connected with the agricultural seasons. A strictly lunar year would cause these festivals, as fixed by the calender, to constantly recede from their appropriate season. It was necessary to bring the lunar year into correspondence with the solar year of 365 days. This was accomplished by the intercalation of blank days at the end of the year, although the custom is not mentioned in the Bible. The year began with the month Abib or Nisan,

> "To you let this month be the first, the month with which your year begins: Keep the feast of unleavened bread; for seven days you shall eat unleavened bread at the appointed time, the month Abib, because in it you came out of Egypt: In the first month, the month Nisan, in the twelfth year of King Ahasuerus, they cast the lot (pur), before Haman, and so each day from month to month until the twelfth month, named Adar." (Exodus 12:2; 23:5; Esther 3:7),

with the new moon next before or next after the vernal equinox; and there was from the earliest times an agricultural year which ended in the autumn.

> "Also keep the harvest feast, the first fruits or your toil, of what you sowed in the field. Then, keep the feast of ingath-

ering at the end of the year, when you are through gathering the fruits of your field work." (Exodus 23:16, 34:22; Leviticus 25:4, 9).

It was convenient for a people devoted to horticulture and agriculture to begin the year with the season of plowing and sowing, and to close it with harvest. In practice they frequently preferred to indicate the time of year by the particular harvest or agricultural occupation than by the number or name of the month,

> *"See what the land is like, whether it is fertile or barren, and whether it is covered with trees or not. Moreover, do your best to bring back some fruit from the land, for this was at the season when the grapes first ripened:" "Naomi and Ruth, the Moabitess, her daughter-in-law, who had come with her from the land of Moab, arrived in Bethlehem at the beginning of barley harvest." (Numbers 13:20; Ruth 1:22).*

Months and Seasons

Month 1: Abib or Nisan
Exodus 23:15; Nehemiah 2:1
Approx. 15 March – 15 April
Spring Equinox

1. New Moon.

Festival: 14. An annual sabbath; Passover in the evening, beginning at sundown the 13th till sundown the 14th day, the preparation day for the feast of unleavened bread (Exodus 7:18, 19; 8:3-10, introducing

15-21. 15 and 21, annual sabbaths; Feast of Unleavened Bread in the evening, beginning at sundown the 14th till sundown the 21st day (Leviticus 23:6).

16. Sheaf of first fruits (Barley) of the harvest presented (Leviticus 23:10-14; cp. Joshua 5:11).

Season: Latter or spring rain. Flax harvest at Jericho (Joshua 2:6). Jordan at Flood (Joshua 3:15; 1 Chronicles 12:15; Ecclesiastes 24:26).
Barley harvest in the maritime plain. Wheat ripe in the hot Jordan valley.

21

Pods on the carob tree.

Dry season begins, continuing to Ethanim or early October, with prevailing wind from the northwest.

ɾ ɾ ɾ

Month 2: Kiv or Iyar
1 Kings 6:1, 37
Approx. 15 April – 15 May

1.   New Moon.

Festival: 14.   Passover for those who could not keep regular one (Numbers 9:10, 11).

Season: Barley harvest in uplands.
Wheat harvest in lowlands.

ɾ ɾ ɾ

Month 3: Sivan
Esther 8:9
Approx. 15 May – 15 June

1.   New Moon.

Festival: 6.   An annual sabbath; Pentecost, or Feast of Weeks or of Harvest, or Day of First Fruits.
Loaves as first fruits of gathered harvest presented (Exodus 23:16; 32:22; Leviticus 23:15-21; Numbers 28:26; Deuteronomy 16:9, 10).

Season: Apples on sea coast.
Early figs general
Oleander in bloom.
Almonds ripe.
Intense heat.

ɾ ɾ ɾ

Month 4: Thamus
Approx. 15 June – 15 July

1.   New Moon.

Festival: None.

Season: Wheat harvest in high mountains.
First grapes ripe.

❧ ❧ ❧

Month 5: Ab
Approx. 15 July – 15 August

1.   New Moon.

Festival: None.

Season: Olives in lowlands.

❧ ❧ ❧

Month 6: Elul
Nehemiah 6:15

Approx. 15 August – 15 September

1.   New Moon.

Festival: None.

Season: Dates and summer figs.

           Vintage general.

❧ ❧ ❧

Month 7: Ethanim or Tishri
1 Kings 8:2

Approx. 15 September – 15 October

Festival: 1.   New Moon. An annual sabbath; Memorial of Trumpet blowing (Numbers 29:1).

10.   Day of Atonement (Leviticus 16:29).

15-21. 15. annual sabbath.

Feast of ingathering or Tabernacles.

First fruits of wine and oil (Exodus 23:16; Leviticus 16:13).

22.   An annual sabbath; Solemn Assembly (Leviticus 23:36; Numbers 29:35; Nehemiah 8:18; cp. John 7:37).

Season: Pomegranates ripe.

Season changing to the winter or rainy season, with prevailing wind from west and southwest.

Former or early rains.

Pistachio nuts ripe.

Plowing.

23

‫‪≈ ≈ ≈‬

Month 8: Bul or Marcheslev
1 Kings 6:38
Approx. 15 October – 15 November

1.   New Moon.

Festival: None
Season: Barley and wheat sown.
Olives gathered in northern Galilee.

≈ ≈ ≈

Month 9: Chislev
Zechariah 7:1
Approx. 15 November – 15 December

1.   New Moon.

Festival: None
Season: Winter figs on trees.
Rainfall increases (cp. Ezra 10:9, 13).

≈ ≈ ≈

Month 10: Tebeth
Esther 2:16
Approx. 15 December – 15 January

1.   New Moon.

Festival: None
Season: Hail; snow on higher hills and occasionally in
Jerusalem. In lowlands grain fields and pastures green,
wild flowers abundant.

≈ ≈ ≈

Month 11: Shebat
Zechariah 1:7
Approx. 15 January – 15 February

1.   New Moon.

Festival: None
Season: Almond trees in bloom.
Appearance of young fruit, or rather blossom, of the fig.

24

Carob tree in bloom.

Oranges and lemons ripe in the lowlands.

Storax blossoming and pomegranates showing their first flowers.

Barley harvest at Jericho.

≈ ≈ ≈

Month 12: Adar
Approx. 15 February – 15 March

1.   New Moon.

Festival: None

Season:

Events: Date set by Haman for massacre of the Jews. Esther 3:7, 13.

Date adopted for Purim. Esther 9:19, 21.

Date of completion of temple. Ezra 6:15.

≈ ≈ ≈

Now that you have discovered the calender of God, turn the pages to discover His Passion Play in the wilderness. But first a look at world history.

4

World History Foretold

"Inflation." "Welfare Rolls Burgeon." "What Does Russia Want?" "Trick Weapons on Increase." "Energy Crisis." Do you recognize the headlines? Who does not? We are lead to inquire, "What will happen next?" That is the great question in which all people are interested, both in their own personal lives and in the events of the world. Today that question seems more important than ever as the world passes through one tense period after another. As each crisis seems to be worked out there are others to take its place. This world tension has become a shadow that enshrouds the individual life of every living creature.

As we leaf through the pages of history, we find manifold times when certain men, nations, and groups of nations have tried to bring all other peoples under their thumb of justice.

Today, the world is divided into great camps. Though overtures for peace continue to be pursued, Bible students know that we can expect the tension to continue to increase between these powers until the "Battle of that great day of God Almighty." Revelation 16:14.

In spite of all attempts to bring this world under one ruler, none have succeeded. Efforts to bring world peace by any means has fallen far short of the goals. Students of Bible prophecy know and have been predicting for years that all these efforts at world rule and world peace will fail. How could they know? Is there a source of knowledge where this information is given?

The source of knowledge is God's Word, the Holy Bible. It is the purpose of this treatise to point out certain of these prophecies that pertain to past, present, and future world events and conditions. We will note that the nations, kindreds, and peoples mentioned compose those nations and powers having direct involvement with the people of God.

World History: The first chapter of the book of Daniel describes the capture of Jerusalem by Nebu-chad-nezzar, King of Babylon. Certain of the Jewish royal family were taken by the Babylonian king to train for positions of special service. Among these was Daniel, who became one of the special advisors to the king.

Before considering the dream of Chapter two, let us notice the time when it was given and what previously had taken place in recorded history. The earliest definite records of history are from the land of Egypt. About a thousand years before the time of Daniel, the Israelites had gone down to Egypt and there became a great nation, then slaves to the Egyptians.

Assyria (Syria) was the next powerful empire to arise as the splendor of Egypt declined. In c. 3250A.S., 721 B.C. Israel was taken captive by Assyria, while Judah payed tribute. In c. 3350 A.S. 607 B.C. Babylon conquered the Assyrians empire. Judah was subdued and the people began to be transported to Babylon.

Daniel was in Babylon as one of the Jewish captives, and it was under these circumstances that God revealed the dream of Nebu-chad-nezzar to him.

The Great Image: The second chapter of the book of Daniel immediately captures our attention by telling us of an unusual dream which the king had and which he believed had special meaning but he had forgotten it. His "wise men" were unable to tell him the dream or the interpretation, with the result that a decree was made to kill them all.

But the God of dreams was at work. In a night vision Nebu-chad-nezzar's dream was revealed to Daniel, who the following day appeared before the king and gave all glory to God for the revelation. It is yet true that fortune tellers and astrologers have no supernatural powers, "But there is a God in heaven that reveals secrets." Now let us consider the dream as told by Daniel to the king:

You, O king looked and behold, there stood before you a mighty image, huge and of unsurpassing brilliance, and it was terrible to look upon: The head of the image was of fine gold; its breast and arms of silver; its belly and thigh of bronze; its legs of iron and its feet partly of iron and partly of clay. You kept looking at it until you saw a Stone, cut without hands, from a mountain, strike the image on its feet of iron and clay, breaking them to pieces – the iron, the clay, the bronze, the silver, and the gold, so pulverized that they became like chaff of the summer threshing floor, which the wind carries away, and not a trace of them could be found. But the Stone that struck the image became a great mountain and filled the whole earth." (Daniel 2:31-35).

It must be understood that the statue which the king saw was only a covering for the red dragon, Satan, in his efforts to undo the plan of salvation that God set into motion when mankind failed in their effort to conform to His will. The beast powers of this chapter, the little horn power, the first beast with its many heads and second beast of Revelation 13 that follow this chapter have the same characteristic, a dragon in the skins of animals which stand for prophetic nations and powers.

Daniel told the king that the dream was symbolic and that its purpose was to reveal events to come.

"You, O king, as you lay in bed, were thinking of the future, speculating as to what should come to pass hereafter, and He who reveals secrets disclosed to you what is going to happen." (Daniel 2:28).

The dream did not reveal the entire history of the world, but rather the history of events from the time of Nebu-chad-nezzar and on to the end. And so, beginning with Babylon, the dream was to reveal certain important facts about world history to the end of the world as we know it.

Of great importance to note is this: The dream was not revealed for the benefit of Nebu-chad-nezzar, but rather for the benefit of the people of God. The dream revealed important world events as they were to relate to God's people – first to physical Israel, and later in a wider scope to the many who have become followers of the Christ in all nations, kindreds, tongues, and peoples, Spiritual Israel. All the world powers which are included in the dreams had a direct relationship with God's chosen people throughout the centuries, even to the end of all things.

In verses 37 and 38, Daniel speaks of the glory and the power, and he said, "You are the head of gold!" In c. 3350 A.S., 606 B.C. the Babylonian empire came into supremacy. It was not the only empire existing in its time. But the fame and glory of Babylon far exceeded the other nations then existing. However, the most important factor to consider is that only Babylon had direct dealings with God's people, physical Israel, during that time.

Verse 39 very briefly brings us the interpretation of the body of the great image. Babylon, strong and proud though it was at the moment, would not last forever. Said Daniel, "After you another kingdom shall arise, less forceful than you." The year c. 3450 A.S., 538 B.C. found the Medes and Persians victorious over Babylon.

The Medes, at first the stronger part of the new empire, soon became the weaker. That empire has become known simply as the Persian Empire. Again we must point out the fact that it was not the only empire then existing in its time. But in its time it was the greatest empire in the world. Further, it was the empire that had primary association with physical Israel at the time.

Concerning the next part of the image, verse 39 interprets, "… Then a third kingdom of bronze, which shall also have sway over all the earth." At the fateful battle of Arbela in c. 3650 A.S., 331 B.C. Alexander the Great and the Grecians defeated the Persians. With this victory Greece was the first world empire. Then Alexander extended his conquests into much of the civilized world.

"The Fourth kingdom shall be strong as iron," explained Daniel. Verse 40. At the battle of Pydna, c. 3800 A.S., 168 B.D., the great iron monarchy of Rome takes over as world leader.

The legs of the image were of iron and Daniel tells us that they represent the nation which followed Greece. This nation would "Crush all peoples." Made of iron, it was a very powerful empire. The Greek empire was followed by the most extensive empire this world has ever known (both in people and in duration). That empire was the Pagan Roman Empire.

As the feet and toes were "Partly of potter's clay and partly of iron," verse 41, so the fourth kingdom was divided into several divisions.

The "feet condition" of the image represents the civil history of the ten nations, not the whole world, until the second coming of the Christ. No single power conquered pagan Rome, but its various provinces were taken over by different barbarian tribes. Eventually these areas became nations or parts of other nations. Much of the time they are at war with each other. Even in the nations of modern Europe seven of these divisions are easily traceable.

In verse 43 the development of the various nations by the mingling of the peoples is described. The people would mix, and spread abroad, nations would rise and fall with yet other nations arising. But only the nations of the great image have been and continue to be like the iron and clay – partly strong and partly weak and never able to hold together. These nations of Europe will still be in this deplorable state when the Christ comes in the clouds of glory.

The Beast Nations: Daniel was but a youth when God revealed to him the future as symbolized by the great image of Nebu-chad-nezzar's dream in Daniel 2. Fifty years (603 B.C. to 553 B.C.) elapsed between Chapters 2 and 7.

In Daniel 7 is a similarly symbolic prophecy. It was given to Daniel in a night vision or dream. This prophecy serves to offer more detail to the vision of Daniel 2. It should be noted that the heart of the beasts is the red dragon, Satan. Daniel said,

"I saw in my vision by night and behold, the four winds of heaven were stirring up the great sea. Out of the sea rose four large animals, different one from another. The first was like a lion and had two wings like an eagle. As I looked, its wings were plucked off and it was lifted from the ground and made to stand on two feet like a man, and the mind of a man was given to it. And behold, a second animal came up, like a bear, having its paw raised, ready to strike, and with three ribs in its mouth between its teeth, and it was told 'Arise, devour much

flesh.' After this I looked, and see: There was another like a leopard, with four wings like those of a bird on its back; it had four heads, and dominion was given to it. After this I saw in the vision of the night, and note, there was a fourth animal dreadful, terrible, and exceedingly powerful, with huge iron teeth; it devoured and tore its victims in pieces, and stamped the remaining portions of it with its feet. It was different from all the animals that were before it. It had ten horns. These horns I studied, and while I was contemplating them attentively, behold, up rose another horn, a little one and a marvel, by which three of the ten were uprooted. This little horn had eyes of a man and a mouth ever boasting of great deeds and uttering proud words. These huge animals, he said, being four in all, are the four kingdoms which shall arise out of the earth. "He said this: 'The fourth animal shall be a fourth kingdom on earth, which shall be different from all other kingdoms; it shall devour the whole earth, and trample it down, breaking it as grain is broken on the threshing floor. For out of its ten horns shall arise ten kings and after them shall arise another, who shall be different from the former kings, and shall put down three of them. He shall speak words against the Most High; he shall plan to change the sacred seasons and the Law, and they shall be given over to him for a year, two years, and half a year." (Daniel 7:2-8, 17, 23-25).

The description of the four huge animals is brief as they march through time, and clearly are those kingdoms of Chapter 2, but in connection with the fourth we are given information of vital interest to us today as the future unfolds.

In many ways the prophecy of Daniel 2, along with Daniel 7, are the key to understanding all Bible prophecy in both the Old and New Testaments. They are given in symbols and then those symbols are clearly interpreted for us. We need not guess at their meaning. Pages of history fully bear out the fulfillment of the prophecies.

With the outline of world history established, as it effects God's people, we are ready to study deeper into Bible prophecy. Daniel mentions his special desire to "know the truth of the fourth beast."

If you wish to know the truth, keep turning the pages.

5

The Little Horn, The Roman Catholic Church, Fifth and Eighth Heads

31 A.D.	538 A.D.	1281 A.D.	1798 A.D.
4999 A.S.	5569 A.S.	6312 A.S.	6829 A.S.
	*You are here		

While Daniel was observing the fourth beast with its ten horns, (Daniel 7), another horn grew up among them. It is this "little" horn, with the heart of the dragon, Satan, which we now wish to understand.

From the ten barbarian tribes that overran Pagan Rome, came the nations of Europe which shall continue in a divided condition and go into the fire of eternal death. They shall be in this deplorable state when the Christ comes in the clouds of glory. This fact is stated in order that we may correctly identify the added feature here mentioned – the little horn.

Before attempting to explain, let us read the Biblical explanation:

> "Concerning the ten horns which were in its head, and the other horn which came up, and before which three of them fell, – the horn which had eyes and a mouth speaking great things; the horn that seemed stronger than its fellows. This horn I saw making war against the saints, and it was prevailing against them until the Ancient of Days came, (the cleaning of the heavenly Temple), and the court took its seat, and dominion was given to the saints of the Most High, and the time came for the saints to possess the kingdom.

> "He said this: 'The fourth animal shall be a fourth kingdom on earth, which shall be different from all other kingdoms; it shall devour the whole earth, and trample it down, breaking it as grain is broken on the threshing floor. His ten horns are ten

kings that shall rise out of his empire and after them shall rise another, who shall be different, more brutal, from the former kings, and shall destroy three of them. He shall defy and speak words against the Most High God, wear down the saints with persecution, and think to change the times and the Law. God's people shall be helpless in his hands for three and a half years. Then the judgement (the cleansing of the heavenly Temple) shall sit and his dominion shall be taken away, to be consumed and destroyed for all times. For the kingdom, the dominion, and the greatness of the kingdoms under the whole heaven shall be given to the people of the saints of the Most High God; their kingdom shall be an everlasting kingdom, and all dominions shall serve and obey them." (Daniel 7:29-27).

Thus far it is clearly explained that the ten horns are ten kingdoms to arise at the fall of the great beast kingdom, the Pagan Roman Empire. The ten horns are not great kingdoms, powers, or nations, but rulers who were strong for a time. They are the barbarian tribes which overran pagan Rome. From the barbarian tribes came the nations of Europe which continue in a divided condition. This fact has been developed in order that we may correctly identify the added feature here mentioned – the little horn. He also is a king – but different from the others. As he arises, three of the ten are at once overthrown. This took place while the ten barbarian kingdoms were such, or after the fall and while the Pagan Roman Empire was still falling.

Every student of history knows that there is just one new and unlike power which arose as the Pagan Roman Empire fell and that power was the Papacy, the Roman Catholic Church. It had been developing during the later years of the Empire. Christendom, so called, had been ruled by five bishops – the Bishop of Alexander, the Bishop of Antioch, the Bishop of Constantinople, the Bishop of Jerusalem, and the Bishop of Rome. As the Empire fell before the attacks of the barbarians and when the last emperor was driven from Rome in 476 A.D., the Bishop of Rome was the only authority left in that city. The world looked to Rome as the leading city and so the power of its bishop grew very rapidly. The christianity of papal Rome was nominally accepted by the barbarians in general, and the Bishop of Rome (the Pope) became the chief power in Europe. The barbarian invaders overran Italy, but with the rise of papal power three of these were driven out, destroyed.

Any interpretation of prophetic symbols must fit not only one part but all parts of the prophecy. And so we notice the additional description of the little horn power.

Four very definite prophecies are given:

First, this power was to speak great words against the Most High. From the Roman Catholic Church point of view the Papacy has not spoken against God, but from a truly scriptural point of view the pope's claims are blasphemy. He speaks great swelling words and claims powers which the Bible ascribes to God alone. Claiming to be the supreme leader of the people of God and yet teaching traditions which are contrary to the Bible is surely against God.

Secondly, this power was to "wear out the saints of the Most High." If Roman Catholics of the Middle Ages were the "saints" then this description would not fit the pope. But if the thousands of devoted men and women who refused to recognize the authority of the pope and who were persecuted even to death because of their refusal were the saints, we find the description most fitting. Yes, for centuries when the Papacy was in absolute power in Europe, the true saints of God were literally "worn out" until they could exist only by hiding and worshiping in secret.

The next point is more specific: "… think to change times and laws …" Evidently this must refer to times and laws established by the Creator, the God of heaven. No power has tried to change the laws and times established by God as the pope has. The ecclesiastical laws of the Catholic church are put above the laws of God as given in the Bible. The day, according to the Bible teaching, is from "evening until evening."

> *"It shall be for you a perfect Sabbath. You will humble your souls on the ninth of the month at eventide; from one evening to the next you will celebrate your Sabbath." Leviticus 23:32.*

But the Papacy recognizes the day as being from midnight to midnight. The year originally began in the spring, (new moon next to the spring equinox), but the "Gregorian" calendar designed by Pope Gregory set the beginning in midwinter.

Fourth, the Ten Commandment Law of God declares that the seventh day of the week is the Sabbath; the papacy teaches that the first day of the week should be observed in lieu of the Sabbath. This is the most outstanding example of an attempt to change a God-given Law. Although the Roman emperor Constantine legalized the "venerable day of the sun as a day of rest, it was the Roman Catholic power and its supreme control of Europe during the dark and middle ages, which perpetrated the observance of Sunday as a day of worship. The Roman church has a large number of so called "canon laws" which it substitutes for the few clear and simple precepts found in the Word of God. The Bible is written for all the world and the Roman church, the Papacy is the only universally known power which has attempted to establish the observance of its own times and laws among the people of the world.

An excellent proof of prophecy is its accurate prediction of the time to be occupied by those things described. The last part of Daniel 7:25 tells us: "And they shall be given over to him, for a year, two years, and a half a year." The pronoun "they" might refer to the saints or to the time and laws, or to both. Since so many things have pointed to the papacy as the power fulfilling this prophecy, a study of its history perhaps would make this time-prophecy clearer. In Revelation there is a prophecy, nearly identical with the description of the little horn, and it unquestionably points to the same time when the apostate papal church, the Roman Catholic Church of the Middle and Dark Ages, began to dominate the state. Paul, looking forward to the time when this "falling away" from truth would arise, referred to this power as "man of sin", the "mystery of iniquity".

"Let no man in anyway deceive you; for the apostasy is to come first, and the man of sin is to be revealed, the one doomed to Hell, the adversary who opposes and rises up against all that is God and what is worshiped as God, so that he seats himself in the temple of God with the claim that he himself is God." (2 Thessalonians 2:3, 4).

But first let us introduce John's Revelation 13 which explains in great detail two organizations, or systems of government, that Satan is especially using in his final attempt to destroy God's end time people:

As Daniel and John stood on the beach, so many years apart in time, they both saw a startling sight. We have already discussed what Daniel saw and now we will look at what John saw.

"And I saw a beast (the heart of the beast is the dragon, Satan) coming up out of the sea with ten horns and seven heads, with ten diadems on his horns, and a blasphemous name upon his heads. The beast I saw resembled a leopard, and his feet were like those of a bear, and his mouth like that of a lion. The dragon invested him with his (the dragon's) power and his (the dragon's) throne and great authority. One of his heads (the fifth) seemed fatally wounded. His mortal wound was healed, however, and the whole earth followed the beat in wonder. They worshiped the dragon, because he had bestowed authority on the beast; they also worshiped the beast, saying, "Who matches the beast, and who is able to war against him?" He was also given a mouth to speak proud words, to utter blasphemies, and he was granted the power to exercise authority for forty-two months. So he opened his mouth to utter blasphemies against God, to blaspheme His name, His abode, and those who dwell in heaven. And he was allowed to make war against the saints and to conquer them, and authority was given him over every tribe, people, language, and nation. All those who lie on the earth, whose names are not recorded in the Book of Life of the Lamb that was slain from the foundation of the world, will worship him. Whoever has an ear, let him hear. Whoever leads into captivity will be led into captivity; whoever kills with the sword must be killed by the sword. In this way the saints exercise their endurance and their faith." (Revelation 13:1-10).

These symbols are based on Daniel 7, as we have seen in reading Chapter 2, which depicted history in terms of four great powers that were to dominate history during their time.

It must be noted that at the time of the writing of the Book of Revelation that John was living in the time of the Pagan Roman Empire, the fourth head. The fifth head is the Papal Roman

Empire, the Roman Catholic Church directed by the dragon heart of the beast. The last two heads whose power is derived from the dragon heart of the beast are explained in following chapters.

> "... while the woman fled into the wilderness, where God had a retreat prepared for her to be cared for there during twelve hundred sixty days." "... but to the woman were granted two wings of a giant eagle, so that she might fly to her retreat in the wilderness where, away from the presence of the serpent, she will be cared for during a time, times, and half a time." (Revelation 12:6, 14).

In prophetic time a day stands for a year.

> "The forty years during which you must pay the penalty for your sins shall be determined by the number of days which you spent spying out the land; that is, forty days – a year for each day; ..." "When you have completed these, you shall lie down a second time, on your right side, and take on you the punishment of the house of Judah. I assign to you forty days, one day for each year." (Numbers 14:34; Ezekiel 4:6).

This method is Biblical and proves itself in practice.

The legally recognized supremacy of the pope began in 538 A.D., was to continue for 1260 years, or to 1798 A.D.

After the fall of the pagan Roman Empire in the west in 476 A.D., the papacy had a rather difficult time maintaining itself in the face of barbarian invasions. Those which caused the most trouble were the Heruli, the Vandals, and the Ostrogoths. During the reign of the Eastern Roman Emperor Justinian, these three were overcome and destroyed. The Bishop of Rome had appealed to Justinian, and thus it was through the Bishop of Rome that these three "horns" were plucked up, the last in the spring of 538 A.D. Justinian not only did this, but in 533 A.D., he also recognized the Bishop of Rome as the supreme head of all Christians, the definer of doctrine, and the corrector of heretics. Before that time the popes had made great claims, but bishops in other cities shared in the power and often contested the claims of the pope. But after Justinian gave secular approval to the pope as the world leader of religion, the power of the pope was established and continued to increase.

From that time on no one openly dared to condemn the pope or to deny the papal power in world affairs until the time of Napoleon Bonaparte. The pope condemned Napoleon, but Napoleon not only refused to recognize the authority of the pope, but through a series of events he greatly weakened the Papal power.

In the spring of 1798 A.D., just 1260 years from 538 A.D., the French general Berthier took the pope prisoner and he died in French exile eighteen months later. The Papacy had received a "deadly wound". The power that led the saints of God into captivity was itself led into captivity.

Yes, the power and dominion was taken away but was later to be restored, healed. The papacy is coming back into full power again even as this is written.

In drawing a parallel between the Little Horn of Daniel 7 and the fifth head of the Leopard Beast of Revelation 13 we find they are identical. From this comparison they symbolize the same power, the papacy. Six points identify their identity:

1. They are a blasphemous power. (Daniel 7:25; Revelation 13:6).
2. They make war against the saints and conquer them. (Daniel 7:21; Revelation 13:7).
3. They speak great things. (Daniel 7:8, 20; Revelation 13:5).
4. They arose on the cessation of the pagan Roman Empire. (Daniel 7:8; Revelation 13:2).
5. They continued in power for 1260 years. (Daniel 7:25; Revelation 13:5).
6. They lost their power at the end of 1260 years. (Daniel 7:25; Revelation 13:10).

When there are in prophecy two symbols representing powers that come upon the stage at the same time, occupy the same territory, maintain the same character, do the same work, exist the same length of time, and meet the same fate, these symbols represent the same identical power.

After describing the rise of the various world powers, including the Papal power, temporarily broken in 1798 A.D., the inspired prophet writes that God's judgment shall be set, and His heavenly Sanctuary made clean. God's judgments are against the wicked powers of earth and the dragon who gives them his power, his throne, and much authority, and especially against that power which makes such great claims in the name of Christianity. It is still a power and shall have a very important part to play in the final ending of this age's history. But his power shall be consumed and the consummation of this age shall see that power's ultimate destruction.

It should be emphasized that the little horn power, the Papacy, the fifth head represents a system, a church-state combination, a religious power that grasps civil authority to enforce certain church doctrine and practices. Because the Romans Catholic Church does use civil power as prophecy predicted does not by any means bring all individual Roman Catholics under condemnation. Multitudes of Roman Catholics have and are following the Christ as best they know how, and many have exhibited a true devotion to God, the Christ, and the cross. But the papal system during its years of supremacy, and now, is singularly fulfilling the prophecies of Daniel and Revelation and shall continue to do so to the end. This power shall be in this deplorable state when the Christ, as King of kings and Lord of lords, returns.

This church-state system, just as other powers before it, fails to unite mankind. And this is what the Word of God brings out. Satan, through man's attempts to create peace through force of arms, legislation, and coercion of the conscience, is doomed to failure.

Having determined that the fifth head, of the first beast power of Revelation 13, and the Little Horn of Daniel 7, is the Papacy we will now turn our attention to the sixth and seventh head, the second beast, noting that the vision is for the benefit of the people of God. The vision reveals important events a they are to relate to God's people, Spiritual Israel. All the powers which are included in the visions have a direct relationship with the people of God throughout the centuries past, the present, and the years to come.

Turn these pages and be surprised to see who the second beast of Revelation 13 is.

6

Mr. 666

The Number: In past centuries, numerology has been a common part of many religions. Numerologists study the mystical hidden "spiritual" significance of numbers. Even in the Bible, numbers have become invested with spiritual significance. The numbers seven and twelve have acquired the connotation of perfection and completeness.

Revelation 13:18 says, "Here is wisdom. Let him that has understanding count the number of the beast: For it is the number of a man; and his number is 666." It is declared to be the number of a man. We have seen that the fifth head of the first beast of Revelation 13 is a prophetic symbol of the Papacy, the Roman Catholic Church. And in verse 18 we read that another clue identifying the beast is the number 666. We learn that this is the number of a man who represents the beast, the Papacy, the Roman Catholic Church.

The great man of the papacy is the Pope. From the book, *Manual of Christian Doctrine*, page 123, and from the *New Catholic Encyclopedia*, page 962, 1967 Edition we find the following: That every Pope is crowned, "Vicarius Filii Dei," the "Vicar of the Son of God," and by virture of his primatial office, "infallible when defining solemnly some doctrine to be held by the universal church."

From the Catholic weekly magazine, *Our Sunday Visitor*, of 18 April 1915, we read: "The letters inscribed in the pope's miter are these: 'Vicarius Filii Dei,' which is Latin for 'Vicar of the Son of God ...' " The numerical letters of the name add up to the number 666. Latin is the official language of the church of Rome and would naturally be used in calculating the number. (Other names might add up too, but the "beast" must not only have a name whose numbers add up to 666 but also must be a religious-political power which held sway for twelve hundred sixty years, was dethroned, and is ruling from Caesar's seat – Rome; which claims power to forgive sins; and which took on titles of Deity.

V	...	5
I	...	1
C	...	100
A	...	0
R	...	0
I	...	1
U	...	5
S	...	0
F	...	0
I	...	1
L	...	50
I	...	1
I	...	1
D	...	500
E	...	0
I	...	1
	...	
		666

You have now discovered who is Mr. 666. Master Andreas Helwig (c. 1572-1643), of Freidland, Germany, is considered the first to compute the numerical values of the Latin letters from the title VICARIUS FILII DEI (Vicar of the Son of God), to yield the number 666. In his book *Antichristus Romanus* (Roman Antichrist), Helwig points out that the Greek word for "Latin man" or "Latin church," equals 666; and the Hebrew word, Romith, "Roman kingdom" equals 666.

Joseph Berg, in *Papal Rome*, page 216 says, "Now we challenge the world to find another name in these languages: Greek Hebrew, and Latin, which shall designate the same number."

The 1914 edition of the *Catholic Douay Bible* (in a note on Revelation 13:18) states that "the numeral letters of his name shall make up this number" – "666."

7

The United States of America and American Protestantism

1776 A.D.	1798 A.D.	1967 A.D.	2000 A.D.	2031 A.D.
6745 A.S.	6767 A.S.	6896 A.S.	6968 A.S.	6999 A.S.

*You are here

Following his vision of the beast from the sea, John saw another animal, this one "who came up from the land."

"Then I saw another beast who came up from the land. He had two horns like a lamb and spoke like a dragon. He exercises the full authority of the first beast in his presence, and he makes the earth and those living in it worship the first beast, whose mortal wound had been healed. He also performs impressive miracles; for instance, he causes fire to descend from heaven to the earth in the presence of the people. By means of the wonders he is allowed to perform in the presence of the beast, he leads those living on the earth astray, telling the earth's inhabitants to make an image, a likeness, to the beast that had the wound by the sword and came back to life.

He was further permitted to infuse life into the beast's likeness, so that the beast's likeness might speak and bring it about that those who did not worship the beast's likeness should be killed. He also compelled all, the small and the great, the rich and the poor, the freemen and the slaves, to receive a mark in their right hands or in their foreheads, so that no one might be able to buy or sell unless he bore the mark of the beast's name or the number corresponding to his name. Here intelligence comes in. Let him who has the mind for it calculate the number of the beast, for it is a man's number, and his number is 666." Revelation 13:11-18.

Later in the Book of Revelation this beast is described as a "false prophet", a highly successful imposter.

"Then I saw coming out of the mouth of the dragon and from the mouth of the beast and from the mouth of the false prophet, three unclean spirits like frogs. For they are spirits, demonic spirits that work miracles. They go out to the kings of the whole world to muster them for battle on that great day of God Almighty," "And the beast was seized, and with him the false prophet who performed miracles in his presence, by means of which he led astray those who received the mark of the beast and who worshiped his image. Both of them were flung alive into the lake of fire that burns with sulphur."
Revelation 16:13, 14; 19:20.

Verses 11-18 before us bring to view a third great symbol, the two horned beast. The dragon, the heart of the beat nations, papal Rome, represented to us by the fifth head, presents before us great world powers standing as the representatives of two great systems of false religion. Analogy would seem to require that the remaining symbol, the two horned beast, have a similar application, and find its fulfillment in some nation which is the representative of still another great system of religion. The only remaining system which is exercising a controlling influence in the world today is Protestantism. Abstractly considered, paganism embraces all heathen lands, containing more than half the population of the world. Catholicism, with its many sects, belongs to nations which compose a large part of Christendom. Mohammedanism and Judaism and their influence is given in other prophecies. But Protestantism is the religion of nations which constitute the vanguard of the world in religious and secular liberty, enlightenment, progress, and power.

At least four points identify this power:

One, this beast power must arise at the end of the 1260 year rule of the Apostate beast from the sea, and its fifth head, the Roman Catholic Church (verse12). In addition, in its final dragon like stage it is contemporary with the Apostate sea beast and its fifth head, the revived Roman Catholic Church (verse 14). Thus, it must begin about the 1798 A.D., and rule until Jesus' return, the spring of 2036 A.D. (see Revelation 19:20).

Two, the first Apostate beast of Revelation 13 and all the beast powers of Daniel 7 arose from the "sea," which, according to Revelation 17:15, represents "people" and "nations." "Then he said to me, 'The waters you saw, where the harlot sits, are people and nations and languages.' " (Revelation 17:15).

In obvious contrast the second beast, mentioned in Revelation 13, comes up from the earth – a term used in Chapter 12 to indicate a sparsely populated wilderness region. The original Greek word in verse 11 and translated "came up" indicates that John saw this power springing up like a plant.

Only one nation, or power, fits these two specifications: the United States of America. It alone, of all the major world powers, emerged in the late 1700's A.D. in a wilderness area.

The United States was not built upon the ruins of older empires. As someone has suggested, "Its natal day does not commemorate a victory of armed forces so much as it does a great moral idea." All Europe marveled to see this nation coming forth from vacancy. The historian Townsend expressed it in these words: "Like a silent seed we grew into an Empire."

Three, the animal from the land exercises an international influence. The whole world follows its example (see verses 12, 16, 17). Again the specification fits the United States of America.

> *"He exercises the full authority of the first beast in his presence, and he makes the earth and those living in it to worship the first beast, whose mortal wound had been healed. He also compelled all, the small and the great, the rich and the poor, the freemen and the slave, to have a mark in their right hands or in their foreheads, so that no one might be able to buy or sell unless he bore the mark of the beast's name or the number corresponding to his name."* (Revelation 13:12, 16, 17).

Four, throughout the Book of Revelation the figure of a lamb represents Jesus, the Christ. The lamb is an innocent, peaceful animal – a sharp contrast to the beasts that represent the other powers used by Satan. The animal from the land, strangely, has "two horns like a lamb" – it appears at first sight to be lamblike, innocent, even Christ-like in appearance. Those who founded the United States of America based the nation's Constitution on two great principles, civil and religious liberty. These two principles are inseparably connected with the republican form of government, which allows the people to rule through their chosen representatives, and the Protestant understanding of the principle of religious liberty.

If, then, Protestantism is the religion to which we are to look, to what nation as the representative of that religion does the prophecy have application? A careful investigation leads to the conclusion that it applies to the United States of America, both civil and religious.

Today this giant republic lifts its head among the nations, and is in many respects still without a peer. It would be strange indeed if the God who sees the end from the beginning would fail to give a place in prophecy to the nation He has used not only to be a haven of rest for the politically and religiously oppressed, but the nation foremost in promulgating the gospel in all the world.

At what time does prophecy place the beast with lamb like horns in world history? This fact is laid out for us, set forth in the facts regarding the Apostate leopard beast. It was at the time the little horn, the fifth head of the Apostate leopard beast, received a mortal wound that John saw the two horned beast coming up. We have conclusively shown that the little horn power, the fifth head of the Apostate beast is symbolic of the papacy, and its captivity by the French in 1798 A.D. met the fulfillment giving us the definite time for the rise of this power. The United States of America was but newly organized, and the only nation that was then just "coming up" into prominence and influence.

America's independence began in 1775 A.D., declared themselves free in 1776 A.D., adopted Articles of Confederation in 1777 A.D., and in 1783 A.D. signed a treaty of peace with Great Britain. In 1787 A.D., the Constitution was framed, and by 26 July 1788 A.D., it was ratified; going into effect 1 March 1789 A.D. With this we come to the year 1798 A.D., when this nation, the United States of America, is introduced into prophecy.

45

In 1754 A.D. in his notes on Revelation 13, concerning the two horned beast, John Wesley says: "He has not yet come, though he cannot be far off. For he is to appear at the end of the forty-two months of the first beast."

There is good evidence in this prophecy to demonstrate that the power symbolized by the two horned beast is introduced in the early part of its career while a youthful nation. John's words are, "two horns" "like a lamb." It is for the purpose of denoting the character and youthfulness of this beast power, showing that it is young, with an innocent and harmless demeanor; for the horns of a lamb are horns that have barely begun to grow.

Keep in mind the date of the fall of the first beast, the Roman Catholic Church, and what notable power was at that time coming into prominence, but still in its youth. Finding nothing in Europe or Asia of a young and rising power at that time period, we can only turn our eyes to the New World. When our eyes turn in that direction, they rest inevitably upon the United States of America as the power in question. No other power fits the description.

One announcement is adequate to direct us to important and correct conclusions on this point. The prophecy calls it "another beast." The beast and the power symbolized by it, the United States of America, is no part of the fifth head (the Papacy) of the Apostate first beast, but is the sixth and seventh head. This statement is fatal to those who claim otherwise.

In other words, all the Eastern Hemisphere known to history and civilization is covered by prophetic symbols respecting the application of which there is scarcely and room for doubt. Since the prophecy is "another" beast, "who came up from the land," it must be found in some territory not covered by other symbols.

In the Western Hemisphere there is a mighty nation, worth, as has been seen, of being portrayed in prophecy. Of all the symbols mentioned in the prophecies, one alone, the two horned beast of Revelation 13, is left. Of all the countries, of all the nations of the earth, respecting any reason why they should be mentioned in prophecy, one alone, the United States of

America, remains. The two horned beast represents the United States, and all the symbols find an application, and all the ground is covered. If it does not represent the United States of America in prophecy, the prophecy is left without a nation to which it applies.

Today this giant republic lifts its head among the nations, and is without peer.

It should be emphasized that the lamb like beast power, the United States of America, the sixth and seventh heads represent a system in two phases. The first phase is one of civil and religious liberty, the second, a church-state combination, a religious power that grasps civil authority to enforce certain church doctrines and practices. Because the Church of the United States of America does use civil power as prophecy predicted, does not, by any means, bring all individual Protestants under condemnation. Multitudes of Protestants have and are following the Christ as best they can, and many exhibit a true devotion to God, the Christ, and the Cross. But the Protestant system during these years of its supremacy, is singularly fulfilling the prophecies of Revelation and shall continue to do so to the end. This nation shall be in this abominable state when the Christ returns.

This great nation is becoming an Apostate church-state system, joining its two horns of liberty into one mighty weapon, and just as other powers, it too shall enforce religion by civil authority, it too shall fail to unite mankind. That is what this prophecy brings out. This power shall be in this deplorable state when the Christ returns in spring of 2036 A.D. as a Warrior King, Harvester, and King of kings and Lord of lords. Satan, through man's attempts to create peace through force of arms, legislation, and coercion of the conscience, is doomed to failure.

Now that the stage has been set, turn the page and let us look at the countdown according to the calender God uses for His countdown.

8

The Dragon Heads

Dan. 2 – Image   Rev. 12 – Seven Headed Dragon
Dan. 7 – Beasts   Rev. 13 – Seven Headed Leopard Beast
                    Rev. 17 –Seven Headed Scarlet Beast

The heart of the image and the beast powers is the seven headed red dragon, Satan, the devil.

606 B.C.	538 B.C.	331 B.C.	168 B.C.	476 A.D.
4362 A.S.	4430 A.S.	4637 A.S.	4800 A.S.	5445 A.S.
Lion	Bear	Leopard	Terrible	Barbarian Tribes
1st Head	2nd Head	3rd Head	4th Head	10 Horns
Image head. Babylon. Dan. 2:7				
	Image Arms Persia. Ram. Dan. 8 Dan. 2:7.			
		Image Belly, Dan. 2:7 Greece. Goat, Dan. 8. Dan. 2:7.		
			Image Legs Rome. Daniel 2:7	
				10 Horns. Dan. 7.

538 A.D.	1776 A.D.	2000 A.D.	2036 A.D.

5507 A.S.   5745 A.S.   5969 A.S.   6005 A.S.
                          *You are here

5th Head   6th Head   7th Head   8th Head
Little Horn.
Papacy.
Whore.
Antichrist.
Dan. 7; Rev. 13: 17: 18.

            Buffalo calf.
            Lamb like.
            United States of America.
            Rev. 13.

                        Buffalo bull.
                        Apostate.
                        United States of America
                        False prophet.
                        Whore.
                        Rev. 13: 14: 17: 18.

                                      10 Horns.
                                      Muslim nations
                                      Rev. 12: 13: 17.
                                          Antichrist
                                          Papacy.
                                          Whore.
                                        Rev. 12: 13: 17: 18.

9

The Passion Play in the Desert

The Passion Play! words that ring with strange fascination! The Dramatic events it portrays – events surrounding the trial, crucifixion, death, and resurrection of our Lord – have for nearly two thousand years held captive the hearts and loyalties of millions. History itself converges about those unforgettable events.

But centuries before the great passion on Calvary's hill in old Palestine, a miniature passion play was enacted daily in physical Israel's ancient church in the desert.

Have you ever wondered what people did about their sins before the Son of God gave His life on Calvary? What provision was made for their forgiveness? Today we can pray, "Lord, I have sinned, but You died for me. I accept that sacrifice and claim forgiveness." All well and good – for us. But what about the people who lived before Jesus died? Was there one plan of forgiveness and salvation for them, and another for us? We look back to the cross. But they did not have a cross to look back to. How, then, were they forgiven? As we draw aside the curtain and watch the spectacle of God's passion play in the desert, we shall discover the answers to these vital questions.

It was back in the Garden, eastward in Eden, that God had first demonstrated Calvary. An altar had been built, upon which a lamb, representing the Christ, was slain, one for Adam and one for Eve. Thus all through those early centuries He had kept before the people the saving fact that the innocent Son of God would one day die for guilty humanity. But now, as a race of slaves led out by the hand of God from Egyptian bondage was about to become a nation, God instructed the people,

"... I want the people of Israel to make Me a sacred Temple where I can live among them." (Exodus 25:8).

The God of heaven was to dwell among His people. Great care was taken to prepare a fit dwelling place. Thirteen chapters of the Bible describe the building of the sanctuary. The entire Book of Leviticus describes its services. And one entire book in the New Testament – the Book of Hebrews – presses home the vital significance of this distant drama to Christians in our day.

"... I want the people of Israel to make Me a sacred Temple where I can live among them." In other words, God set up a judicial department on earth in temporary quarters until Jesus would come to fulfill His part in the redemption of mankind.

We soon discover in Scriptures that there are two sanctuaries. There was the one on earth, built by Moses. The New Testament makes it clear that there is one in heaven, built by God. For a moment let us look into the heavenly sanctuary described in the Book of Hebrews:

> "...: We have such a High Priest, who is seated at the right hand of the throne of the Majesty in the heavens, as a minister in the sanctuary; yes, of the true tabernacle, which the Lord pitched, not man." Hebrews 8:1, 2.

Now in Hebrews 9:9 we learn that the earthly sanctuary is "a figure, a type, for the time then present." You see, the sanctuary in the desert was only a model, a figure, of the true heavenly sanctuary.

As we learn the operations of the earthly sanctuary, we can begin to understand how the heavenly sanctuary operates – where our High Priest, the Lord, Jesus, the Christ, now officiates in our behalf. Think of the thrilling prospects as we let this truth unfold.

But first, what was the sanctuary? What was it like? In Hebrews 9:1-5 we read:

> "To be sure, the first covenant had its worship regulations and its earthly sanctuary; for the first tabernacle was furnished in this way: In what was called the Holy Place were the lampstand, the table and the presentation loaves, and the golden alter of incense before the second curtain. Behind the second curtain was the tabernacle called the Holy of Holies containing the Ark of the Covenant completely covered with

gold; inside it the golden jar of manna, Aaron's rod that sprouted, and the tablets of the covenant. Above it were the cherubim of glory overshadowing the mercy seat, – about which we cannot now go into detail." (Hebrews 9:1-5).

Here is pictured a most unusual building, with most unusual furniture. To see how it operates, let me take you back over the centuries to a day some fifteen hundred years before the Christ. On the vast plain rolling out before majestic Mount Sinai is the tent city of the twelve tribes of the children of Israel. In the midst of the camp is a courtyard. And nestled in the western end of the courtyard is the sanctuary of God.

As the courtyard is entered, the first article to meet the eyes is the huge altar of brunt offering. It is made of brass. Beyond, but still in the open courtyard, stands the laver, where priests wash before carrying out their sacred duties.

The tabernacle itself is a beautiful portable building made of upright boards overlaid with pure gold; it is covered with various materials to protect it from the weather. At the far end of the first apartment, called the Holy Place, there hangs a door of gorgeous curtains, beyond which lies the Holy of Holies.

As the priest steps into the first room, he faces on the right side the table of showbread, a type of the Bread of Life. On the left side stands the magnificent even-branched candlestick, beaten from one piece of solid gold, representing the work of the Holy Spirit. Beyond these pieces of furniture is the altar of incense, its ever-ascending smoke representing the prayers of God's people. God Himself kindled the fire there. Whenever the high priest stepped beyond the curtain into the Holy of Holies, into the very presence of God, he was instructed to shield himself from the blinding glory of God by a cloud of incense.

Stepping into the Most Holy place, we discover only one article of furniture – the Ark, a chest overlaid with gold, above which are two golden angels, their faces looking reverently downward to the mercy seat, representing the reverence with which the heavenly host regard God. It was here in the Ark of the

Covenant, under the mercy seat, that the Ten Commandment law, written by the finger of God on two tablets of stone, was placed.

Now notice, if you will, another law, written on a scroll and placed on a shelf on the outside of the Ark. It is this scroll that contained the ceremonial law which describes the sacrifices. On it, too, is recorded the civil code for the camp of Israel. This law – significantly – lies in a place of secondary importance – just outside the Ark on a shelf.

At the entrance of the sanctuary, in the courtyard, was the Altar of Burnt offering. And between it and the tabernacle was the Laver where the priests washed before entering the House of God.

The Lord appointed the Levites as priests, and one of them was appointed high priest. Only the high priest was permitted to enter the Most Holy place.

The primary purpose of the sanctuary was to teach the Plan of Salvation in the scenario of sin and salvation. Here the animal sacrifices were offered, which typified Jesus "the Lamb of God who takes away the sin of the world." John 1:29.

You may ask, "Why was all this necessary?"

That question takes us to the heart of the Gospel, the Good News of the kingdom of God, centered in the Christ. Without the heart of the Gospel, there can be no redemption, no forgiveness, no moral power. Without it, religion becomes cold and formal, a mere outward display that mocks the soul with emptiness.

To touch the heart of the gospel we touch life – the life of the Son of God. On the cross Jesus poured out His life – His blood – for us.

Gruesome? Unlovely? Yes, the cross that brought salvation for the human heart was not lovely. It was the ugliest, most dev- ilish contrivance of the ages. On that gruesome cross the Son of God died. Yet that death was necessary if we are to escape eter- nal death, for "without blood shedding there is no forgiveness." (Hebrews 9:22). "All have sinned and fall short of God's moral excellence." (Romans 3:23).

What is sin? God's definition, you remember, is this: "Everyone who commits sin is guilty of lawbreaking; sin is law-

53

breaking." (1 John 3:4). I repeat it. Sin is not a mistake in judgment. Sin is not merely human weakness or personality deficiency. Sin is the breaking of God's law. Can we not now better understand the words of Romans 6:23 – "For the wages of sin is death, but the gift of God is eternal life in the Christ, Jesus, the Lord."

The wages, or penalty, of sin – of breaking God's law – is eternal death. So if we have all sinned – and we have – then are we not all under the death penalty? Jesus, however, consented to die in our place. And that vicarious death settles the account. He sets us free, if we wish to be set free, from the curse of eternal death. God cannot excuse sin. But He made provision to forgive it.

There is no other way, no other gate, no other avenue, into eternal life except by way of the cross of our Lord, Jesus, the Christ.

But again you ask, "What were these people who lived before the cross to do? Are they forever lost?"

No. God provided that these people bring a lamb and take its life. He laid his hand on the animal's head, confessed his sin, and cut its throat. In other words, an innocent substitute was to be offered to show the faith of the sinner in the coming death of the Son of God – the Lamb of God – who would die as man's innocent substitute.

Each day the people brought their sin offerings. Each day, in the morning and in the afternoon, the priest offered a lamb for all the people and for himself. He repeats the procedure followed by the people, but he carries it a step further. He takes the blood into the sanctuary. Passing through, he stands before the curtain beyond which is the presence of God. He sprinkles the blood before the curtain, thus in illustration bringing the sins of the people, and himself, to the mercy seat, to the law that has been broken and that can only be healed by the blood of the Christ.

The sins of physical Israel were thus transferred, symbolically to the sanctuary, through the blood of the lamb. Here the sins of the people remained through the year, and a special work became necessary for their removal. God commanded that once each year an atonement be made for each of the sacred apartments, and the sanctuary be made clean, free from sin. "Thus he shall make the atonement for the holy place because of the uncleanness of the Israelites, all their sinful transgressions. He shall do the same for the dwelling, which stays with them in the midst of their impurities." An atonement was also to be made for the altar, to "cleanse, and sanctify it from the uncleanness of the Israelites." (Leviticus 4:27-35; 16:16, 19).

This service continued daily, and yearly, through the long centuries until one day some nineteen hundred sixty three years ago. That afternoon, as usual, a lamb had been brought, and the priest was about to take its life. But at that crucial moment, on a lonely hill just outside the city, the Lamb of God was giving His life to save the world. Notice what happened:

"Jesus, once more crying with aloud voice, dismissed His spirit. And the veil of the temple was torn in two from top to bottom; the earth shook; the rocks were split." Matthew 27:50, 51.

Do you see the significance of it all? No longer did mankind need to bring lambs, for the Son of the living God had made the supreme sacrifice once for all.

A Lamb broke your fall! A Lamb broke mine – the Lamb of God that takes away the sin of the world.

For more detail turn the page and enjoy the Feasts.

10

The Feasts

We may agree that the Bible does not teach and Christians should not observe, the holidays of pagan origin. We may agree that the Bible does teach observance of the seventh-day Sabbath. But what about the annual festivals which physical Israel was commanded to observe? There are people who are teaching that in Old Testament times God commanded the observance of seven annual days or periods, and that these have been carried over into the Christian age, so Christians should practice and teach the observance of these events.

In the following pages it will be shown from the Bible that (1) physical Israel was commanded to keep just three annual "feasts" – each kept for a designated period of time – and two other special days, each with a special significance; and, (2) none of these annual feasts or special days are to be kept by Christians. There is no Bible record that any Christian since the death of the Christ ever kept them, and no Bible record of instruction to keep them. It is important that we, as Christians, be faithful in practicing what God has commanded us to do, and equally important that we refrain from doing and teaching as sacred duty anything which God has not commanded us to do or has strictly forbade.

The Value of Types and Illustrations: There are many types and illustrations in the Bible. The study of these is interesting and profitable. The sacrificial lamb, goat, and etc. were always a type of the Christ, the Lamb of God. The near sacrifice of Isaac by Abraham was a type of the sacrifice of the Christ. The ark which Noah built is a type of our salvation. The journey of physical Israel in the wilderness is a type of spiritual Israel's journey, our Christian journey. Such types and illustrations are good, and they are explained in the Bible. One such explanation is found in 1 Corinthians 10:1-11. These "examples" were types. To study them is for our interest and profit.

> *"I want you to know, brothers, that although our fathers were all under the cloud, and all passed through the sea, and all as followers of Moses were baptized in the cloud and the sea, and all ate the same spiritual food and drank the same spiritual drink, for they drank from the spiritual Rock which accompanied them, which Rock was the Christ. Nevertheless, God was not pleased with the majority of them, for they were struck down in the wilderness.*
>
> *These things occurred as examples for us, so that we may not lust after evil as they lusted, neither be idol-worshipers as some of them were, as it is written, "The people sat down to eat and to drink and got up to dance." Neither should we do immoral deeds as some of them did, when twenty-three thousand fell in one day. Neither should we become a trial to the Lord as some of them tried Him and were destroyed by serpents. Do not grumble, either, as some of them grumbled, and they were put out of the way by the destroyer. These experiences came to them as a lesson for us and were written as a warning to us, on whom the end of the age has come." (1 Corinthians 10:1-11).*

In the Bible we have found the purpose of each festival clearly given. The main festivals were memorials by which physical Israel was to remember God's dealings with their fathers in connection with the deliverance from Egypt and their prosperity in the promised land. The festivals are also symbolic of God's dealings with spiritual Israel in connection with our deliverance from sin and our prosperity in the Promised Land. The symbolic work of the generations of physical Israel came to an end with the coming of the Messiah, the Christ, and His sacrificial death, a type met antitype, on the cross of Calvary.

The Passover and the Festival Of Unleavened Bread: The cycle of Temple festivals appropriately opens, in the first month, Nisan, with 'the Passover' and 'Feast of Unleavened Bread.' The first of the annual days which physical Israel was commanded to observe. For, properly speaking, these two are quite distinct, the 'Passover' taking place on the 14th of Abid, (March-April), called Nisan at a later date, and the 'Feast of Unleavened Bread' commencing on the 15th, and lasting for seven days, to the 21st of the month.

The passover was the first of the three Feasts on which all males in Israel were bound to appear before the Lord in the place which He would choose (the two others being the Feast of Weeks and that of Tabernacles). All three great festivals bore a threefold reference.

First, to the season of the year, the latter rain, and the enjoyment of the fruits of the good land which the Lord had given them.

Second, their deliverance as a nation, miraculously preserved and set free, for they first became a people, and that by the direct interposition of God.

Third, the bearing of all the festivals is typical. Every reader of the New Testament knows how frequent are such allusions to the Exodus, the Paschal Supper, and the Feast of Unleavened Bread. And that this meaning was intended from the first, appears from the whole design of the Old Testament, and from the exact correspondence between the types and the antitypes. Indeed, it is, so to speak, impressed upon the Old Testament by a law of internal necessity. For when God bound up the future of all nations in the history of Abraham and his seed, He made the history prophetic; and each event and every rite became, as it were, a bud, destined to open in blossom and ripen into fruit on that tree under the shadow of which all nations were to be gathered. Thus physical Israel celebrated the spring-time of their history, and each year their national birthday; and the spring-time of grace, their grand national deliverance pointing forward to the birth of spiritual Israel, true Israel, and the Passover sacrifice of that 'Lamb of God which takes away the sin of the world.'

Before type met antitype in the sacrifice of the Christ the people of God were justified, or considered righteous in the sight of God, by obedience to the Law. There was, however, no complete justification or real salvation until type met antitype. People living before the Christ had to accept Him as their coming Saviour just as we must accept Him as the One who came and died, shedding His blood for the sins of the world. The sheaf of grain offered, Leviticus 23:10, was symbolic of the Son of God, raised from the grave to eternal life.

"Tell the Israelites: When you have come into the land which I give you and you harvest its crop, bring the first sheaf of your harvest to the priest." (Leviticus 23:10)

We are harvested from the world as grain is harvested from the fields. Therefore, since the Christ has fulfilled all sacrifices, and the waving of the sheaf, the Passover and Festival of Unleavened Bread are not to be observed by Christians.

The Festival of Pentecost: The next annual festival, in the month of Ziv (April-May), and later called Iyar, as recorded in Leviticus 23, is the Festival of Weeks, or Pentecost, when all males were to appear before Jehovah in his sanctuary, and the appointed sacrifices and offerings to be brought. Its character is expressed by the term 'feast of harvest' and 'day of firstfruits.'

The instruction was that each family present two loaves before God. (Leviticus 23:17). The observance of this festival depended on the people being engaged in agriculture in the land of promise, symbolic of the first fruits of the resurrection of the saints. As the dedication of the harvest, commencing with the presentation of the first barley sheaf, being the first ripe corn in the land, on the Passover, was completed in the thank-offering of the two wave-loaves, prepared from wheat at Pentecost. This memorial of physical Israel's deliverance appropriately terminated in their harvesting the grain in the land of Canaan and storing it in their barns. The loaves offered were symbolic of the saints resurrection with the Christ and taken with Him to the very throne of God, put in the Lord's garner, at His ascension (Matthew 27:52, 53; Ephesians 4:8). Therefore, since the Christ has fulfilled all sacrifices and the sheaf offering, the saints, the souls whose graves were opened at the Christ's death and were resurrected after Him on the third day (Matthew 27:52, 53) and ascended to the heavenly with Him, fulfill the waving of the loaves, the Festival of Weeks is not to be observed by Christians.

"Bring along from your homes two loaves to be waved, made from fifth bushel of fine flour; they shall be baked with leaven, the firstfruits to the Lord." (Leviticus 23:17).

"The tombs were opened and many of the buried saints were raised and after His resurrection they left their tombs, entered the holy city and appeared to many." (Matthew 27:52, 53).

"Wherefore he says, 'When He ascended up on high, He led captivity captive, and gave gifts unto men.' " (Ephesians 4:8).

The Blowing Of Trumpets: While the Blowing of Trumpets is listed among the festivals of Leviticus 23 it is not officially called a festival there or in any other place in the Bible. It was one of the annual sabbaths but should not be listed as a festival. It called attention to and prepared physical Israel for the Day of Atonement, symbolic of the Great Awakening that called to attention and prepared spiritual Israel for the heavenly Day of Atonement. Therefore, since the Great Awakening has fulfilled the calling to attention and preparing of spiritual Israel for the heavenly Day of Atonement and the act of cleansing, the Blowing of Trumpets is not to be observed by Christians.

"Tell the Israelites: In the seventh month, on the first day of the month, enjoy a day of complete rest, a memorial day, announced by the blowing of trumpets, a sacred convocation." (Leviticus 23:24).

Day of Atonement: One of the most sacred days of physical Israel was the Day of Atonement as is the heavenly Day of Atonement is today to spiritual Israel. It is not called a feast, a festival, or a fast, but simply a "holy convocation" or sabbath (Leviticus 23) taking place the 10th day of Ethanim (September-October), later called Tishri.

Very little description of the events of the Day of Atonement is given in this chapter. In verse 28 it is mentioned that the day's purpose is for the making of atonement for the people before God, but no details are given. The details of those special activities that were to be done in observance of this day are given in Leviticus 16. Here is found that once a year, on the great Day of Atonement, symbolic of the heavenly Day of Atonement, was the one day in the year in which the High Priest entered the Most Holy Place for the cleansing of the tabernacle or temple. The work there performed completed the yearly round of ministration. On the Day of Atonement two kids of the goats were brought to the door of the tabernacle, or temple, and lots were cast upon them, "one lot for the Lord, and the other lot for the scapegoat, or the Azazel goat." Verse 8. The goat upon which fell the lot for the Lord was slain as a sin offering for the people. And the high priest brought his blood within the veil. He alone was in the sanctuary, he alone entered this place three times, twice with the blood for the priests and himself, and third with the blood of the goat which he sprinkled on the mercy seat for the sins of the people. After that, the sins of the people were confessed by the High Priest with his hands on the head of the live goat. Then this goat was taken away and let go in an uninhabited place, the wilderness. Thus, in the act of a moment, the sanctuary was cleansed of sin. (Leviticus 16).

> *"And Aaron shall lay both his hands on the head of the live goat and confess over it all the iniquities of the Israelites, all their transgressions and all their sins; he shall lay them on the head of the goat and send it away into the desert by a man at hand. The goat shall carry away upon itself all their iniquities to a desolate region and in the desert he shall let the he-goat go free."*

The placing of the sins upon the goat for removal occurred at one-thirty in the afternoon, the act of a moment.

The whole ceremony impressed the Israelites with the holiness of God and His abhorrence of sin; and, further, to show them that they could not come in contact with sin without becoming polluted. Every man was required to afflict his soul while this work of atonement was going forward. All business was to be laid aside, and the whole congregation of Israel were to spend the day in solemn humiliation before their God, with prayer, fasting, and deep searching of heart.

After the service of atonement and cleansing was complete, the sin sacrifices continued. Those who brought sacrifices for sin were accepted till the going down of the sun, and atonement made retroactive to one-thirty.

Those individuals whose sins were not covered by the blood of the lamb by the going down of the sun were not atoned for, bringing judgment upon themselves, and were put out of the camp.

These unique functions were done each year on the Day of Atonement while physical Israel had the tabernacle, and later, the temple. No one need try to make up ideas about the meaning of the type because the Bible gives the explanation. This explanation is found in the book of Hebrews, Chapters 9 and 10. Chapter 9 is a description of the tabernacle with its Holy and Most Holy Places, along with the golden Ark and other sacred furnishings. The services of the Day of Atonement are carefully described.

The Bible refers to these events as in the past and tells us they were a type for that time, thereby indicating that they are no longer to be practiced. Reading on in Chapter 10, we find it further explained that the ceremonies and sacrifices which made up the Day of Atonement were brought to an end when the Lamb of God, the Christ, made the great sacrifice of Himself. The type, symbolic of the heavenly Day of Atonement, was fulfilled and we all wait the end of the heavenly Day of Atonement.

There was a five day waiting time between the Day of Atonement and the Feast of Tabernacles. During this time the unrepentant of Israel were put out of the camp. Sin, having been put out of the camp, allowed the children of Israel to celebrate with joy and gladness.

The Feast of Tabernacles: The most joyous of all festive seasons in physical Israel was that of the 'Feast of Tabernacles.' It fell at a time of year when the hearts of the people would naturally be full of thankfulness, gladness, and expectancy, the 15th day of the seventh month, Ethanim, later called Tishri. All the crops had been long stored; and now all fruits were gathered, the vintage past, and the land only waited the 'former rain' to prepare it for a new crop. It was appropriate that, when the commencement of the harvest had been consecrated by offering the first ripe sheaf of barley, and the full ingathering of the corn by the two wave-loaves, there would now be a harvest feast of thankfulness and gladness unto the Lord. But that was not all. As they looked around on the goodly land, the fruits of which had just enriched them, they remembered that by miraculous interposition the Lord their God had brought them to this land and given it to them, and that He ever claimed it as peculiarly His own. For the land was strictly connected with the history of the people; and both the land and the history were linked with the mission of physical Israel. The beginning of the harvest pointed back to the birth of physical Israel in their Exodus from Egypt, and forward to the true Passover sacrifice and His resurrection in the future. The corn harvest was connected with the giving of the Law on Mount Sinai and Moses' ascending to receive the two tables of the Law in the past, and forward to the Christ and the saints ascending with Him and the outpouring of the Holy Spirit on the Day of Pentecost. The harvest-thanksgiving of the Feast of Tabernacles reminded physical Israel, on the one hand, of their dwelling in booths in the wilderness, while, on the other hand, it pointed to the final harvest when spiritual Israel's mission shall be completed, and all nations gathered unto the Lord.

Thus, the first of the three great annual feasts, Passover and the Feast of Unleavened Bread, spoke, in the presentation of the first sheaf, of the resurrection and the Christ presenting Himself to the Father. The second, the Feast of Weeks, or Pentecost, the ascension of the Christ and the saints, the first fruits of those secured to eternal life by the blood of the Lamb, presented as two leavened wave-loaves; and the founding of the New Testament Church. The third, the Feast of Harvest, pointed forward to the celebration of the full harvest, when all the redeemed of the Lord shall be taken to Zion, Armageddon, the Mount of the Congregation, without spot or blemish, when 'On this mountain the Lord of Hosts shall make for all people a feast of rich food; ... And He shall destroy in this mountain the veil which is upon all peoples and the shroud that covers all nations. He shall swallow up death forever, and the Lord God shall wipe away tears from their faces: He shall remove from all the earth the reproach of His people (spiritual Israel), for the Lord has spoken it.' (Isaiah 25:6-8; comp. Revelation 21:40).

There is yet another important point to be noticed. The Feast followed closely on the Day of Atonement. Both took place in the seventh month; one on the 10th, the other on the 15th of Tishri. What the seventh day, or Sabbath, is in reference to the week, the seventh month was in reference to the year. It closed not only the sacred cycle, but also the agricultural or working year. It also marked the change of seasons, the approach of the former rain and of the winter equinox. The Feast of Harvest appropriately followed five days after the Day of Atonement, at time of sifting, in which the sinners of physical Israel was removed and its covenant relation to God restored. Thus, a sanctified nation could keep a holy Feast of Harvest joyfully unto the Lord, just as in the truest sense it will be 'in that day' when the meaning of the Feast shall be a reality.

The time setter, the heavenly Day of Atonement is next, please turn the pages.

11

The Heavenly Day of Atonement

Spring				Spring
1031 A.D.	1281 A.D.	1531 A.D.	1844 A.D.	2031 A.D.
5001 A.S.	5251 A.S.	5501 A.S.	5814 A.S.	6001 A.S.

*You are here

We are now living in the time of the great heavenly Day of Atonement, the spring of 1031 A.D., 1 Nisan, 5001 A.S., to the spring of 2031 A.D., 1 Nisan, 6001 A.S. In the typical service, while the high priest was making the atonement for physical Israel, all were required to afflict their souls by repentance of sin in humiliation before the Lord, least they be cut off from among the people.

In like manner, all who would have their names retained in the Lamb's Book of Life should now, in the few remaining years of their probation, afflict their souls before God by repentance of sin in humiliation. There must be deep, faithful searching of the heart. The light, frivolous spirit indulged by so many professed Christians, cultural Christians, must be put away. There is earnest warfare for all who would subdue the evil tendencies that strive for the mastery. The work of preparation is an individual work. We are not saved in groups. The purity and devotion of one will not offset the want of these qualities in another. We stand before God as if there were no other being upon the face of the earth.

As anciently the sins of the people were by faith placed upon the sin offering and through its blood transferred, in figure, to the earthly sanctuary, so in the new covenant the sins of the repentant are by faith placed upon the Christ and transferred, in fact, to the heavenly sanctuary.

65

As the typical cleansing of the earthly was accomplished by the removal of the sins by which it had been polluted, so the actual cleansing of the Heavenly was accomplished by the removal, or blotting out, of the sins which were there recorded. The cleansing of the Heavenly sanctuary, at the termination of the 2300 years, involved the Christ removing the sins of the repentants and placing them upon the head of Satan. 22 October 1844 A.D., the act of a moment, and the heavenly sanctuary was cleansed. This work of removal has been preformed and we wait for the coming of the Christ to take us, the redeemed, to our Father's house; for when He comes, His reward is with Him to give to mankind according to their works. To the righteous eternal life, to the wicked eternal death, annihilation. (Revelation 22:12).

It is seen, also, that while the sin offering pointed to the Christ as sacrifice, high priest, and mediator, the scapegoat typified Satan, the author of sin, upon whom the sins of the repentant have been placed. The scapegoat was sent away into a land not inhabited, never to come again into the congregation of Israel. So also will Satan be forever banished from the presence of God and His people, and he will be blotted from existence in the final destruction of sin and sinners.

The Christ's mission was not for judgement, mankind passes judgement upon themselves, but for salvation and atonement. And before the Sanhedrin Jesus declared,

> *"Truly I assure you that he who listens to My message and believes* (obeys) *Him who sent Me has eternal life; he comes under no sentence but has passed over from death into life." (John 5:24).*

Because He tasted the very dregs of human affliction and temptation, and understands the frailties and sins of mankind; because in our behalf He has victoriously withstood the temptations of Satan, and will deal justly and tenderly with the souls that His own blood has been poured out to save – because of this, the Son of man is appointed to execute the judgement of execution. This will occur sometime after the year 3031 A.D., 1 Nisan 7001 A.S., probably 3036 A.D., 1 Nisan 7006 A.S.

Day of Atonement
Leviticus 16
Earthly Day of Atonement
Tenth day, Seventh month
Type

Sunset 6 PM	Midnight 12 AM	Sunrise 6 AM	Sanctuary cleansed 1:30 PM	Sunset 6 PM
I---------------I----------------I------I---------I--------------------I
Spring				Spring
1031 A.D.	1281 A.D.	1531 A.D.	1844 A.D.	2031 A.D.
5001 A.S.	5251 A.S.	5501 A.S.	5814 A.S.	6001 A.S.
Tribulation Matthew 24	Inquisition	Reformation	Sanctuary cleansed Dan. 8:12	Mankinds probation ends Rev. 11:15 Michael stands up Dan. 12:1

Antitype
Heavenly Day of Atonement

The earthly Day of Atonement had 24 hours, 48 half hour segments, form 6 P.M. to 6 P.M. and the heavenly Day of Atonement, of necessity, must be divided into 48 segments to cover the symbolism. 1:30 P.M., the moment of cleansing, is 39 segments and 8125% of 48 segments. 22 October 1844 is 39 segments and 8125% of the heavenly Day of Atonement whose beginning date corresponds to 1 Nisan, 5001 A.S., the spring of year 1031 A.D., the beginning of the sixth millennium of the scenario of sin and salvation. There remains therefore 1875% of the time for both the earthly and the heavenly Day of Atonement. 6 P.M. for the type and 1 Nisan, 6001 A.S., the spring of 2031 A.D., for the antitype.

The Christ came with the truth of heaven, and all who are listening to His voice, the Holy Spirit, are drawn to Him. The worshipers of self belong to Satan's kingdom and are judged from the beginning. In our attitude toward the Christ, all show on which side they stand. And thus we, all of mankind, everyone, pass judgement on ourselves.

The Christ's atoning sacrifice in behalf of mankind was full and complete on Calvary, once for all. The condition of the atonement was fulfilled, once for all. The work for which He had come to this world was accomplished. He had won the kingdom. He wrestled it from Satan and is heir of all things.

Our Lord returned to the throne of God to be honored by the heavenly host. Yet, one thing remained, the removal of the sins of the saints from the heavenly Temple.

As the disciples went out preaching, "The time is fulfilled, the kingdom of God is at hand" so it was proclaimed, in the early 1800s A.D., that the longest prophetic time period brought to view in the Scriptures was about to expire, that the heavenly Temple was to be made clean, free from the sins of the saints, that the judgement of execution was at hand, and the everlasting kingdom to be ushered in. The message given at the turn of the century announced the termination of the 2,300 days of Daniel 8:14.

"He told me, 'For 2,300 evenings and mornings; then the sanctuary shall be restored to its rightful state.' " (Daniel 8:14).

The Lord gave Daniel a vision regarding this important matter. In Daniel 8:13-14 we read:

"How long shall be the vision concerning the daily sacrifice, and the transgression that causes desolation to give both the sanctuary and the host to be trodden under foot? And he said unto me, unto 2300 days; then shall the sanctuary be cleansed."

What are the 2300 days? Since a day stands for a year in the Bible prophecy (Numbers 14:34; Ezekiel 4:6), they represent 2300 years.

When does this time period begin? Daniel 9:23-25 gives us the answer:

> *"Seventy weeks are determined upon your people and upon the holy city ... Know therefore and understand, that from the going forth of the command to restore and to build Jerusalem unto the Messiah the Prince shall be seven weeks, and three-score and two weeks."*

The Hebrew word for "determine" is (chathak) and it means "cut off." Seventy weeks (of seven days each or 490 years), were to be cut off from the 2300 year prophecy for the Jews "to make an end of sins, and ... to bring in everlasting righteousness." (Daniel was careful to point out that during that seventieth week of the prophecy the Messiah would come).

The Book of Ezra records that the commandment to restore and to build Jerusalem was issued by Artaxerxes in the fall of 457 B.D. (Ezra 6:14; 7:7). Thus the prophecy began in that year.

When would the prophecy end? Beginning in the fall of 457 B.C. and counting toward our day, the 2300 years would end in the fall of 1844 A.D.

We can be sure of our dates by checking them with the life of the Christ. Daniel declared that 69 weeks or 483 years would pass from the commandment to restore and to build Jerusalem until the Messiah came. In the fall of 27 A.D., exactly 483 years after the fall of 457 B.C., the Christ was baptized by John the Baptist. At the age of 30 years the Christ began His ministry, preaching, "The time is fulfilled, and the kingdom of God is at hand." (Luke 3:1, 21; Mark 1:15).

In the middle of the seventieth week the Messiah was to be cut off from the living, crucified. This happened in the spring of 31 A.D., when He was 33.5 years of age. The gospel would be preached to the Jews for another half week (three and a half years). This brings us to the fall of 34 A.D. In that year the gospel went to the Gentiles. (Acts 13:46).

Because of the crucifixion of the Lamb of God and the murder of His followers, and their unrepentant hearts, the Jews were cut off at the termination of the 490 years, fall of 34 A.D. The branches were pruned from the Tree of Life, Jesus the Christ, and can only attain salvation through the Blood of the Lamb.

Any concern for the Israelis today is to believe the deceptions of Satan. The true Israel of today is spiritual Israel, the followers of the Lamb of God, Jesus the Christ.

The Messiah came to His people in the fall of 27 A.D., once for all. He returns the spring of 2036 A.D., 1 Nisan, 6006 A.S., not as a redeeming Messiah, but as a Warrior King, King of kings, and Lord of lords, the Harvester King to take the redeemed, spiritual Israel, to His Father's house.

Like the first disciples, the importance of the message given in the late 1700s A.D. was not fully comprehended. Errors that have long been established in the church prevented, and still prevents, the arriving at the correct interpretation of this important point, and others, in prophecy.

The earthly, or old covenant sanctuary was a typical system, which was symbolic, a shadow of the sacrifice and priesthood of the Christ. The cleansing of the sanctuary was the last service preformed by the high priest in the yearly round of ministration. It was performed on the Day of Atonement, the tenth day of the seventh month, Ethanim or Tishri as it was later called. It was the removal, or putting away, of the sins of penitent physical Israel. It prefigured, was symbolic of, the ministration of our Great High Priest in heaven, in the removal or the putting away of the sins of His people, penitent spiritual Israel, those who remain recorded in the Lamb's Book of Life.

As in the typical, the new covenant sanctuary in heaven is antitypical where the Christ made atonement, once for all, one the Cross of Calvary. As in the typical, in the antitypical, the Christ, our Great High Priest, removed or put away the sins of the saints, once for all, from the heavenly and placed them upon the head of Satan, the antitypical scapegoat. This occurred 22 October, 1844 A.D., the act of a moment, and the heavenly Sanctuary is clean, free from the sins of the saints. Satan, the goat for removal, who, in the judgement of execution, must bear the final penalty, shall forever be banished from the presence of God and His people, and will be blotted from existence in the final destruction of sin and sinners. (Hebrews 8).

After the Heavenly was made clean, the act of a moment, free from the sins of the saints, 22 October, 1844 A.D., the court of Heaven is again open to receive the penitent sinner. Those who wash their robes in the blood of the Lamb of God will be accepted until the close of the heavenly Day of Atonement, 1 Nisan, 6001 A.S., spring of 2031 A.D.

While the Day of Atonement is going forward in Heaven, while the sins of penitent believers are being confessed, their Atonement is the Christ on the Cross of Calvary, 14 Nisan, 4001, spring of 31 A.D., their sins are removed retroactive to 22 October, 1844 A.D., 10 Tishri, 5814 A.S.

When the heavenly Day of Atonement shall have ended, then, and not until then, probation will close, the door of mercy will be forever shut. At this time, 1 Nisan, 6001, spring of 2031 A.D., the followers of the Lamb will be ready for His appearing. Then the church, the Church of the First Born, which our Lord at His coming will receive to Himself, will be a glorious church.

"So that He may present the church to Himself gloriously, having no spot or wrinkle or any such things, but holy and blameless." (Ephesians 5:27).

Discover with us the darkest hour of the Christian Age by turning the pages.

12

The Midnight Hour

1031 A.D.	1281 A.D.	1531 A.D.	1844 A.D.	2031 A.D.
5001 A.S.	5251 A.S.	5501 A.S.	5814 A.S.	6001 A.S.
	*You are here.			

The accession of the Roman Church to power in 538 A.D. marked the beginning of the dark ages, the midnight of the first millennium A.D. As her power gradually increased, the darkness deepened. Faith was transferred from the Christ, the true foundation, to the Bishop of Rome, the pope. Thus the minds of the people were turned from God to fallible, erring, and cruel men, no, more, to Satan himself, the prince of darkness, who exercises his power through them. With the elevation of human laws and traditions is manifested the corruption that ever results from setting aside the law of God.

Those were days of peril for the church of the Lamb of God. The faithful standard bearers were few indeed. Though the truth was not left without witnesses, at times it seemed that error, tradition, and superstition would totally prevail, and God centered religion would be banished from the earth. The gospel was lost from view, but the forms of religion were multiplied, and the people were burdened with rigorous exactions.

Notwithstanding that vice prevailed and continued to escalate over the years, even among the leaders of the Roman Church, her influence steadily increased. The church had rejected the truth of God and greedily accepted the deceptions of Satan.

The darkness seemed to grow more dense. In the evening of the second millennium another step in papal assumption was taken, when, in the eleventh century A.D., Pope Gregory VII proclaimed the perfection of the Roman Church, and the evening of the heavenly Day of Atonement began, 1 Nisan, 5001, spring of 1031 A.D.

The advancing centuries witnessed a constant increase of error in the doctrines put forth from Rome. Even before the establishment of the papacy the teachings of heathen philosophers had received attention and exerted an influence in the church. This prepared the way for the introduction of many of the inventions of paganism, which the Roman Church employs to terrify the credulose and superstitious multitudes.

In the thirteenth century was established that most terrible of all the engines of the papacy – the Inquisition. This truly was the Midnight hour for the chosen of the Lord, 1281 A.D. The prince of darkness wrought it through the leaders of the papal hierarchy. In their secret councils Satan and his angels controlled the minds of evil men, while unseen in the midst stood an angel of God, taking the fearful record of their iniquitous decrees and writing the history of deeds too horrible to appear to human eyes. The "Little Horn" of Daniel, the fifth head of the first "Beast" of Revelation 13, spiritual "Babylon" was "drunk with the blood of the saints." The mangled forms of millions of martyrs cry to God for vengeance upon this apostate power.

Popery had become the world's despot. Kings and emperors bowed and still bow to the decrees of the Roman pontiff. The destinies of men, both for time and for eternity, seemed under his control. For hundreds of years the doctrines of Rome have been extensively and implicitly received, it rites reverently performed, its festivals generally observed. Its clergy are honored and liberally sustained. Never since has the Roman Church attained to greater dignity, magnificence or power.

But "the noon of the papacy was the midnight of the world." – J.A. Wylie, *The History of Protestantism*, b. 1, ch. 4. By the sixteenth century A.D. the Scriptures were almost unknown, not only to the people, but to the priests. Like the Pharisees of old, the papal leaders hated the light which would reveal their sins. God's law, the standard of righteousness, having been removed, they exercised power without limit, and practiced vice without restraint. Fraud, avarice, and profligacy prevailed. Men shrank from no crime by which they could gain wealth or position. The palaces of popes and prelates were scenes of the vilest debauchery. Some of the reigning pontiffs were guilty of crimes so revolting that secular rulers endeavored to dispose of them as monsters too vile to be tolerated. For centuries Europe had made no progress in learning, arts, or civilization. A moral and intellectual paralysis had fallen upon Christendom.

The Inquisition has been called may things, from the resolute defender of Catholicism to the earliest version of the Nazi Gestapo. The Inquisition is indeed the midnight hours of the heavenly Day of Atonement in relationship to God's people here on Planet Earth. Its history is often confounded with racialism, religious tyranny, obnoxious legal procedures, the permanent delaying of modernization, and other equally regressive matters. For these reasons readings are selected that exemplify the historiography of the subject, as well as those that describe its workings. Indeed, to this day, the attitudes toward the Inquisition, to Holy Office as it was also named, among professional historians as well as laymen, are frequently an index of broadly liberal or conservative approaches to present-day issues affecting the world in general. Similarly specialized and popular interpretations of such great events as the American Civil War usually cast a long shadow on the present. The Inquisition – indeed, what to make of Europe»s great imperial past, of which the Holy Office was so significant a part – remains a burning coal in the national conscience and consciousness.

Precisely why is the study of this institution not merely an antiquarian endeavor? In a large part: (1) It is because the Inquisition's history so closely paralleled the time of national greatness, although it continued to function well beyond the mid-seventeenth century. Many of the tribunal's defenders, while often regretting its excesses as they saw them, still interpreted its role as a necessary constituent of that lost national supremacy in Europe and much of the world from about 1500 to

1650 A.D. (2) The Inquisition, in some form, will be reinstituted about 1 Nisan, 6001, the spring of 2031 A.D., closely paralleling the time of the United States of America's international greatness and will continue to function to the second coming of the Christ in the spring of 2036 A.D., 1 Nisan, 6006.

During the 1520's and 1530's A.D., the Inquisition acquired new grounds for its investigation which, however, were intimately related to its original jurisdictional reason for being, the scrutiny of the converted's religious sincerity. Illuminism – a peculiar form of mysticism, the most interior kind of religious experience – emerged in the first third of the sixteenth century with particular intensity among devout clergy and laymen (and women, who figured with unusual prominence, foreshadowing a St. Tersa in more ways than sex) of frequently New Christian background. The end of the fifteenth century and first decades of the new one – the classic pre-Reformation period – were marked in Europe by much religious reform and striving.

The outbreak of Protestantism, with its apparent similarities to Illuminism in the eyes of the inquisitors, permitted the inquisitors to tie the two firmly together and brand them as expressions of "Lutheranism."

The story of medieval persecution is a frightful one, and we dread to dwell upon its detail. Yet for a proper understanding it is necessary that some of the happenings of these unhappy times be presented. Albert Barnes, in his comment on the Inquisition remarks: "Can anyone doubt that this is true of the papacy? The Inquisition, the 'persecutions of the Waldenses' the ravages of the Duke of Alva; the fires of Smithfield; the tortures at Goa – indeed, the whole history of the papacy may be appealed to in proof that this is applicable to that power. If anything could have 'worn out the saints of the Most High' – could have cut them off from the earth so that evangelical religion would have become extinct, it would have been the persecutions of the papal power. In the year 1208 A.D., a crusade was proclaimed by Pope Innocent III against the Waldenses and Albigenses, in which a million of men perished. From the

75

beginning of the order of Jesuits, in the years 1540 to 1580 A.D., nine hundred thousand were destroyed. One hundred and fifty thousand perished by the Inquisition in thirty years. In the Low Countries fifty thousand persons were hanged, beheaded, burned, and buried alive, for the crime of heresy, within the space of thirty-eight years from the edict of Charles V against the Protestants, to the peace of Chateau Cambreses in 1559 A.D. Eighteen thousand suffered by the hand of the executioner in the space of five years and a half during the administration of the Duke of Alva. Indeed, the slightest acquaintance with the history of the papacy will convince anyone that what is here said of making war with the saints, and wearing out the saints of the Most High, is strictly applicable to that power, and will accurately describe its history."

These facts are confirmed by the testimony of V. E. H. Lecky. He declares: "That the Church of Rome has shed more innocent blood than any other institution that has ever existed among mankind, will be questioned by no Protestant who has a complete knowledge of history. The memorials, indeed, of many of her persecutions are now so scanty that it is impossible to form a complete conception of the multitude of her victims, and it is quite certain that no powers of imagination can adequately realize their suffering... These atrocities were not perpetrated in the brief paroxysms of a reign of terror, or by the hands of obscure sectaries, but were inflicted by a triumphant church, with every circumstance of solemnity and deliberation."

It makes no difference that in numerous instances the victims were turned over to the civil authorities. It was the church that made the decision upon the question of heresy, and it then passed the offenders over to the secular court. But in those days the secular power was but the tool in the hands of the church. It was under its control and did its bidding. When the church delivered its prisoners to the executioners to be destroyed, with fiendish mockery it made use of the following formula: "And we do leave and deliver thee to the secular arm, and to the power of the secular court; but at the same time do most earnestly beseech

76

that court so to moderate its sentence as not to touch thy blood, or to put thy life in any danger." Then, as intended, the unfortunate victims of popish hate were immediately executed.

The testimony of Lepicier is to the point in this connection: "The civil power can only punish the crime of unbelief in the manner and to the extent that the crime is judicially made known to it by ecclesiastical persons, skilled in the doctrine of the faith. But the church taking cognizance by herself of the crime of unbelief, can by herself decree the sentence of death, yet not execute it; but she hands over the execution of it to the secular arm."

The false claims of some Catholics that their church has never killed dissenters, have been flatly denied by one of their own standard writers, Cardinal Bellarmine, who was born in Tuscany in 1542 A.D., and who, after his death in 1621 A.D., came very near being placed in the calender of saints on account of his great service in behalf of the church. This man, on one occasion, under the spur of controversy, betrayed himself into an admission of the real facts in the case. Luther having said that the church (meaning the true church) never burned heretics. Bellarmine, understanding it of the Roman Catholic Church, made answer: "This argument proves not the sentiment, but the ignorance or impudence of Luther; for as almost an infinite number were either burned or otherwise put to death. Luther either did not know it, and was therefore ignorant; or if he knew it, he is convicted of impudence and falsehood – for that heretics were often burned by the church, may be proved by adducing a few from many examples."

Alfred Baudrillart, rector of the Catholic Institute of Paris, when referring to the attitude of the church toward heresy, remarks: "When confronted by heresy, she does not content herself with persuasion; arguments of an intellectual and moral order appear to her insufficient, and she has recourse to force, to corporal punishment, to torture. She creates tribunals like those of the Inquisition, she calls the laws of state to her aid, if necessary she encourages a crusade, or religious war, and all her 'horror of blood' practically culminates into urging secular power to shed it, which proceeding is almost more odious – for it is less frank – than shedding it herself.

"Especially did she act thus in the sixteenth century with regard to Protestants. Not content to reform morally, to teach by example, to convert people by eloquent and holy missionaries, she lit in Italy, in the Low Countries, and above all in Spain, the funeral piles of the Inquisition. In France under Francis I and Henri II, in England under Mary Tudor, she tortured the heretics, while both in France and Germany, during the second half of the sixteenth, and the first half of the seventeenth centuries, if she did not actually begin, at any rate she encouraged and actively aided the religious wars."

In a letter of Pope Martin V (A.D. 1417-1431), are th following instructions to the King of Poland: " 'Know that the interest of the Holy See, and those of your crown, make it a duty to exterminate the Hussites. Remember that these impious persons date proclaim principles of equality; they maintain that all Christians are brethern, and that God has not given to privileged men the right of ruling the nations; they hold that Christ came on earth to abolish slavery; they call the people to liberty, that is, to the annihilation of kings and priests! Whilst there is still time, then, turn your forces against Bohemia; burn, massacre, make deserts everywhere, for nothing could be more agreeable to God, or more useful to the cause of kings, than the extermination of the Hussites.' "

All this was in harmony with the teaching of the church. Heresy was not to be tolerated, but to be destroyed.

Pagan Rome persecuted the Christian church relentlessly. It is estimated that three million Christians perished in the first three centuries of the Christian Era. Yet it is said that the primitive Christians prayed for the continuance of imperial Rome, for they knew that when this form of government should cease, another far worse persecuting power would arise, which would literally wear out the saints of the Most High. Pagan Rome could slay the infants, but spare the mothers; but papal Rome slew both the mothers and infants together. No age, no sex, no condition in life, was exempt from her relentless rage.

The condition of the world under the Romish power presented a fearful and striking fulfillment of the words of the prophet Hosea:

78

"My people are destroyed for lack of knowledge: Because you have rejected knowledge, I will also reject you: ... seeing you have forgotten the law of your God, I will also forget your children." "There is no truth, nor mercy, nor knowledge of God in the land. By swearing, lying, killing, stealing, and committing adultery, they break out, and blood touches blood." (Hosea 4:6, 1, 2).

Such are the results of banishing the word of God.

With the Reformation the Morning Has Broken, please read on.

13

The Morning Breaks

1031 A.D.	1620 A.D.	1776 A.D.	1798 A.D.	2031 A.D.
5001 A.S.	5590 A.S.	5746 A.S.	5768 A.S.	6001 A.S.
	*You are here.			

The name "Protestant" is a battle-name, Kriegsname — so writes a German professor in Bonn. In the light of the days of the Reformation, this, indeed, is what Protestantism overall came to mean. The times were bad, politically, religiously, ethically, socially – and especially in the precincts of the holy church. One must never forget the almost incredible abyss of tyranny, superstition, cold formalism, bigotry, sanctified authoritarianism, intolerance, corruption into which the Roman church had slumped, nor fail to remember and appreciate the heroism of those who stood out so boldly against everything that is sentimentally dear, even against the corporate promise of eternal salvation of the soul – if one is to understand what Protestantism originally meant.

It is true, that we now like to stress the word "Protestant" as meaning a positive "witness" to a faith. But such charity must not offset the historical realism of the genesis of the Reformation. All institutions with time get set into frozen patterns of belief and behavior and even Protestants suffer from this inexorable law of potential stagnation and decay. It is a law of life that life moves toward death; and it is a corollary law that if life is to retain itself it must undergo vigorous regeneration.

The Catholic church in its own counter Reformation has acknowledged some of the mistakes and evils of that day and would now wish that Luther had had better handling by Pope Leo V, so as to have averted the tragedy to itself of the split from its ranks. But the Reformation is deeper than that. It cut at roots, not branches. It would individualize man before his God and remove some of the machinery that stood in the way in expressing his own inner conscience. It was a fearful and yet great day in the history of Christianity. We will see again the likes of such heroes as fought so willingly with their lives for the recovery of the spirit of the common man.

Protestantism itself, as time went on, proved to be no angel of reform since it took up, in many instances, the very tools of iniquity which plagued those early in the strife. We do well not to extol the warriors of reform unduly for they, too, were men of their times. It would be folly to quote them indiscriminately and approvingly for everything they did. The appeal to their writings and savings as proof-texts is the appeal to authority all over again, a lack of remembrance that the life of the spirit has continually to be recharged as men come to see the errors of the past and to reach out for further illumination in the things that matter most.

Protestantism means fundamentally, eternal vigilance against the forces which continually endeavor to encase the human spirit. It remains a "battle-name" in the core of its heritage and in the essential mission of its general point-of-view. It means protesting not alone against Catholicism but a protesting against any form of Protestantism itself, or any religion, which usurps power over individual conscience and over the spirit of freedom in the realm of man's inner life. It means this today, and in the future, as much as any yesterday. It means reforms, if necessary, down to the roots, of its own traditions. There continues to be Protestants protesting against Protestants after the first guns were fired and its own history, and its future, is full of the tragic accounts of martyrs within its own household.

It is hoped that the impression is created – and historical it is – that other than being a witness to something (and it was) the Protestant spirit essentially is a battle-name against unwholesome infringements of the Word of God (be they of creed, councils, books, catechisms, theology, ecclesiastical polity, confessions, heroes) against the on-moving forces of the spirit of life. The battle is never finished and we must be prepared for neo-Protestants of whatever kind in the days to come – if we are of this historic tradition or pretend to be.

The great movement, the Reformation that Wycliffe inaugurated, and Luther propagated, along with many others, which liberated the conscience and the intellect, and set free the nations so long bound to the triumphal car of Rome, had its spring in the Bible. Here is the source of that stream of blessing, which, like the water of life, flows down the ages, and to us, since the sixteenth century. The Holy Scriptures were accepted with implicit faith as the inspired revelation of God's will, a sufficient rule of faith and practice. Wycliffe had been educated to regard the Roman Catholic Church as the divine, infallible authority, and to accept with unquestioning reverence the established teachings and customs of a thousand years; but he turned away from all these to listen to God's Holy Word. This was the authority which he urged the people to acknowledge. Instead of the church speaking through the pope, he declared the only true authority to be the voice of God speaking through His Word. He taught not only that the Bible is a perfect revelation of God's will, but that the Holy Spirit is its only interpreter, and that ever man is, by the study of its teachings, to learn his duty for himself. Thus the minds of men and women were turned from the pope and the Church of Rome to the Word of God.

The doctrines which had been taught, not only traversed England, but scattered to other lands, carrying the knowledge of the gospel. Now that Wycliffe was removed by the hand of God, the preachers labored with even greater zeal than before, and multitudes flocked to listen to their teachings. Some of the nobility, and even the queen were among the converts. In many places there was marked reform in the manners of the people, and the idolatrous symbols of Romanism were removed from the churches. But soon the pitiless storm of persecution burst upon those who had dared to accept the Bible as their guide. The monarchs, eager to strengthen their power by securing the support of Rome, did not hesitate to sacrifice the Reformers. For the first time in the history of England the stake was decreed against disciples of the gospel. Martyrdom succeeded martyrdom. The advocates of truth, proscribed and tortured, could only pour their cries into the ear of the Lord of Sabaoth. Hunted as foes of the church and traitors to the realm, they continued to preach in secret places, finding shelter as best they could in the humble homes of the poor, and often hiding away even in dens and caves.

One of the noblest testimonies ever uttered for the Reformation was the protest offered by the Christian princes of Germany at the Diet of Spires in 1529 A.D. The courage, faith, and firmness of those men of God gained for succeeding ages liberty of thought and conscience. Their protest gave to the reformed church the name of Protestant; its principles are "the very essence of Protestantism."

It is believed by many that the Reformation ended with Luther in the mid 1500's A.D. It did not. The Reformation is to be continued to the close of this world's history. Luther had a great work to do in reflecting to others the truth which God and permitted to shine upon him; yet he did not receive all the truth which was given to the world. From that time to this, new understanding has been continually shining upon the Scriptures, and new truths are constantly unfolding.

But Satan was not idle in the past, and is not idle today. He now attempts what he has always attempted in every reformatory movement – to deceive and destroy the people by palming off upon them a counterfeit in place of the true work. As there has always been in the body of the people of God, there were false christs and false prophets in the body of the first century Christian church, so there arose false christs and false prophets in the sixteenth century. These false teachers continue to the second coming of the Christ, and go into perdition with the Dragon, the Apostate beast, and the false prophet in 2036 A.D.

The fruit of the new teaching soon became apparent. The people are led to neglect the Bible or to cast it wholly aside. The schools are thrown into confusion. Students, spurning all restraint, abandoned their studies and withdraw from the schools. The men who think themselves competent to revive and control the work of Reformation succeed only in bringing it to the verge of ruin. The Apostates now regain their confidence and exclaim exultingly: "One last struggle, and all will be ours."

Satan is constantly seeking to deceive mankind and lead them to call sin righteousness and righteousness sin. How successful is his work!!! How often censure and reproach are cast upon God's faithful servants because they will stand fearlessly in defense of the truth! Men who are but agents of Satan are praised and flattered, and even looked upon as martyrs, while those who should be respected and sustained for their fidelity to God are left to stand alone, under suspicion and distrust.

In the sixteenth century the Reformation, presenting an open Bible to the people, had sought admission to all the countries of Europe. Some nations welcomed it with gladness, as a messenger of Heaven. In other lands the papacy succeeded to a great extent in preventing its entrance; and the truth of Bible knowledge, with its elevating influences, was almost wholly excluded. In one country, though the light of God's Word found entrance, it was not comprehended by the darkness. For centuries, truth and error struggled for the mastery. At last the evil triumphed, and the truth of Heaven was thrust out.

"This is the condemnation that light is come into the world, and men loved darkness rather than light." John 3:19.

The nation was left to reap the results of the course which she had chosen. The restraint of God's Spirit was removed from a people that had despised the gift of His grace. Evil was permitted to come to maturity. And all the world saw the fruit of willful rejection of the light of truth.

The war against the Bible, carried forward for so many centuries in France, culminated in the scenes of the Revolution. That terrible outbreaking was but the legitimate result of Rome's suppression of the Scriptures. It presented the most striking illustration of the papal policy – and illustration of the results to which for more than a thousand years the teaching of the Roman Church had been tending.

Counterfeit holiness, spurious sanctification, is still doing its work of deception. Under various forms it exhibits the same spirit as in the days of old, diverting minds from the Scriptures and leading men to follow their own feelings and impressions rather than to yield obedience to the law of God. This is one of Satan's most successful devices to cast reproach upon purity and truth.

Had the Reformation, after attaining a degree of success, consented to temporize, to secure favor with the world, it would have been untrue to God and to itself, and would thus have ensured its own destruction. The experience of the noble Reformers contains a lesson for all succeeding ages. Satan's manner of working against God and His Word has not changed; he is still as much opposed to the Scriptures being made the guide of life as in the ages past. Today there is a wide departure, an apostasy from their doctrines and precepts, and there is need of a return to the great Protestant principle – the Bible, and the Bible only, as the rule of faith and duty. Satan is still working through every means which he can control to destroy religious liberty. The antichrist power, which the protesters of Spires rejected, is now with renewed vigor seeking to re-establish its lost supremacy. The same unswerving adherence to the Word of God manifested at that crisis of the Reformation is the only hope for the people of God today.

The Puritans in England, like the Lutherans, Calvinists and Jesuits on the Continent, thought to bring men nearer to the knowledge and service of God as they saw it. Their search for reality and purity in religion shattered the unity of the great Christian church, the Roman Catholic Church of the Dark and the Middle Ages, and destroyed the authority it had exercised over the minds of men for centuries. By the end of the sixteenth century Christians were separated from each other as never before, but there was arising already a new respect for freedom of the individual conscience, and a new desire to discover the essential truths of Christianity which was to lead them into fresh ways of unity in our own times.

It's High Noon as the United States of America comes upon the scene, so turn the pages and enjoy.

14

High Noon,
The Birth of a Nation

1031 A.D.	1776 A.D.	1798 A.D.	2001 A.D.	2031 A.D.
5001 A.S.	5746 A.S.	5768 A.S.	5971 A.S.	6001 A.S.

*You are here.

New nations generally rise by overthrowing other nations, and taking their place. But no other nation was overturned in order to make room for the United States of America.

The United States, after gaining its independence in 1776 A.D., the high noon of the millennium, grew in relative peace over the years as a plant might grow as it springs forth from the earth. It is a remarkable fact that this same figure has been chosen by political writers as the one conveying the best idea of the manner in which the United States has arisen. George Alfred Townsend says: "In this web of islands, the West Indies, began the life of both Americas. There Columbus saw land; there Spain began her baneful and brilliant Western empire: thence Cortez departed for Mexico, De Soto for the Mississippi, Balboa for the Pacific, and Pizarro for Peru. The history of the United States was separated by a beneficent Providence far from this wild and cruel history of the rest of the continents, and like a silent seed we grew into an empire; while empire itself, beginning in the South, was swept by so interminable hurricane that what of its history we can ascertain is read by the very lightenings that devastated it. The growth of English America may be likened to a series of lyrics sung by separate singer, which, coalescing, at last make a vigorous chorus, and this, attracting many from afar, swells and is prolonged, until presently it assumes the dignity and proportions of epic song."

86

A writer in the Dublin Nation spoke of the United States as a wonderful empire which was "emerging," and "amid the silence of the earth daily adding to its power and pride."

Edward Everett, in an oration on the English exiles who founded this government, said: "Did they look for a retired spot, inoffensive for its obscurity, and safe in its remoteness, where the little church of Leyden might enjoy the freedom of conscience? Behold the mighty regions over which, in peaceful conquest – victoria sine clade (victory without strife) – they have borne the banners of the cross."

Will the reader now look at these expressions side by side – "coming up out of the earth," "emerging amid the silence of the earth," "like a silent seed we grew into an empire," "mighty regions" secured by "peaceful conquest." The first is from the prophet, stating what would be when the two-horned beast should arise; the others are from political writers, telling what has been in the history of the United States of America. Can anyone fail to see that the last three are exactly synonymous with the first, and that they record a complete accomplishment of the prediction?

Another inquiry naturally follows: Has the United States "come up" in a manner to meet the specifications of the prophecy? Let us see. A short time before the great Reformation in the days of Martin Luther, more than four centuries ago, this Western hemisphere was discovered. At the mid-night hour of the millennium, the Reformation awoke the nations that were fettered in the galling bonds of superstition and oppression, to the great truth that it is the heaven-born right of every man to worship God according to the dictates of his own conscience. But rulers, spiritual and secular, are loath to lose their power. Under these circumstances, a body of religious heroes at length determined to seek in the wilds of America that measure of civil and religious freedom which they so much desired. In pursuance of their noble purpose, one hundred of these voluntary exiles landed from the "Mayflower" on the coast of New England, December 21, 1620 A.D. "There," said Martyn, "New England was born," and this was "its first baby cry, a prayer and a thanksgiving to the Lord."

Another permanent English settlement had been made at Jamestown, Virginia, in 1606 A.D. In process of time, other settlements were made and colonies organized, which were all subject tot he English crown till the Declaration of Independence, July 4, 1776 A.D.

The population of these colonies amounted in 1701 A.D. to 262,000; in 1749 A.D., to 1,046,000; in 1775 A.D. to 2,803,000. Then came the struggle for independence, the establishment of a united constitutional government, and the proclamation to the world that here all could find an asylum from oppression and intolerance. From the Old World came immigrants by the thousands, adding by peaceful means to the population and prosperity of the new nation. Large territories were purchased or acquired by treaty to make room for all who came to settle. Now, passing over more than 200 years, to the fourth quarter of the twentieth century, the territory of the United States has expanded to more than four million square miles, and its population has exploded to over 6,000,000,000 people.

The growth of the United States in material prosperity and enlightened development is an astonishment to the world, and furnishes an ample basis for the application of the prophecy.

As a power the United States, in the beginning, answered, in respect to its age, to youthfulness, innocence, and gentleness, while no other power can be found to do this. Considered as an index of power and character, it can be decided what constitutes the government, if it can be ascertained what is the secret of its power, and what reveals its character, or constitutes its outward profession. The Hon. J. A. Bingham gives us the clue to the whole matter when he states that the object of those who first sought these shores was to find "what the world had not seen for ages; viz., a church without a pope, and a state without a king." Expressed in other words, this would be a government in which the ecclesiastical should be separate from civil power, and civil and religious liberty would be characteristic.

It needs no argument to show that, in the beginning, this was precisely the profession of the American government.

88

Article IV., sec. 4, of the Constitution of the United States, reads in part: "The United States shall guarantee to every State in this Union a republican form of government." Article VI: "No religious test shall ever be required as a qualification to any office or public trust under the United States." The First Amendment to the Constitution begins as follows: "Congress shall make no law respecting an establishment of religion, or prohibiting the free exercise thereof." These articles profess the amplest guarantee of civil and religious liberty, the entire and perpetual separation of church and state.

There is no crown connected with a nation with a republican form of government. A crown is an appropriate symbol of a kingly or dictatorial form of government, and the absence of crowns, as in this case, suggests a form of government in which the power is not vested in any such ruling member, but is lodged in the hands of the people.

The two-horned beast of Revelation 13 symbolizes a nation which cannot be Roman Catholic in religion. The papacy is a religion that is fundamentally a union of church and state. The Constitution of the United States of America (Article VI) declares that "No religious test shall ever be required as a qualification to any office or public trust..." and thereby establishes a perpetual separation of church and state. Civil and religious liberty is a fundamental principle of Protestantism. The founders of this great land, living close to all of the events that resulted from a union of church and state, were jealous of the liberties that they claimed as the rights of all, and were quick to denounce anything that savored of a union of church and state. From the religious stand-point, therefore, the United States is a Protestant nation, and meets the requirement of the prophecy of Revelation 13 admirably in this respect. Thus again the prophecy points directly to this nation.

Before entering upon a discussion of another aspect of this prophetic symbol, the two-horned beat of Revelation 13, lets review the points already established.

The United States meets the requirement of a nation distinct from the powers of the Old World, whether civil or ecclesiastical.

The United States arose in the Western Hemisphere.

The United States assumed a position of prominence and influence about the year 1798 A.D. She declared her independence 1776 A.D., and confirmed it in 1812 A.D.

The United States rose in a peaceful and quiet manner, not augmenting its power and expanding its territory, as other nations have done, by aggressive wars and successful conquests.

The United States progressed so quickly as to strike the beholder with as much wonder as would the perceptible growth of an animal, or plant, before his eyes.

The United States is republican in its form of government.

The United States is Protestant in its form of religion.

The United States exhibits before the world, as an index of its character these elements of government, two great principles which are in themselves perfectly just, innocent, and lamb-like.

The United States has grown in size and power at a phenomenal rate since her humble beginnings in the 1700s A.D.

As the tidings spread through the countries of Europe, of a land where every man might enjoy the fruit of his own labor and obey the conviction of his own conscience, thousands flocked to the shores of the New World. Colonies rapidly multiplied. Massachusetts, by special law, offered free welcome and aid, at the public cost, to Christians of any nationality who might fly beyond the Atlantic to escape from wars or famine, or the oppression of their persecutors. Thus the fugitive and the downtrodden were, by statute, made the guests of the commonwealth. In twenty years from the first landing at Plymouth, as many as a thousand Pilgrims were settled in New England.

To secure the object which they sought, they were content to earn substance by a life of frugality and toil. They asked nothing from the soil but the reasonable returns of their labor. No golden vision threw a deceitful halo around their path. They were content with the slow but steady progress of their social polity. They patiently endured the privation of the wilderness, watering the tree of liberty with tears, and with the sweat of their brow, till it took deep root in the land.

The Bible was held as the foundation of faith, the source of wisdom, and the charter of liberty. Its principles were diligently taught in the home, in the school, and in the church, and its fruits were manifest in thrift, intelligence, purity, and temperance. One might be for years a dweller in the Puritan settlement, and not see a drunkard, or hear an oath, or meet a beggar. It was demonstrated that the principles of the Bible are the surest safeguards of national greatness. The feeble and isolated colonies grew to a confederation of powerful states, and the world marked with wonder the peace and prosperity of a church without a pope, and a state without a king.

But continually increasing numbers were attracted to the shores of America, actuated by motives widely different from those of the first Pilgrims. Though the primitive faith and purity exerted a widespread and molding power, yet its influence became less and less as the numbers increased of those who sought only worldly advantages.

The regulation adopted by the early colonist, of permitting only members of the church to vote and to hold office in the civil government, led to most pernicious results. This measure had been accepted as a means to preserving the purity of the state, but resulted in the corruption of the church. A profession of religion being the condition of suffrage and office holding, many, actuated solely by motives of worldly policy, united with the church without a change of heart. Thus the churches came to consist, to a considerable extent, of unconverted persons; and even in the ministry were those who not only held errors of doctrine, but who were ignorant of the renewing power of the Holy Spirit. Thus again was demonstrated the civil results, so often witnessed in the history of the church from the days of Constantine to the present, of attempting to build up the church by the aid of the state, of appealing to the secular power in support of the gospel of Him who declared: "My kingdom is not of this world." (John 18:36). The union of the church with the state, be the degree ever so slight, while it may appear to bring the world nearer to the church, does in reality but bring the church nearer to the world.

The great principle so nobly advocated by Robinson and Roger Williams, that truth is progressive, that Christians should stand ready to accept all the truth which shines from God's holy Word, was lost sight of by their descendants. The Protestant churches of America – and those in Europe as well – so highly favored in receiving the blessings of the Reformation, failed to press forward in the path of reform. Though a few faithful men arose, from time to time, to proclaim new truth and expose long cherished error, the majority, like physical Israel in the Christ's day or the papist in the time of Luther, were content to believe as their fathers had believed and to live as they had lived. Therefore religion again degenerated into formalism; and errors and superstitions which would have been cast aside had the church continued to walk in the truth of the Word of God, were retained and cherished in the Protestant churches as in the Roman Church in the time of Luther. There was and is the same worldliness and spiritual stupor, a similar reverence for the opinions of men, and substitution of human theories for the teachings of God's Word.

The wide circulation of the Bible in the early part of the nineteenth century, and the great truths thus shed upon the world was not followed by a corresponding advance in knowledge of this revealed truth, or in experimental religion. Satan could not, as in former ages, keep God's Word from the people; it had been placed within the reach of all; but in order to still accomplish his objective, he led many to value it but lightly. Men neglected to search the Scriptures, and thus they continued to accept false interpretations, and to cherish doctrines which had no foundation in the Bible.

Seeing the failure of his efforts to crush out the truth by persecution, Satan had again resorted to the plan of compromise which led to the great apostasy and the formation of the Church of Rome. He had induced Christians to ally themselves, not now with pagans, but with those who, by their devotion to the things of this world, had proved themselves to be as truly idolaters as were the worshipers of graven images. And the results of this union were no less pernicious now than in former ages; pride and extravagance were fostered under the guise of religion, and the churches became corrupted. Satan continued to pervert the doctrines of the Bible, and traditions that were to ruin millions were taking deep root. The church was upholding and defending these traditions, instead of contending for the faith which was once delivered unto the saints. Thus were degraded the principles for which the Reformers had done and suffered so much.

The second coming of the Lord is the day that all believers should long, hope, and wait for as being the accomplishment of all the work of their redemption, and all the desires and endeavors of their souls. Such was the hope of the apostolic church, of the church in the wilderness, and of the Reformation.

Prophecy not only foretells the manner and object of the Christ's coming, but presents tokens by which men are to know when it is near, even at the door, even the hour. Jesus said: "There will be signs in Jerusalem, the sun, moon, and stars..." (Matthew 24:29; Luke 21:24, 25). "But in those days, after that tribulation, the sun will be darkened and the moon will not shed her light, the stars will be falling from and the heavens will be shaken; and, "...until the period of the Gentiles is completed." Men neglect to search the Scriptures, and thus they continue to accept it but lightly. Then will they see the Son of Man coming in the clouds with great power and glory." (Mark 13:24-26). The revelator thus describes first of the signs preceding the second coming: "I saw a tremendous earthquake occur. The sun turned as black as sackcloth and the full moon became as blood." (Revelation 6:12).

These signs were witnessed before the opening of the nineteenth century. In fulfillment of this prophecy there occurred, in the year 1775 A.D., the most terrible earthquake that has ever been recorded. Though commonly known as the earthquake of Lisbon, it extended to the greater part of Europe, Africa, and

America. It was felt in Greenland, in the West Indies, in the island of Madeira, in Norway and Sweden, Great Britain and Ireland. It pervaded an extent of not less than four million square miles. In Africa the shock was almost as severe as in Europe. A great part of Algiers was destroyed; and a short distance from Morocco, a village containing eight to ten thousand inhabitants was swallowed up. A vast wave swept over the coast of Spain and Africa engulfing cities and causing great destruction.

Twenty-five years later appeared the next sign mentioned in the prophecy – the darkening of the sun and a blood moon. What rendered this more striking was the fact that the time of its fulfillment had been definitely pointed out. In the Christ's conversation with the disciples after describing the long period of tribulation for the church – the 1260 years of papal persecution, concerning which He had promised that the tribulation should be shortened – He thus mentioned certain events to precede His coming, and fixed the time when the first of these should be witnessed: "But in those days, after that tribulation..." (Mark 13:24). The 1260 years terminated in 1798 A.D. Twenty-five years earlier, persecution had almost wholly ceased. Following this persecution, according to the words of the Christ, the sun was to be darkened. On the 19th of May, 1780 A.D., this prophecy was fulfilled.

Said eyewitnesses of the scene: "I could not help conceiving at the time, that if every luminous body in the universe had been shrouded in impenetrable shades, or struck out of existence, the darkness could not have been more complete. Though at nine o'clock that night the moon rose to the full, it had not the least effect to dispel the deathlike shadows. At midnight the darkness disappeared, and the moon, when first visible, had the appearance of blood.

May 19, 1780 A.D., stands in history as "The Dark Day." Since the time of Moses no period of darkness of equal density, extent, and duration, has ever been recorded. The description of this event, as given by witnesses, is but an echo of the words of the Lord, recorded by the prophet Joel, twenty-five hundred years previous to their fulfillment:

"The sun shall be changed into darkness, and the moon into blood, before the coming of the day of the Lord, dark and terrible." (Joel 2:31).

In 1833 A.D. the third of the signs appeared which were promised by the Saviour as a token of His coming. Jesus said, "...The stars will fall from the sky..." (Matthew 24:29). And John in the Revelation declared, as he viewed in vision the scenes that would herald the great day of God Almighty:

"The stars of heaven fell to the earth as when a fig tree, shaken by a violent wind, drops its unripe fruit." (Revelation 6:13).

This prophecy received a striking and impressive fulfillment in the great meteoric shower of November 13, 1833 A.D. That was the most extensive and wonderful display of falling stars which has ever been recorded; the whole sky, over the United States, being then, for hours, in fiery commotion! No celestial phenomenon has ever occurred in this country, since its first settlement, which was viewed with such intense admiration by one class in the community, or with so much dread and alarm by another. For years its sublimity and awful beauty lingered in many minds. Never did rain fall much thicker than the meteors fell toward the earth; east, west, north, and south, it was the same. In a word, the whole heavens seemed in motion. From two o'clock until broad daylight, the sky being perfectly serene and cloudless, an incessant play of dazzlingly brilliant luminosities was kept up in the whole heavens.

The fourth sign came to fruition in 1967 A.D., and with it we come closer in pinpointing the time of His return. The Saviour said concerning physical Israel of His day:

"They will fall by the edge of the sword and will be carried off as prisoners to all nations. And Jerusalem will be trampled down by the Gentiles until the period of the Gentiles is completed." (Luke 21:24).

The Christ had bidden His people to watch for the signs, the markers, of His return and rejoice as they should behold the tokens of their coming King. He said:

"When these things begin to occur, straighten up and lift up your heads, because your deliverance is near." (Luke 21:28)

He referred to the budding trees of spring, and said:

"When they are fully budding, you know by looking at them that summer is in the offing. Similarly when you notice these things taking place, be assured that the kingdom of God is near." (Luke 21:30-31).

He further adds:

"...And Jerusalem will be trampled down by the Gentiles, until the period of the Gentiles is completed." "I assure you that all this will happen before this generation passes away." (Luke 21:24, 32).

As you turn the pages you will learn more about this wonderful country we live in.

15

The Chronology of
The United States of America

1031 A.D.	1492 A.D.	1776 A.D.	1798 A.D.	2031 A.D.
5001 A.S.	5462 A.S.	5746 A.S.	5768 A.S.	6001 A.S.

*You are here.

1492-1504	Columbus' four voyages to the New World.
1497-1498	John Cabot explores Newfoundland, Labrador, and Nova Scotia, and establishes English claim to North America.
1508-1509	Sebastian Cabot explores Hudson Bay.
1509-1547	Henry VIII.
1513	Ponce de Leon discovers mainland of Florida.
1523	Verrazano explores coast of North America, establishing French claim.
1534	Cartier's explorations established French claim to St. Lawrence basin.
1539-1541	De Soto explores southeastern United States and discovers the Mississippi.
1540-1542	Coronado seeks legendary cities of wealth in North American Southwest.
1558-1603	Elizabeth I.
1574	Gilbert leads expedition to Hudson Bay.
1585-1587	Raleigh's Roanoke Colony fails.
1603-1625	James I.
1607	Virginia Company establishes Jamestown settlement.
1619	First Africans arrive in Virginia; First representative assembly meets.
1620	Mayflower Compact signed; Pilgrims establish Plymouth Colony.

1624	Virginia Company charter annulled; English crown takes control of Virginia; First settlements in New Netherlands by Dutch.
1625-1649	Charles I.
1629	Massachusetts Bay founded.
1630	Puritan emigration from England begins.
1632	Cecilius Calvert, Lord Baltimore, receives charter for Maryland colony.
1634	First settlement in Maryland.
1635	Roger Williams banished from Bay Colony.
1636	Harvard College founded; First permanent English settlement in Connecticut and Rhode Island.
1638	Anne Hutchinson convicted of heresy in Massachusetts; flees to Rhode Island.
1643	Confederation of New England.
1644	Rhode Island receives patent.
1647	Law requiring towns to maintain schools passed in Massachusetts Bay Colony
1649	Charles I beheaded; Maryland Toleration Act.
1660-1685	Charles II.
1663	Carolina charter granted to eight proprietors; Rhode Island granted charter.
1664	English take over New Netherlands; Grant of New Jersey to two proprietors.
1670	Settlement of Charleston.
1675-1676	King Philip's War in New England.
1676	Bacon's Rebellion.
1677	Culpeper's Rebellion in Carolina.
1680	New Hampshire given royal charter.
1681	Pennsylvania charter granted to William Penn; First settlement in 1682.
1686	Dominion of New England.
1688	Glorious Revolution in England drives out James II (1685-88) in favor of William and Mary.
1689-1691	Leisler's Rebellion, New York.

1692	Witchcraft hysteria in Salem, Massachusetts; nineteen "witches" hanged, one pressed to death.
1696	English government establishes Board of Trade and Plantations; passage of comprehensive navigation act, extending admiralty courts to America.
1699	Woolen Act.
1732	Georgia established to furnish buffer against Spanish and as philanthropic effort to locate England's paupers; Hat Act.
1733	Molasses Act restricts colonial importation of sugar goods from French West Indies.
1734-1735	Jonathan Edward's evangelical revival in Northampton, Massachusetts and Connecticut River Valley.
1735	New York jury acquits John Peter Zenger of charges of seditious libel on grounds that printing truth can be no libel.
1739-1740	George Whitefield tours America and brings major phase of Great Awakening.
1750	Iron Act, limiting production of finished iron goods in colonies, passed by Parliament.
1751	Currency Act, restricting issuance of paper money in New England colonies, passed by Parliament; Publication of Franklin's Experiment and Observations on Electricity.
1754	Albany Congress and Plan of Union.
1754-1763	French and Indian War (colonial phase of Europe's Seven Year's War. 1756-63).
1759	Quebec falls to British army.
1760-1820	George III.
1763	Treaty of Paris ends Seven Year's War between Great Britain, and France and Spain; Pontiac's rebellion, uprising of Indians in Ohio Valley; Proclamation line drawn along Appalachians by British forbids settlement in West; Paxton uprising by Scotch-Irish settlers in Western Pennsylvania.

1764	Sugar Act; Currency Act prohibits issues of legal-tender currency in the colonies.
1765	Stamp Act; Stamp Act Congress meets in New York; Quartering Act.
1766	Stamp Act repealed by Parliament, which adopts Declaratory Act asserting its authority to bind the colonies "in all cases whatsoever."
1767	Townshend Duties passed; American Board of Customs established; John Dickinson's Letters from a Farmer in Pennsylvania.
1768	British troops sent to Boston.
1770	Lord North's ministry; Townshend duties repealed, except for duty on tea; Boston massacre.
1772	British schooner Gaspee burned in Rhode Island; Boston committee of Correspondence formed.
1773	Tea Act imposed; Boston Tea Party.
1774	Coercive or Intolerable Acts; Continental Congress meets in Philadelphia; Galloway's Plan of Union.
1775	Battle of Lexington and Concord; Fort Ticonderoga taken by American forces; Second Continental Congress meets in Philadelphia; George Washington appointed commander in chief of Continental army; Battle of Bunker Hill; Congress adopts its "Declaration of the Causes and Necessities of Taking Up Arms."
1776	Thomas Paine's Common Sense; Declaration of Independence; British troops evacuate Boston; Battle of Long Island, New York; British take New York City; Battle of Trenton.
1777	Battle of Princeton; Battle of Monmouth; Battle of Brandywine, Pennsylvania; British occupy Philadelphia; Battle of Germantown; Burgoyne surrenders at Saratoga; Articles of Confederation adopted by Continental Congress, but not ratified by all states until 1781; Washington retires to Valley Forge for winter.

1778	United States concludes military alliance and commercial treaty with France; British evacuate Philadelphia; Seize Savannah, Georgia.
1779	Spain enters the war against Britain; George Rogers Clark captures Vincennes and ends British rule in Northwest.
1780	Americans surrender 5500 men and the city of Charleston, South Carolina; Battle of Camden, South Carolina; Battle of King's Mountain, South Carolina.
1781	Battle of Cowpens, South Carolina; British under Tarleton defeated by Morgan; Battle of Guilford Courthouse, North Carolina; Cornwallis withdraws to coast; Cornwallis surrenders to Washington at Yorktown, Virginia.
1782	Fall of Lord North's ministry.
1783	Treat of Paris with Britain signed.
1785	Land Ordinance for Northwest Territory adopted by Congress.
1786	Jay-Gardoqui Treaty rejected by Congress; Virginia Statute for religious Freedom; Shay's Rebellion in western Massachusetts; Annapolis Convention adopts plan to meet in Philadelphia to revise Articles of Confederation.
1787	Federal Constitutional Convention meets in Philadelphia; Northwest Ordinance enacted by Congress; The Federalist Papers by Madison, Hamilton, and Jay.
1788	Ratification of United States Constitution by all states except Rhode Island and North Carolina.
1789	First session of Congress meets; Washington inaugurated as first President; Outbreak of French Revolution.
1790	Hamilton's Report on Public Credit; Father John Carrol made first Roman Catholic bishop of United States.

1791	Bank of the United States established; First ten amendments to Constitution (Bill of Rights) adopted.
1792	Washington reelected.
1793	Citizen Genet Affair; Samuel Slater erects first cotton mill at Pawtucket, Rhode Island; Eli Whitney applies for patent on cotton gin.
1794	Whiskey Rebellion in western Pennsylvania; Battle of Fallen Timbers, Ohio; General Anthony Wayne defeats Indians.
1796	Washington's Farewell Address, warning against foreign entanglements and domestic factions; John Adams elected President.
1798	XYZ Affair reported by Adams to Congress; Quasi-war with France on high seas; Alien and Sedition Acts enacted by Federalists in Congress; Virginia and Kentucky resolutions.
1800	Washington, D.C., becomes capital; Thomas Jefferson elected President.
1801	War with Barbary states; John Marshall becomes chief justice.
1803	Marbury v. Madison, Supreme Court upholds right of judicial review; Louisiana Purchase; Lewis and Clark expedition begun.
1804	Hamilton killed by Vice-President Raymond Burr in duel; Jefferson reelected.
1807	Embargo Act; Robert Fulton's steamboat travels on Hudson River from albany to New York in 30 hours.
1808	Congress prohibits Americans from participating in African slave trade; James Madison elected President.
1809	Embargo repealed; Nonintercourse Act passed, prohibiting trade with Britain and France.
1810	Macon's Bill No. 2 passed, restoring trade with Britain and France, but providing for trade restrictions to be reimposed on one of the powers if other should abandon its seizure of American ships.

1811	Madison, believing Napoleon has removed restrictions of American commerce, prohibits trade with Britain; Battle of Tippecanoe, Indiana, in which William Henry Harrison defeats Tecumseh and prevents formation of Indian confederacy.
1812	Congress declares war against Britain; Americans surrender Detroit to British; Madison reelected.
1813	Battle of Lake Erie, Captain Oliver Perry defeats British navel forces; Battle of the Thames; General Harrison defeats British and their Indian allies.
1814	Battle of Horseshoe Bend, Alabama; General Andrew Jackson defeats Creek Indians fighting for British; British burn Washington, D.C.; Commander Thomas Macdonough defeats British fleet on lake Champlain; invading British turned back at Plattsburgh, New York; Hartford, Convention of Federalist delegates from New England; Treaty of Ghent signed between United States and Great Britain.
1815	Battle of New Orleans, Jackson defeats British; North American Review founded in Boston.
1816	Second Bank of the United States chartered by Congress; Protective tariff passed; James Monroe elected President.
1818	General Jackson invades Florida to end Seminole War; Rush-Bagot Convention between British and United States Established fishing rights and Canadian boundary.
1819	Depression begins; Adams-Onis Treaty; Spain cedes Florida; Dartmouth College Case; McCulloch v. Maryland.
1820	Missouri Compromise; Re-election of James Monroe without opposition, "Era of Good Feelings."
1822	Denmark Vesey's Conspiracy.
1823	President issues Monroe Doctrine.
1824	John Quincy Adams elected President by House of

	Representatives after failure of any candidate to win electoral majority.
1828	John C. Calhoun's anonymous South Carolina Exposition and Protest; Congress passes "Tariff of Abominations"; Election of Andrew Jackson as President brings victory to new Democratic Party.
1830	Jackson vetoes Maysville Road Bill; Anti-Masonic Party holds first national party convention.
1831	Natt Turner's slave insurrection in Virginia.
1832	Beginning of Jackson's "war" against Second Bank of the United States (BUS); Special convention in South Carolina nullifies new protective tariff; Jackson reelected President.
1833	Congress provides for a gradual lowering of tariffs, but passes Force Bill authorizing Jackson to enforce federal law in South Carolina.
1836	Jackson's "specie circular"; Martin Van Buren elected President.
1838	Aroostook War.
1840	Congress passes Van Buren's Independent Treasury Act; William H. Harrison elected President; Whigs in power; World antislavery convention; American Female Moral Reform Society organized as first national female reform association.
1841	John Tyler becomes President upon Harrison's death.
1842	Webster-Ashburton Treaty settles disputed U.S.-Canada boundary.
1843	First overland caravans to Oregon.
1844	Senate rejects Calhoun's Texas annexation treaty; James K. Polk elected President; Lowell Female Reform Association organized.
1845	Texas enters Union as slave state; John Slidell's unsuccessful mission to Mexico to negotiate purchase of New Mexico and California; Margaret Filler published *Woman in the Nineteenth Century*.
1846	Beginning of Mexican War; General Zachary Taylor

invades Mexico from the North; Treaty with Britain divides Oregon Territory along 49th parallel.

1847   General Winfield Scott captures Vera Cruz and Mexico City.

1848   Gold discovered in California; Van Buren, running for President on Free-Soil ticket, receives 10 percent of popular vote; Zachary Taylor elected President; Treaty of Guadalupe Hidalgo ends Mexican War, establishes Rio Grande as border; First Women's Rights Convention at Seneca Falls, New York; Elizabeth Cady Stanton drafts "Declaration of Sentiments."

1849   California gold rush.

1850   In Congress, sectional debate culminates in Compromise of 1850; Fugitive Slave Law requires federal agents to recover escaped slaves from sanctuaries in the North; Taylor's death makes Millard Fillmore President.

1851   Herman Melville's *Moby Dick*.

1852   Franklin Pierce elected President.

1853   Upsurge of political nativism, the Know-Nothing Party.

1854   Spectacular Know-Nothing election victories; Collapse of Whigs; New Republican Party; Commodore Perry opens Japan to American trade; Kansas-Nebraska Act rekindle sectional controversy over slavery; "Bleeding Kansas."

1856   John Brown's raid at Pottawatomie Creek; James Buchanan elected President.

1857   Dred Scott v. Sanford; In Kansas, proslavery Lecompton Constitution ratified as free-state men refuse to vote.

1858   Lincoln-Douglas debates.

1859   John Brown's raid on Harpers Ferry.

1860   Democratic Party, deadlocked at Charleston convention, divides along sectional lines at Baltimore;

	Abraham Lincoln elected President; South Carolina secedes from Union.
1861	Secession of remaining states of deep South (Texas, Louisiana, Mississippi, Alabama, Georgia, and Florida); Jefferson Davis begins serving as President of the Confederate States of America; Firing on Fort Sumter precipitates war; Secession of Virginia, North Carolina, Tennessee, and Arkansas; Union army routed at first Battle of Bull Run (Manassas); McCellan heads Union Forces; Trent affair; Vassar College founded.
1862	Both Union and Confederacy adopt paper money; Union general, U.S. Grant, captures Fort Henry and Fort Donelson; Battle of the ironclads; Virginia (Merrimack) vs. Monitor; McCellan's army to outskirts of Richmond, the Confederate capital; Robert E. Lee becomes commander of army of northern Virginia; Confederate victory at second battle of Bull Run; Stalemate between Lee and McCellan at Antietam; Confederate invasion of Kentucky; Lincoln issues preliminary Emancipation Proclamation; Confederate victory at Fredericksburg.
1863	Lincoln issues final Emancipation Proclamation; Confederates defeat Union army under Hooker at Chancellorsville; Lee's invasion of North checked by Union army under Meade at Gettysburg; Grant captures Vicksburg; Draft riots in the North; Confederate army under Bragg defeats Union forces at Chickamauga; Union victory at Chattanooga (Lookout Mountain and Missionary Ridge); Lincoln offers lenient reconstruction program.
1864	Grant named Union general in chief; Grant's direct advance on Richmond checked at the Wilderness, Spotsylvanis, and Cold Harbor; Lincoln reelected President; Sherman marches from Atlanta to the sea.

1865	Sherman pushes northward through South Carolina and North Carolina; Lee gives up Petersburg and Richmond; Lee surrenders at Appomattox; Lincoln assassinated; Andrew Johnson becomes President; Johnson moves for speedy, lenient restoration of southern states to Union; Thirteenth Amendment ratified.
1866	Johnson breaks with Republican majority in Congress by vetoing Freedoman's Bureau bill and Civil Rights bill (passed over his veto); Congress approves Fourteenth Amendment; Ku Klux Klan formed.
1867	Congress passes Military Reconstruction Act over John's veto; Congress passes Tenure of Office Act and Command of Army Act to reduce Johnson's power.
1868	Former Confederate states hold constitutional conventions, for which former slaves are allowed to vote, and adopt new constitutions guaranteeing universal suffrage; President Johnson impeached; escapes conviction by one vote; Republican Ulysses S. Grant elected President.
1869	Congress passes Fifteenth Amendment; National Women Suffrage Association founded by Elizabeth Cady Stanton and Susan B. Anthony; American Women Suffrage Association founded by Lucy Stone and Henry Blackwell.
1870	First Ku Klux Klan (or enforcement) Act gives Grant power to move against white Terrorist in South.
1874	Women's Christian Temperance Union organized by Annie Wittenmeyer.
1876	Republicans nominate Rutherford B. Hayes for President; Democrats nominate Samuel J. Tilden. Tilden secures majority of popular vote but electoral vote is in doubt because of disputed returns from three southern states; General Custer's defeat at Little Bighorn; Alexander Graham Bell transmits first telephone message; End of Reconstruction;

Declaration of Women's Rights read at Centennial Exposition, Philadelphia.

1877   After political and economic bargaining, Congress creates an electoral commission, which rules that all disputed ballots belong to Hayes, who is inaugurated; Munn v. Illinois.

1878   Bland-Allison Act; Greenback Labor Movement; "Anthony Amendment" first introduced in Congress.

1879   Frances Willard gains presidency of Women's Christian Temperance Union.

1880   Garfield elected President.

1881   Helen Hunt Jackson, a *Century of Dishonor*; Garfield assassinated; Arthur becomes President.

1882   Pendleton Civil Service Act.

1884   Cleveland elected President.

1885   Josiah Strong, *Our Country*.

1886   AFL organized; Haymarket Massacre.

1887   Interstate Commerce Act; Dawes Severalty Act; Edward Bellamy, Looking Backward, 2000-1887.

1888   Harrison elected President.

1890   Sherman Antitrust Act; Sherman Silver Purchase Act: "Battle" of Wounded Knee; McKinley Tariff; Alfred Thayer Mahan, The Influence of Sea Power Upon History; National Woman Suffrage Association and American Woman Suffrage Association merge to form National American Woman Suffrage Association.

1892   Cleveland elected to Presidency again; Homestead Strike; General Federation of Women's Clubs established.

1893-1897   Depression.

1894   "Cosey's Army"; Pullman Strikes; Coin's Financial School.

1895   Venezuelan boundary dispute; United States v. E. C. Knight.

108

1896	McKinley elected President; Plessy v. Ferguson; National Association of Colored Women founded.
1898	Spanish-American War; Hawaiian Islands annexed.
1899	Thorarein Veblen, *The Theory of the Leisure Class*; National Consumer's League founded.
1899-1900	Open Door Notes.
1900	Gold Standard; McKinley reelected.
1901	United States Steel Corporation formed; Platt Amendment; Assassination of McKinley; Theodore Roosevelt becomes President; Hay-Pauncefote Treaty.
1902	Newlands Act.
1903	Departments of Commerce and Labor established; Elkins Antirebate Act; Hay-Bunau-Varilla Treaty; Women's Trade Union League founded.
1904	Roosevelt Corollary to Monroe Doctrine; Roosevelt elected President; Northern Securities Company v. United States.
1905	Portamouth Peace Conference; Lochner v. New York.
1906	Hepburn Act; Pure Food and Drug Act; Meat Inspection Act; Algeciras Conference.
1907	Gentleman's Agreement with Japan.
1908	White House Conservation Conference; Muller v. Oregon; Taft elected President.
1909	Payne-Aldrich Tariff.
1910	Mann-Elkins Act; Ballinger-Pinchot Controversy.
1911	Triangle Shirtwaist Company fire.
1912	Socialist nominate Eugene Debs for President; Progressives nominate Theodore Roosevelt on Bull-Moose Ticket; Wilson elected President.
1913	Sixteenth Amendment, Popular Election of United States Senators; Underwood Tariff; Federal Reserve Act; Charles Beard, An Economic Interpretation of the Constitution of the United States; Congressional Union funded by Alice Paul and Lucy Burns.

1914	Federal Trade Commission Act; Clayton Antitrust Act; Margaret Sanger writes *Family Limitation*.
1915	Sinking of the Lusitania; National Birth Control League founded by Mary Ware Dennett to include wide middle-class membership.
1916	Adamson Act; Federal Farm Loan Act; Jones Act; Wilson reelected President; Sinking of Sussex; National Woman's Party founded as outgrowth of Congressional union and split-off from NAWSA.
1917	United States enters World War I on April 6; Espionage Act; Lever Food and Fuel Control Act; Russian Revolution.
1918	Wilson's Fourteen Points; Sedition Act; War Finance Corporation; Republicans gain control of Congress; Armistice Day, November 11.
1919	League of Women Voters founded.
1919-1920	Red Scare.
1920	Palmer Raids, January 2; Harding elected President; Nineteenth Amendment; Women acquire the right to vote; Women's Bureau of the Department of Labor founded; Transportation Act; Sinclair Lewis, Main Street.
1921-22	Washington Armament Conference.
1923	President Harding dies, August 2; Calvin Coolidge becomes President; Equal Rights Amendment first introduced by National Women's Party.
1924	Immigration Restriction Act; Dawes Plan; Coolidge elected President.
1925	F. Scott Fitzgerald, *The Great Gatsby*; Scopes trial.
1927	Charles Lindbergh flies solo across the Atlantic; Sacco and Vanzetti executed.
1928	Hoover elected President.
1929	Black Thursday, October 24 (stock market crash); Young Plan; Ernest Hemingway, *A Farewell to Arms*; Agricultural Marketing Act.
1930	London Naval Conference; Hawley-Smoot Tariff.

1931	Hoover Debt Moratorium; Japanese invasion of Manchuria.
1932	Stimson Doctrine, Reconstruction Finance Corporation; Glass-Steagall Act; Bonus Army; Roosevelt elected President.
1933	"Hundred Days" session of Congress; Agricultural Adjustment Acts; Emergency Banking Act; Tennessee Valley Authority; Civilian Conservation Corps; National Industrial Recovery Act; United States recognizes Soviet Union; Twenty-first Amendment ratified, repealing prohibition.
1934	Gold Reserve Act; Securities and Exchange Act; Platt Amendment abrogated.
1935	National Labor Relations Act; Social Security Act; Works Progress Administration.
1936	Roosevelt reelected; Butler v. United States.
1937	Administrative Reorganization Act; Congress of Industrial Organizations (CIO).
1938	Munich Agreement.
1939	War breaks out in Europe, September 1.
1940	United States preparedness and defense measures; Battle of Britain; Roosevelt reelected.
1941	Battle of the Atlantic; Lend-Lease Act; Atlantic Charter; Japanese attack Pearl Harbor, December 7.
1942	Battle of Coral Sea; Allied campaign in North Africa.
1943	Casablanca Conference; Allies invade Italy; Terheran Conference.
1944	Invasion of Europe; landing at Normandy, June 6; Roosevelt reelected; Battle of the Bulge.
1945	Yalta Conference; Germany surrenders; Atomic Bomb dropped on Hiroshima, August 6; Japan surrenders; United Nations formed; Roosevelt dies; Truman becomes President; Potsdam Conference.
1947	Marshall Plan proposed; Taft-Hartley Act; Truman Doctrine.

1948	Truman elected President; Berlin Blockade; Creation of State of Israel.
1949	North Atlantic Treaty Organization.
1950	Korean War; McCarran Act; Rise of Senator Joseph McCarthy as popular anti-Communist.
1951	General Douglas MacArthur fired by Truman.
1952	Eisenhower elected President.
1953	Stalin dies; Korean ceasefire.
1954	Southeast Asia Treaty Organization; Geneva Conference on Indochina; Senate censure of Joseph F. McCarthy; Brown v. Board of Education of Topeka; Communist Control Act; Atomic Energy Act.
1955	Geneva Summit Meeting.
1956	Suez Crisis; Eisenhower reelected President; Hungarian Revolt.
1957	Eisenhower Doctrine; Sputnik; Eisenhower sends paratroopers to Little Rock.
1958	National Defense Education Act.
1959	Eisenhower and Khrushchev meet at Camp David.
1960	Kennedy elected President.
1961	Bay of Pigs; Berlin Wall; Peace Corps.
1962	Cuban missile Crisis; President Kennedy appoints Commission on the Status of Women; Prayer removed from schools, 25 June.
1963	Test Ban Treaty; Kennedy is assassinated, November 22; Lyndon B. Johnson becomes President; Betty Friedan publishes *The Feminine Mystique*.
1964	Gulf of Tonkin Resolution passes Senate with two votes against it; Johnson elected President; Civil Rights Act.
1965	Voting Rights Act; Medicare; Elementary and Secondary Education Act.
1966	National Organization for Women (NOW) formed.
1968	Tet offensive in Vietnam, January-February; Martin Luther King assassinated, 4 April; Nixon elected President.

1969	Moon landing, Apollo 11.
1970	American invasion of Cambodia.
1971	Kissinger's secret trip to Peking.
1972	Nixon reelected; Congress passes the Equal Rights Amendment.
1974	Nixon resigns Presidency; Ford becomes President.
1976	Carter elected President.
1977	Panama Canal Treaties.
1978	Camp David Agreements.
1979	Three Mile Island Nuclear Accident.
1980	Reagan elected President.
1980-1981	Iranian hostage crisis.
1982	Equal Rights Amendment fails to gain ratification.
1983	Soviets shoot down Korean Airlines jet over Russian airspace; 241 United States Marines killed in airport compound, Beirut, Lebanon; United States invades Grenada.
1984	Reagan reelected President.
1986	Tax Reform Act.
1988	George Bush elected President.
1990	Air Quality Act.
1991-1992	Crisis in the Gulf.
1992	Los Angeles riots; Bush reelected President.
1994	Bill Clinton elected President; Gay Rights Act; Abortion Act.
1995	? ? ? ? ? ? ? ? ? ? ? ?
1996	? ? ? ? ? ? ? ? ? ? ? ?

16

The United States, a Christian Nation?

1031 A.D.	1776 A.D.	1798 A.D.	2001 A.D.	2031 A.D.
5001 A.S.	5746 A.S.	5768 A.S.	5971 A.S.	6001 A.S.
	*You are here.			

The concept of America as a "Christian nation" has been with this country since its origins. Most often, the term has sparked controversy and ill will because it has been used to elevate the role of one faith over others and to further the politics of exclusion on the basis of religious belief. This explains why so many Americans are offended when public officials use the term today.

The idea that the United States should be officially Christian was explicitly rejected by James Madison and the other formers of the Constitution. Instead, they provided for a system of separation of church and state that guarantees religious freedom for all individuals and groups – Christian and non-Christian alike.

Nevertheless, the concept of America as a Christian society has been strongly advocated by religious conservatives since the colonial period, and the movement reoccurs frequently in history. Over the years, even some judges and assorted government officials have expressed sympathy for that viewpoint.

No God In The Constitution: To the modern-day Religious Right, these assertions are proof that the United States is, or once was, officially a "Christian nation." Most constitutional scholars believe otherwise. They point out that the Constitution contains no references to God, Jesus the Christ, or Christianity – a deliberate move on the part of the framers who thought government should be given no power to intrude into religious matters. (During the debates surrounding the drafting and ratification of the Constitution, a minority faction argued for some

114

sort of official recognition of Christianity, but its views were rejected.) Had a Christian nation been the intent of the framers, historians point out, the concept would have been featured prominently in the Constitution.

U.S. Not Founded On Christianity: Many Religious Right boosters are also unaware that officials of the early U.S. government on at least one occasion formally declared that the United States was not founded on the Christian faith. The treaty of Tripoli, a trade agreement signed between the United States and the Muslim region of North Africa in 1797 A.D., bluntly states that "the Government of the United States is not, in any sense, founded on the Christian religion."

The language was inserted into the document by trade negotiator Joel Barlow. The Senate approved the agreement indicating that they saw the provision as non-controversial and in line with the character of the new nation's government. (The treaty was signed by John Adams, the second president, and the provision cited above remained in it for eight years until the agreement was renegotiated.)

Unable to find much support for the "Christian nation" concept in post-Revolutionary War America, Religious Right activists look to a different period of history as their model for a Christian republic – a period that began before the Civil War and extended well into the 20th century.

State Courts Speak Out: Church-state matters during these decades were left chiefly to state legislators, and disputes, if they occurred at all, were usually resolved by state court. Judges at this level were often appointed through political patronage systems. As a result, decisions sometimes emerged that today are seen as at odds with religious freedom and separation of church and state.

Many state courts in the 19th century did refer to the United States as a "Christian nation" or implied that Christianity should receive some type of special favor from the state. James Kent, a New York Supreme Court justice, declared in an 1811 A.D. blasphemy case, "The people of this state, in common with the people of this country, profess the general principles of Christianity as the rule of their faith and practice; and to scandalize the author of these doctrines is not only a religious point of view, extremely impious, but even in respect to the obligations due to society, is a gross violation of decency and good order."

Arguments From the Supreme Court: The U.S. Supreme Court even fell victim to this "Christian nation" mentality on one occasion. Religious Right activists frequently cite 1892 A.D.'s Holy Trinity Church v. United States decision as proof that the high court considered the United States to have a religious foundation. However, they usually do not tell the whole story.

In the ruling, Justice David Brewer flatly declared "this is a Christian nation." To this day, historians debate what Brewer meant by the term. It is unclear whether he meant to say the country's laws should reflect Christian moral principles or was simply acknowledging the fact that most Americans are Christians and that Christianity has played a prominent role in American life.

A strong argument can be made for the latter proposition by examining a case that came along five years after the Holy Trinity ruling. The dispute centered on legalized prostitution in New Orleans, insisting that the activity is inconsistent with Christianity "which the Supreme Court of the United States says is the foundation of our government ... "

Writing for a unanimous court, Brewer completely ignored the congregation's argument and upheld the New Orleans policy. Brewer's bypass suggests that he did not mean to imply in Holy Trinity that the United States should enforce the dictates of Christianity by law. Had that been the justice's intention, he surely would have upheld the Methodist's claim.

Possibly because his phrase was being taken out of context, Brewer felt compelled to explain his views in greater detail. In 1905 A.D., he published a short book titled *The United States A Christian Nation*. In that volume Brewer elaborates on what he meant in the famous Holy Trinity passage. "But in what sense can (the United States) be called a Christian nation?" asked Brewer. "Not in the sense that Christianity is the established religion or the people are compelled in any manner to support it. On the contrary, the Constitution specifically provides that 'Congress shall make no law respecting an establishment of religion or prohibiting the free exercise thereof.' Neither is it Christian in the sense that all its citizens are either in fact or in name Christians. On the contrary, all religions have free scope within its borders. Numbers of our people profess other religions, and many reject all."

Continued Brewer, "Nor is it Christian in the sense that a profession of Christianity is a condition of holding office or otherwise engaging in public service, or essential to recognition either politically or socially. In fact, the government as a legal organization is independent of all religion."

The passage strongly suggests that Brewer simply meant that the United States is "Christian" in the sense that many of its people belong to Christian denominations and many of the country's customs and traditions have roots in Christianity. Brewer expounds on this theme for the rest of his 98-page book, predicting that Christianity will one day unify the American masses and make the United States a leader in world affairs.

Whatever Brewer's intent, it is important to realize that the Christian nation concept has never been embraced by the Supreme Court as officially binding judicial policy. The Holy Trinity ruling, for example, is a legal anomaly that has been cited as precedent only once by the Supreme Court since it was handed down.

American Government Is Not Religiously Grounded: It is also important to note that not all 19th century courts saw the American government as religiously grounded. As early as the 1840s A.D., judges began questioning the legal basis for the doctrine. In 1872 A.D., the Ohio Supreme Court expressly rejected a claim grounded on the Christian nation concept. "Those who make this assertion (that America is a Christian nation) can hardly be serious, and intend the real import of their language," the court wrote. "If Christianity is a law of the State, like every other law, it must have a sanction. ...No one seriously contends for any such doctrine in this country, or I might say, in this age of the world."

Moving Toward A Constitutional Amendment: With judicial rulings falling on both sides of the issue, 19th century precursors of today's Religious Right organizations sought to promote the Christian nation concept by securing passage of a constitutional amendment that would grant official endorsement to Christianity.

The movement was spearheaded by the National Reform Association (NRA), a coalition formed in 1863 A.D. by representatives from 11 Protestant denominations. One of the group's stated goals was "to secure such an amendment to the Constitution of the United States as will declare the nation's allegiance to Jesus, the Christ, and its acceptance of the moral laws of the Christian religion, and so indicate that this is a Christian nation..."

In 1864 A.D. the group petitioned Congress to amend the preamble of the Constitution, adding a section "humbly acknowledging Almighty God as the source of all authority and power in civil government, the Lord Jesus Christ as the Ruler among the nations, His revealed will as the supreme law of the land, in order to constitute a Christian government."

Precursor To Sabbath Laws And Religious Tests: Critics charge that the "Christian amendment" was clearly designed to be the first step in a broader NRA agenda. The group also advocated strict enforcement of blasphemy and Sabbath laws, religious tests for public officeholders, limits on divorce, and an increase in the religious content in the nation's public schools.

The NRA's Christian nation amendment languished in Congress for years, occasionally being reintroduced in different versions. Finally in 1874 the House Judiciary Committee voted against its adoption. The congressional panel said it took the action "in full realization of the dangers which the union between church and state had imposed upon so many nations of the Old World, with great unanimity that it was inexpedient to put anything into the Constitution or frame of government which might be construed to be a reference to any religious creed or doctrine."

Other "Christian America" amendments resurfaced periodically, and such proposals were introduced in Congress as late as 1965

A.D. This time the proposed addition to the Constitution would have had the United States "devoutly" recognize "the authority and law of Jesus Christ, savior and ruler of nations, through whom are bestowed the blessings of almighty God." One of the measure's sponsors was U.S. Rep. John Anderson (R-Ill.). When Anderson ran for president as an independent in 1980 A.D., he dismissed the effort as a foolish move by a young congressman. "It was a dumb thing to do," he said, "and I should not have introduced it."

A Secular Government: Indiana State University history professor Richard V. Pierard says today's Religious Right activists push the Christian nation concept because they dislike the idea of a secular government. "The Religious Right sees America almost in a sacred sense," observed Pierard. "They are not willing to accept the idea that we have a secular state. They are still living in a 19th century vision of America. That's were this comes from."

Pierard points out that fundamentalist Christian influence over government and society was at its peak in the 19th century. Public schools reflected generic Protestantism, communities enforced laws curtailing commerce and other activities on Sunday and religious based censorship of the arts was common. "They want to go back to that," he said. "But in the 20th century we've come to realize America is a much more complex society. The genius of the American system is that in religious matters the government remains neutral. This environment allows all to practice their religious faiths freely and not impose them through government."

The Christian Right: In a fund-raising letter (1992 A.D.), religious broadcaster Pat Robertson resurrected the Holy Trinity decision as part of an appeal for donations for his legal arm, the American Center for Law and Justice. The politically influential evangelist noted that "One hundred years ago, a landmark Supreme Court ruling reaffirmed America's identity as a Christian nation."

Other Religious Right leaders have made comments that the United States is or ought to be a Christian nation. In his autobiography *Right From The Beginning*, conservative commentator Pat Buchanan refers to the United States as "A once-Christian country that has been force-fed the poisons of paganism."

Christian Right propagandist David Barton takes a similar tack in his widely circulated book *The Myth Of Separation*. "Our Father intended," he argues, "that this nation should be a Christian nation; not because all who lived in it were Christians, but because it was founded on, and would be governed and guided by Christian principles."

Generally speaking, when Religious Right leaders use the term "Christian nation," they are referring to their desire to see the nation's laws reflect the narrow sectarian principles they themselves hold – not simply saying that most Americans identify with Christian denominations. These misguided activists want to send a signal that only those individuals with the "correct" religious views are real Americans.

Mainstream American religious denominations do not use the term "Christian nation" or speak of such a concept as desirable, recognizing that it offends and excludes those Americans who are not affiliated with the Christian faith. Thus, the term is closely tied to the Religious Right and its extreme religio-political goals. Today, as in previous eras of American life, it is unmistakably a term of exclusion, not inclusion.

Turn the pages to read of the spiritual freedom of the United States of America in its infancy and enjoy what remains.

17

Spiritual History of
The United States of America

1031 A.D.	1614 A.D.	1776 A.D.	1798 A.D.	2031 A.D.
5001 A.S.	5584 A.S.	5746 A.S.	5768 A.S.	6001 A.S.

*You are here.

The New England Puritans: In 1607 A.D., as the first Englishmen reached the Jamestown peninsula, some of their countrymen were being thrown into jail for their religious practices. In Lincolnshire, William Brewster, leader of a group of religious dissenters known as Separatists, and his young friend, seventeen year old William Bradford, were among those imprisoned for several months. Separatists, so called for their desire to separate from the Church of England, incurred the wrath of King James I, Elizabeth's successor (1603-1625 A.D.) and the first of the Scottish Stuart monarchs, who declared that a Separatist was like "a rat to be trapped and tossed away."

Brewster, Bradford, and a small group of Separatists fled to the Nether lands in 1611 A.D., and in 1620 A.D. cemented an agreement with the London Company of Virginia to finance their emigration to America. In September 1620 A.D. the 180-ton bark Mayflower left Plymouth Sound with 102 colonists, and after a voyage of 65 days they reached Cape Cod on November 9.

In New England in 1620 A.D. at least one Indian spoke English. Squanto, or Tisquantum as he called himself, was a pawtuxet Indian who years before had been taken to England by English explorers, converted to Christianity, and returned to find that his entire tribe had succumbed to smallpox. Settling among the Wampanoags near the coast, Squanto befriended the

121

Pilgrims, served as their interpreter in negotiations with the Wampanoag chief Massassoit, and showed them how to fish and "set their corn". The grateful Pilgrims, who celebrated their first Thanksgiving in October 1621 A.D., viewed Squanto as "a special instrument sent of God."

To secure their government in this unknown land, the leaders of these Separatists had drafted on shipboard an agreement that has come to be known as the Mayflower Compact, embodying the principle of government by majority rule. Every adult male who intended to be a part of the Separatist community signed it, and it has held a special place in the American imagination ever since as a model for the formation of government by free consent. And since the Mayflower landed outside the boundaries prescribed by the Virginia Company charter, the Company document would have no authority to serve on its own as the form of government for the settlement. With William Brewster as their first governor, the Pilgrims named their colony Plymouth, after the English seaport they had left behind. In 1691 Plymouth colony would become part of the larger Puritan colony of Massachusetts.

Boston: The Massachusetts Bay Company, organized in 1629 A.D. by a group of well-to-do English Puritans, received from the King a charter granting it land in present-day New England and elsewhere to the South. Members of the Company signed a document, known as the Cambridge Agreement, to settle with their families in the new land, provided that they be allowed to take the charter and government of the Company with them. Nothing in the charter required the Company to maintain headquarters in England, and the transfer was arranged. The Company elected as its governor John Winthrop, a solid country squire. Within the year, Winthrop and ten other members of the Company had set sail for America with a fleet of eleven ships carrying 800 adults and children with them. They arrived in Massachusetts in July 1630 A.D. In the next decade, as persecutions of Puritans increased, more than 20,000 would come to New England in what has been called the Puritan

Migration. From the start, the immigration of families distinguished the settlement of New England. The presence of as nearly as many women as men among the Puritans guaranteed that the settlement would grow in population. Women's presence further guaranteed the accomplishment of basic domestic tasks necessary for survival. Perhaps because of that, these New England colonists, with the exception of those at Plymouth the first winter, did not suffer the dreadful mortality of Virginia's early years. By the end of 1630 the Puritans had established six settlements besides Boston.

While they saw themselves as a religious people specially chosen by God and believed that "God sifted as a whole nation that He might bring choice grain over into the wilderness," they realized that not everyone had come to New England for religious reasons.

The Puritan government enacted into law the Biblical injunctions against drunkenness, adultery, murder, theft, and violations of the Sabbath, and otherwise attempted to regulate the religion and morality of the people. Yet Massachusetts Bay was not a theocracy; its ministers did not run the government. And as the colony developed in the seventeenth century, it was by no means a guilt-ridden, pleasure-denying society. Its members engaged in lively and profitable commerce; they developed a bright if decorous social life and did not prohibit alcohol; and well-educated Puritans read secular as well as religious literature. Government of the church was the domain of the members of the congregation; and the government of the town was also the domain of the members of the local church.

Puritan Theology: Economic ambition had combined with religion in the founding of the colony, and many settlers had land or opportunity as their motive. The prevailing creed, however, was Puritan. This creed was heavily John Calvin, best known for his belief in predestination; that those who were to be saved had been so chosen from the beginning of time. Calvin's premise might be taken to mean that there was no need to make any effort to be moral and good since salvation had already been granted. Not so; orthodox ministers in Massachusetts observed that religious conversion, an intense personal experience of salvation would be attended by diligent pursuit of a "calling" or earthly occupation and a life of fervent prayer and good works. Industriousness, charity, and the other virtues were considered a consequence of salvation, a continuing act of gratitude, a joyful expression of faith of the saved, as Calvinists called them, the elect.

Not all Puritans reasoned the same way from these premises, and not all agreed even on the principle of cooperation among congregations. One who shared none of the Puritans' values was Thomas Morton, an adventurer whose followers fraternized with the Indians and enjoyed drinking freely and dancing around a maypole at Mt. Wollaston, near Plymouth. The Puritans disapproved of his conduct and shipped him back to England in 1628 A.D. Settlers who shared Puritan values but disputed specific points of the colony's religious practices were a good deal more troublesome.

Rhode Island: In 1631 A.D., Roger Williams, a clergyman of great personal charm, arrived in Massachusetts and became minister of the congregation at Salem. He began immediately to point out the numerous defects he saw in the Massachusetts scheme of things, declared the colony's charter invalid because it had not purchased the land from the Indians, and delivered such seditious doctrines as that no government should have authority over religious matters. When large numbers began to share those views the government found it necessary to banish him, least the foundation for all authority in Massachusetts be undermined. In 1636 A.D., he went down the coast to Narragansett Bay, established a settlement he named Providence, which he said would be a "shelter for persons distressed of conscience," and for almost half a century presided as the spiritual head of what became the colony of Rhode Island and Providence Plantations – a haven for religious nonconformists. Roger Williams is sometimes mistaken for an early secular liberal. He was not. His opposition to government coercion of conscience was founded in his intense religiosity, not his concern for civil liberties. Williams was a Separatist. This group wished not to control and reform the church established and enforced by government, but to separate themselves from all state religion as a sinful worldly institution.

In 1638 A.D. the colony's authorities tried and banished another religious dissident. Anne Hutchinson, the daughter of a minister, wife of a prosperous cloth-merchant, and mother of eleven children, had arrived with her family in 1634 A.D. She soon emerged as a charismatic amateur theologian. Holding informal meetings in her home to discuss the Sunday sermons, she began to attack leading ministers, accusing them of teaching the doctrine that good works are the means to redemption. She started to propound on beliefs, commonly called Antinomianism, which by a rough translation from the Greek means "against the law". It amounts to the belief that the Christian, where love of the Christ burns in the human spirit, is no longer under the cold law of reason, custom, and government. More specifically, Anne Hutchinson rejected the authority of the Puritan ministers.

The words of this formidable early New England woman found a receptive audience among some women who were conscious of regularly risking their lives – and confronting eternity – in childbirth, and among those merchants who favored the development of a more mobile and commercial society in the new world. Even the most learned ministers had difficulty in countering the hair-splitting logic of her reasoning. As increasing numbers of Bostonians embraced Anne Hutchinson's doctrines, she became even more dangerous to the established authorities than Roger Williams had been. John Winthrop described her as "a woman of a haughty and free carriage, of a nimble wit and active spirit ... more bold than a man." Spurred on by Winthrop, the authorities reacted sharply, accusing her and her followers of heresy. She was condemned by both civil and religious authorities and banished. She and her family, along with a number of loyal followers, moved to Rhode Island.

In the 1630s A.D. other Massachusetts colonists settled elsewhere, many simply out of an urge to have room to move around in, physically and politically. In 1635 A.D. a group settled along the Connecticut River. The Reverend Thomas Hooker led his flock west also, to establish Hartford. In 1639 these new towns, choosing to place themselves outside the jurisdiction of Massachusetts, drew up an agreement called the Fundamental Orders. They established their own government, which differed from the one in Massachusetts in a single important feature: suffrage was not confined to church members only.

Maryland: In the 1630s A.D. religion was a primary motive for the founding of another colony to the south of the Puritans. Roman Catholics were isolated within an England of Protestants – Anglican, Puritan, and Separatist. One of these Catholics was Sir George Calvert, Lord Baltimore, who wanted to expand his land holdings. The charter of 1632 A.D., by which the Crown granted to his son, Cecilius, the vast estate that would become the colony of Maryland constituted the fulfillment of the plans George Calvert had begun.

Roman Catholics never settled in Maryland in large numbers, and Protestants soon sought greater influence. During the 1640s A.D. the militant Protestants of the period of the English Civil War put the Calvert family on the defensive. In 1649 A.D. the Maryland assembly adopted an act, framed by Lord Baltimore in response to pressure in England and America and in response to his own conscience, that guaranteed religious toleration to the Christians. Maryland, like the New England colonies and Virginia, felt the shock waves from Civil War and revolution in England.

The Beginnings of "Salutary Neglect": In 1642 A.D., the Puritan Parliament in England began open civil warfare with the Anglican Royalists.

From the Civil War until the restoration of the Stuarts, England was occupied with argument, war, and experiment, and the colonies were orphaned, virtually independent of the mother country. During these times they nurtured institutionally and socially.

In the Spanish empire, government financed all of the overseas colonies and supervised them closely. The governing body of Spain's New World empire was the Council of Indies, which was directly subordinate to the Spanish monarchy. The Council was directly responsible for all religious, political, and civil activities of the crown officials in the Americas and in the Philippines.

The British empire was quite different. The first of the British colonies were financed by private joint-stock companies; the English government had little to do with funding or operating them. The Chesapeake colonies of Virginia and Maryland, and the settlements in New England, evolved largely on their own, and then during the twenty years of the English Civil War the government largely ignored them. With little outside interference, the early British colonies developed a powerful sense of independence and self-sufficiency. Their size and population growth made Virginia and Massachusetts especially strong-willed. When the British government attempted to impose central controls over the highly independent North American colonies in the 1760s A.D. and 1770s A.D., the result would be revolution. Virginia and Massachusetts being the leaders.

New England vs. Virginia: From the beginning the settlers in New England differed fundamentally from those in Virginia. The New Englanders (Rhode Island always excepted) had a tight cooperative community, based upon a shared devotion and a shared theology. A spirit of adventure and a quest for private fortune had prompted Virginians, by and large to move to America. Natural conditions strongly reinforced the initial tendencies of both groups of settlers. In New England a rocky soil and a lack of navigable streams discouraged large-scale agriculture, and small subsistence-farming communities, each with its church, were the form of settlement. In Virginia, fertile soil intersected by rivers and tidal creeks encouraged the cultivation of tobacco as a cash crop. In the 1604s the experience of isolation that resulted from the English Civil War drove the two groups of colonies into courses of development at once different and similar.

When the war broke out, the Puritan magistrates in New England formally dissolved their connections with the Crown. Various of the colonies formed the New England Confederation for mutual defense and general cooperation. Rhode Island was excluded, on the grounds that it was a sinkhole of depravity and heresy. The sense of a common identity among the members of the Confederation hardened through their isolation from England and their sense of being surrounded by enemies.

In Virginia the colonial government likewise separated itself from England, but for the opposite reason. Virginia proclaimed loyalty to Charles I, and when the Puritan Parliamentarians won the Civil War Virginia declared its allegiance to the Stuart heir in exile, Charles II.

When the Civil War broke out in England the flow of Puritan immigrants to New England stopped, but by the time the war was over in 1647 A.D. the population of the colonies was increasing as fast as ever. In New England the increase derived from an extremely high birth rate; in Virginia it sprang from new immigration, first in trickles and then in waves, of fugitives from Puritanical repression that was unfolding in England.

After about 1650 A.D., New England's economy began to boom. This quickening of economic activity turned heads away from the original purpose of the founder, John Winthrop, and attracted profit seekers who remained outside the religious community. And by the 1650s A.D. Puritans uneasily noticed that many of their children were not undergoing the conversion experience required for church membership. If the trend continued, Puritans feared, a dangerously large portion of the population would soon be outside the church.

In 1662 A.D., a meeting of Puritan ministers arrived at a solution to the problem of declining church membership. The ministers agreed to admit the grown children of church members into partial fellowship even though they could not give evidence of grace. To preserve the church's purity, the ministers excluded these "halfway" members from participation in the sacraments of Holy Communion. This Half-Way Covenant did revive lagging church membership, but it also showed that the Puritans' early dreams were yielding to practicality. Churches must be kept filled, even though, as one Concord man complained, "In the extreme seasons of heat and cold we were ready to say of the Sabbath, 'Behold what a weariness.' " The Massachusetts Bay colony was no longer a community of saints.

New England Democracy: It is easy, and in part correct, to trace American democracy to early New England institutions. But the Mayflower Compact, the government of Massachusetts Bay, and the church polity of the New England congregations did not spring from anything close to a conscious modern democratic theory. Each of the three came out of its own special circumstances and needs.

The Mayflower colonists were going to be far beyond the reach of established authority, and therefore the Pilgrim leaders feared that some of the settlers might "use their own liberty, for none had the power to command them." A need for law and order, not a desire for democratic government, inspired the Mayflower Compact. To agree among themselves to have a government was a simple, necessary act. And the Compact did not project an independent government; it specifically declared allegiance to the King of England.

The suffrage in Massachusetts Bay represented the fusion of the organization of a business company with that of the New England Puritan congregations. That English joint-stock companies gave a vote to each shareholder for the conduct of business was a practical arrangement among people who had chosen to pool their resources for some enterprise. The purpose of such companies was not to establish a democracy, nor was democracy the purpose of the settlers who turned the shareholder voting system into a political system for the colony. Seventeenth century Massachusetts Bay had few if an advocates of democracy. "If the people be governors," said Puritan divine John Cotton, "who shall be governed?"

Within the Puritan and the Separatist congregations, members were spiritual equals, of a sort. While women could be of the elect and therefore could be full members of the congrega-

129

tions, they could not be ministers or members of the governing body of the church, and they could not voice their opinions loudly, as Anne Hutchinson had proved. The Puritan concept of equality derived from the doctrine, which no modern democrat would accept, that the members of the church congregations must be confined to the elect, selected for salvation from the beginning of time. Members were spiritual equals, but only because there can be no inequality among saints.

Yet even if the early institutions of New England did not derive from any philosophical notions of equality or democracy, they deserve a place in the history of American Democracy. The manner of their formation represents the way in which many of the nation's political and social institutions came into being – either by theory nor by ancient custom but by matter-of-fact response to conditions and needs.

New Colonies

While the Virginia and the Puritans were establishing settlements other colonies were taking shape – some founded for religious reasons and some for a variety of other motives. Early in the seventeenth century lands lying within the present states of New Hampshire and Maine had gone to individual proprietors receiving authority from the Crown, but that authority was shadowy and from time to time Massachusetts Bay had extended its government to settlers there. By 1679 A.D. New Hampshire became a royal colony, while Maine stayed with Massachusetts until 1820 A.D.

Connecticut and Rhode Island were quickly provided for. In 1662 A.D., the towns in Connecticut Valley received a charter from Charles. The charter, to the displeasure of New Havenites, placed the strict Puritan town of New Haven within the same colony as the more liberal settlements of the Connecticut Valley. The Puritan government of England at Roger Williams' urging had granted a patent to Rhode Island. In 1663 A.D., Charles granted a charter to that democratic collection of towns. The grant confirmed the policy of religious freedom that had made

Rhode Island a haven for religious dissenters. Their charters gave to Connecticut and Rhode Island the privilege of governing themselves. Therein appeared a colonial form, the charter colony, taking its place alongside the proprietary colony such as Maryland, owned by a single individual or small group, and the colony owned by a joint-stock company, like Massachusetts. Before long the British American mainland would contain more royal colonies, with governors appointed by the Crown.

The Salem Witches: In 1692 A.D., the Devil assaulted the seaport town of Salem, Massachusetts, north of Boston, with an unparalleled fury. This village of a few hundred people was invaded by scores of warlocks and witches, men and women who had covenanted with the Devil to make mischief, to drive little children mad, to sicken and kill livestock and people. One witch, it seemed, had caused the death of fourteen members of a single family. The jails bulged with over a hundred prisoners awaiting trial, including a four-year-old child bound for nine months in heavy iron chains. Twenty-seven people eventually came to trial; the court hanged nineteen – fourteen women and five men as witches. One man refused to enter a plea, and suffered peine forte et dure: Heavy weights were laid on Giles Cory's body, still refusing to plea, he was pressed to death.

The trouble had begun innocently enough: "Conjuration with sieves and keys, and peas, and nails, and horseshoes" at first seemed harmless activities with which to pass the New England winter. But these games turned serious when grim-visaged parents tried to discover what was causing their children's "fits" and "distempers".

Everyone knew about witchcraft. Witches and their male counterparts, the warlocks, had made a pact with the Devil. They "wrote in his book," joining his legions for the thrill of conjuration, midnight frolics, obscure or perhaps obscene rituals, and the power to harm their neighbors. Waves of witchcraft had swept across Europe for nearly the past two centuries as the Protestant Reformation inspired a direct struggle between the Christ and the Devil. Do not "suffer a witch to live," the Bible commanded, and tens of thousands, mostly women but many men as well, had been executed as the Evil One's followers.

Before 1692 A.D., the Devil had paid small attention to New England. Forty-four cases, three hangings, no burnings – such was the entire history of New England witchcraft before the malady spread to nine adolescent girls in Salem. Under intense questioning, and responding to the attention with yet further manifestations of demoniac possessions, the girls named three women as the source of their sufferings. These were likely candidates. Sarah Goode, daughter of a well-to-do innkeeper, had steadily tumbled down the social ladder; she was in 1692 A.D. a surely, pipe-smoking beggar whose "muttering and scolding" seemed to cause cows to die. Sarah Osborne's name swirled in contention and scandal. Her battle with her own sons for control of her first husband's estate, her liaison with the Irish indentured servant who became her second husband. And there was Tituba, the slave woman who had introduced the practices of voodoo she had learned in the West Indies. At the pretrial examination, Tituba readily and noisily told the audience of townspeople and "possessed" girls what they wanted to hear. For three days, she regaled them with stories of her comporting with the Devil and with witches Sarah Goode and Sarah Osborne, of midnight sabbaths and rides through the air with Satan, whom she described as "a thing all over hairy, all the face hairy, and a long nose." She had seen the Devil's "book" and although she could not read, she had counted nine names in it. Nine names! There were more witches. Soon the girls, shrieking, contorting, sobbing hysterically, dredged up still more names. Not all were outcasts like Sarah Goode, Sarah Osborne, and Tituba; not all were from Salem. The jails groaned; the gallows rope snapped. The madness, for the better part of a year, infected a whole society. When the accusers began to name prominent citizens – some Boston clergymen, for instance, and the governor's wife – the Reverend Cotton Mather, his father, the Reverend Increase Mather, and some other ministers recommended the cessation

132

of the trials. (Cotton Mather, like everyone else in the seventeenth century, believed in witches, but he also believed in science. He would have his day in 1721 A.D., when to combat popular fears of the new medical practice of inoculation for smallpox, he allowed his son to be inoculated.) In 1692 A.D., reason returned to Salem; probing questions were asked; the jailed were sent home and pardoned.

The girls part in it is easiest to explain. The life of young girls in Massachusetts Bay was dull in the best of times. "I am not fond," wrote Cotton Mather, foremost Puritan minister, "of proposing Play to children, as a Reward of any diligent Application to learn what is good; lest they should think Diversion to be better and nobler Thing than Diligence." While young men, sent to school and taught to pray and work, could at least look forward to the adventure of choosing careers, girls could do little more than wonder "what trade their sweethearts should be of". It is understandable that when the little girls dabbled in magic with Tituba, their slightly older friends and relatives joined the only excitement midwinter had to offer. (Many teenaged girls – including most of the "afflicted" ones did not live at home where parents might spoil them, but were sent to relatives or neighbors houses to learn their adult roles and to be evenly disciplined.) Once the adults began to fuss over their fits, how could the young resist pursuing their adventure and showing their power over the adult community, particularly over married women who laid on endless chores and discipline? Even these antics would have been relatively harmless had not the adults panicked.

In Salem the witchcraft epidemic had fed upon local conflicts as people from different political and clerical factions hurled accusations black and forth. For Salem was an angry place. Town and countryside were sharply diverging. Conservative back country farmers smarted under the growth of commercial capitalism and its accompanying secular style. Sons coming of age found difficulty establishing themselves as land became increasingly scarce. The values of Puritanism itself seemed more and more in question as ministers bemoaned the "declension" from the piety of the colony's founders three generations before. And from 1684 to 1691 the colony of Massachusetts had been without a charter. Would the old land claims be valid under a new one? Would voting still be restricted to church members? Nearly every adult must have been startled at a changing world crowding in on what had been for two generations a largely fixed culture. Men and women who were supposed to practice Christian unity engaged year after year in lawsuits over boundaries and legacies. Like the witches, they were at war with their neighbors, disrupting the church and government, bursting the old molds. Were they too possessed? How much easier it must have been to blame everything on the literal bewitchment of enemies rather than on their own bewitchment with the new and perhaps dubious values and goals that were transforming John Winthrop's "Citty upon a Hille" into a secular society.

Finally a new study, Carol Karlson's *Devil in the Shape of a Woman*, correlates the witchcraft scare with an Indian War that began in 1689. Here was a main cause of dislocation. People who survived the frontier massacres abandoned their exposed positions and retreated to older settlements. Fear of Indian attack spurred by French Catholics to the north was quite thoroughly mixed up with fear of the devil in the minds of seventeenth century Protestants. Massachusetts a few years later passed an act reversing the conviction of those executed. Though this did not help the victims, it lifted a stigma from the townspeople. No community before had ever issued a repentance for destroying witches.

There was after the events mentioned a spiritual awakening that overflowed the United States so turn the pages and discover the Awakening.

18

The Great Awakening

1031 A.D.	1776 A.D.	1798 A.D.	2001 A.D.	2031 A.D.
5001 A.S.	5746 A.S.	5768 A.S.	5971 A.S.	6001 A.S.
	*You are here.			

In the 1730s A.D., a fervent new religious movement – Pietism on the Continent, Wesleyanism in Britain, and the Great Awakening in America – began to spread rapidly everywhere. A new enthusiasm for religion and moral reform appeared almost simultaneously in continental Europe, Great Britain, and the colonies. The message of the new religion was essentially the same, whatever its form: That the way to salvation lay not in faithful performance of sacraments and rituals as the Catholics and Anglicans had always maintained, or a life of good works, but simply in opening the heart to God through prayer. A simple and total act of faith in God's goodness and mercy would bring to the faithful an unspeakably profound experience of personal conversion and salvation.

As John Winthrop and those who banished Anne Hutchinson had argued in the 1630s A.D., any such doctrine is potentially dangerous to an established social order, for it implicitly vests in the individual alone the capacity to judge the moral rectitude of his own behavior. The new pietist faith of Anglo-America was disruptive. It advocated the separation of converts from others and their formation into small groups, and aimed at the immediate reform and the final transformation of all of man's ways – to serve the coming of the Kingdom of Heaven on earth.

In the colonies the Great Awakening had its beginnings in 1734 A.D., when the Reverend Jonathan Edwards, pastor of the church in the small frontier town of Northampton, Massachusetts, a community of about 200 families, noticed a "religious concern on people's minds." As the winter of 1734 A.D. progressed, Edwards noticed that "There was scarcely a single person in the town, either old or young, that was left unconcerned about the great things of the eternal world. Those that were wont to be the vainest, and loosest, and those that had been most disposed to think and speak slightly of vital and experimental religion, were now generally subject to great awakening." Edward's account of the Northampton revival, *A Faithful Narrative of the Surprising Work of God*, published in 1737 A.D., may have prepared the way for the preaching of George Whitefield, the eloquent young English clergyman who arrived in America in 1739 A.D.

Various French, German, and Dutch ministers were associated with revivalism, and John and Charles Wesley were the most important figures in England. The most influential of all in British America was George Whitefield.

After receiving some training at Oxford, Whitefield had persuaded the bishop to ordain him before he was of canonical age. In his maiden sermon, this restless, charismatic preacher raved and exhorted, sang and shouted, wept and thundered and, it is said, drove fifteen people mad.

Whitefield made his first evangelical tour to America in 1739 A.D. at age twenty-five, preaching under the open air and converting hundreds in Georgia, and returned two years later to conduct a great revival in New England. The New England and mid-Atlantic tour was the great triumph of Whitefield's career, though he made several successful trips to America during the next thirty years. In 1740 A.D., the populace was ready for him, if only out of restlessness, boredom, or economic troubles. The brief revival that Jonathan Edwards had conducted five years earlier in Northampton, Massachusetts, had already primed New England. Edwards had carried the right message, and with Whitefield's personal magnetism and style might have set the region aflame himself.

In Philadelphia Whitefield managed to affect even that lover of reason, Benjamin Franklin, who recorded in his autobiography:

"I happened ... to attend one of his sermons, in the course of which I perceived he intended to finish with a collection, and I silently resolved he should get nothing from me. I had in my pocket a handful of copper money, three or four silver dollars, and five pistoles in gold. As he proceeded I began to soften, and concluded to give the coppers. Another stroke of his oratory made me ashamed of that, and determined me to give the silver; and he finished so admirably, that I empty'd my pocket wholly into the collector's dish, gold and all."

"Enthusiastic" Religion: The impact of the Great Awakening was not quite what the ministry that welcomed Whitefield had expected. The number of active participants in church affairs doubled, tripled, and quadrupled, and for the first time in years religion attracted the enthusiasm of the young. But much of New England, for example, became divided into fiercely hostile camps of "Old Lights," or defenders of the existing order, and "New Lights," who embraced the new piety.

The Great Awakening had its philosophical connections with more sober forms of Protestantism that had preceded it. Puritans, like other Protestants, had taken the conversion experience very seriously, and even after the Half-Way Covenant of 1662 a conversion experience was a requirement for admission to full church membership among New England Puritans. But the Puritan congregations had not demanded the violent outpourings of emotion that revivalism usually identifies with religious experience. The Great Awakening was the earliest instance of a revivalism that has become a recurrent phenomenon in American Protestantism. Like the Great Awakening, moreover, American religion since has emphasized the experiential component of religion. In breaking open churches that had been stable and undivided, the Awakening is suggestive of the tendency within Protestantism to multiply churches and sects. And the Awakening introduced America to a movement that John and Charles Wesley were spreading within the Church of England: Methodism, a faith that stressed both religious feeling and a morality of self-discipline and hard work. In the nineteenth century the Methodist and Baptist church, well adapted in structure, practice, and belief to spread to the frontier and the back country, would become two of the largest denominations both in cities and in the countryside and a notable influence on American ideas of morality.

Land, Slavery, and Religion: Major changes occurred in the pattern of land ownership after the war. By 1778 A.D. all thirteen states had confiscated the property of those who "took refuge with the British tyrant." Some 100,000 already had left the country, most for Canada or England, and their estates were sold for money to support the patriot cause.

The Revolution also made for a rhetoric of liberty that stumbled against the reality of human bondage. A group of blacks in Boston announced to the General Court that their race looked for "great things from men who have made such a noble stand against the designs of their fellow men to enslave them." Soon a voluble antislavery movement emerged. Philadelphia Quakers had formed the first antislavery society in 1775 A.D.

The Revolution also affected religion. Most states "disestablished" churches, ending the special privileges or civil functions of particular sects. Only Massachusetts and Connecticut still collected taxes to fund a state church; the other states viewed competing religions as equal in the eyes of the law. Tolerance did not extend to atheists, however, and most state legislatures established a religious test for holding public office. Blasphemy remained a crime punishable by imprisonment. Documents like Thomas Jefferson's Statute of Religious Freedom in Virginia, fully enacted by the Virginia legislature in 1786 A.D., granted tolerance for the free practice of religion, not a guarantee of rights for nonbelievers. If narrow by twentieth-century standards, the statute was for its time a model, proclaiming to the rest of the world an example of the nation's new freedom.

Religious Movements

The Second Great Awakening: During the first part of the nineteenth century, America experienced a second Great Awakening of religious enthusiasm. Relying on the excitement of revival meetings, a wide variety of evangelical sects sought to turn the masses toward spiritual regeneration. Evangelist like Charles G. Finney rejected the harsh traditional Calvinist view of original sin and predestination and preached that any good Christian could attain eternal salvation. Their teachings generally involved a literal interpretation of the Bible. Many emphasized the Second Coming of the Christ and believed that God's Kingdom would establish itself on earth. This religious resurgence reflected distinctly American values and attitudes. Its intensely democratic message stressed individual free will and immediate salvation; it breathed optimism; it brought religion to the people in language they could understand. These common people wanted sermons devoid of "literary quibbles and philosophical speculations." As one spiritual put it to music, every person wanted to "see bright angels stand waiting to receive me."

The characteristic doctrine of the Second Great Awakening was perfectionism, the idea that human beings could not merely achieve salvation, but overcome sin altogether. Perfectionism's Scriptural basis lay in the New Testament account of Jesus telling His disciples that they were to be "perfect, even as your Heavenly Father is perfect." Charles Grandison Finney, the most successful of the revivalists of the day, read this text literally. Jesus did not tell His followers to try to be perfect, he reasoned. He told them to be perfect. Since He had, Finney argued, He must have also supplied the means for them to do so. There must be a special form of divine assistance, a special grace, available to the converted, which would enable them to transcend their sinful natures and achieve moral perfection. Here was a doctrine matched to the American belief that this truly was a New World and that Americans could avoid the ills of the Old. Like the first Great Awakening of a century before, the new evangelicalism was more than a religious movement. And The spirit of perfectionism animated the many reform movements of the era.

The Second Great Awakening has been called "a women's awakening." Men certainly responded to the religious enthusiasm, but women far outnumbered them among converts and played a decisive part in leading men either back to established churches, or into new ones. Historians have shown that male conversions frequently followed the conversion of one or more female members of the family. Mothers often proved especially influential in converting their sons and husbands. But the most characteristic converts were adolescent girls. An affirmation, or reaffirmation, of religious belief and commitment seems to have offered young women a powerful sense of identity and purpose at a time in which their brothers and male peers could look forward to identifying themselves with jobs or careers, while women were expected to prepare for a life of secluded domesticity.

Religious enthusiasm rapidly increased the membership of most Protestant denominations, Methodist and Baptists increasing the fastest, but new sects also arose. Each new prophet, interpreter, or mystic found followers willing to join in anticipating the literal fulfillment of even the most outlandish prophecies. For a time the poor farming district of upstate New York burned with religious emotions. "Enthusiastic" sects, sects cultivating emotion, flourished in this "burned-over district," as it was called; whatever the ultimate derivation of the phrase, it came to signify a region seared by fires of religious enthusiasm.

Some of the fervent young religious movements of the early 1800s encouraged believers to join together in exclusive communities of the faithful. The more distinctive the tenants of their faith, leaders reasoned, the more necessary the intensive instruction and supervision that community living made possible. This often lead to communal property-holding and cooperative economic enterprise. Many of the religious communities barely survived the death of their founders; others, such as the Shaker Society, lasted a century or more.

The Shakers and the Mormons: The Shaker faith, brought to this country by Ann Lee in 1774 A.D., received its name from one of its most distinctive practices, a sacred dance during which the members "shook" their bodies free of sin through their fingertips. "Mother Ann," as she was called, believed that she had received direct revelations from God and, since she preached millennialism – that is, the imminent coming of the millennium, the period of the Christ's rule on earth – she saw no need for the Shakers to have children. The members therefore practiced celibacy. After reaching a membership of some six thousand in the 1830s A.D., the Shakers gradually died out. Their furniture and housing arrangements, which were simplicity itself, are their best remembered achievements.

By far the most important of the religious communitarians were the Mormons. Mormonism strikingly elaborated the new theology of free will, direct revelation, universal salvation, the expectation of the Christ's imminent return, and the establishment of a millennial Kingdom.

In 1830 A.D., at the age of twenty-five, Joseph Smith of Palmyra, New York, published the *Book of Mormon*. He had transcribed it, he claimed, from gold plates that had lain undisturbed in a nearby hillside for more than a thousand years. The angel Moroni directed him to the spot where the plates were buried. Using two magis "seeing stones" fixed in silver bows, Smith translated the ancient script into readable text. The book was a curious mixture of Old Testament theology, popular history, and social beliefs of the times.

One young man would recall this account of the doings of Joseph Smith:

"It was adjoining one of the farms where the farce of walking on the water was enacted. It was in haying time and the Cornwalls were mowing near the river and they discovered tracks through the brush to its bank. The boys made an examination which developed a plank bridge just under the water which extended across a level branch of the river to its opposite side. The planks were supported by legs driven into the ground, upon which they were supported, and a tall straight tree was plainly visible in its line. The mowers procured a saw and weakened the third plank so that no one could step upon it without going into the river to its bottom. That night from a good vantage point the boys watched for its development. After dark on came Smith with a number of his proselytes to see walking on the water verified. Smith stepped forth with confidence and turned to address his hearers, telling them that this performance was wholly a matter of faith and that their faith for its success was as necessary as was his own, and continuing we will all thus continue our faith – and walking onward until coming to the weakened legs, down went the prophet breast deep into the river. He clambered out of the water with the answer that their faith had weakened and that this alone was not sufficient to support him alone on the water."

(Jemimah Wilkinson, the "Universal Friend" of Penn Yan, New York, also took followers to water, but she asked them if any doubted that she could walk on it. When no one spoke, she left, saying that it would therefore not be necessary to perform the miracle.)

Although Mormonism borrowed freely from the convictions and practices of evangelical Protestantism, it offered a simple alternative to the confusing proliferation of Christian sects. By extending salvation to all adherents and clerical status to each adult white male, and by stressing the sanctity of secular accomplishments and the need for a community of "saints" (the church's official name was and is "The Church of Jesus Christ of Latter-Day Saints", the new faith tapped the energies and talents of the unsuccessful and the neglected. In Joseph Smith, a prophet who was believed to receive revelation directly from God, Mormonism provided theological truths and authoritarian leadership to whoever craved practical and spiritual guidance.

After converting a small group of relatives and friends, Smith moved his flock to Ohio and then to Missouri in an attempt to establish a commonwealth of believers. In each place, nonbelievers persecuted the Mormons and drove them from their lands. In 1839 A.D., Smith lead his followers to Illinois. After securing political authority from state officials, he founded a city, called Nauvoo, which became a self-sufficient religious community. The success of Nauvoo, which grew to fifteen thousand inhabitants by 1844 A.D., as well as its voting power in state elections, brought envy and hostility of outsiders. Smith's increasingly eccentric behavior (he declared himself a candidate for President in 1844 A.D.) also generated unfavorable publicity. When a disgruntled Mormon confirmed that Smith and other members of the church's elite practiced polygamy, state officials arrested him and his brother. Soon after their confinement at Carthage, a mob of disbanded militia murdered them both.

When the harassment and violence continued, Brigham young, Smith's successor to the presidency of the church, led the Mormons on the long difficult exodus from Illinois to uninhabited Mexican territory beyond the Rocky Mountains. Under Young's stern but effective leadership, the Mormons established a thriving agricultural community near the Great Salt Lake. Believers recall a miracle that saved that first band. After a desperate winter, the Mormons had planted a small crop and irrigated it by hand, a back breaking task. Then, just as harvest time approached, a horde of locusts swept down upon the fields. Near despair as they watched the insects devouring the only food available for next winter, the Mormons suddenly heard the calls of hundreds of seagulls. The mysterious visitors, a thousand miles away from any ocean, ate the locusts and saved the community. The story freshened the vision of a new Zion. By 1877 A.D., the year of Young's death, the commonwealth numbered some 350 settlements with a total population of 140,000.

Organized like a medieval kingdom, the church collected from each individual an annual tithe in goods, labor, or money, and channeled this surplus into projects that benefited everyone. Banning or discouraging the use of tea, coffee, tobacco, liquor, fashionable clothing, and elegant furniture, the church curtailed wasteful spending and assured the development of an industrious community. This mixture of collectivism and private enterprise saved the community from worst evils of uncontrolled capitalism and prevented Utah from becoming dependent on imports from the industrial East.

Although the Mormons wished to be self-sufficient and independent, they also considered themselves Americans and asked for Utah's admission to the Union. Congress, however, balked at the Mormon practice of polygamy, which the Republican Party had linked to slavery. In fact, only a small percentage of the community participated in this patriarchal institution; but most of the American public though that Brigham Young's twenty-seven wives and fifty-six children were typical. In 1890 A.D., the church formally renounced polygamy. Mormonism was retreating from the attempt to establish a society operating in entire accordance with religious principles and communal ideals. Mormons continued, however, to integrate themselves tightly into the life of their church and community. Congress admitted Utah to the Union in 1896 A.D.

Millennialism: Not content with establishing an earthly paradise, the Americans looked to the fulfillment in their own time of the New Testament prophecy of the Christ's Second Coming. The foremost exponents of millennialism was William Miller, a hard working farmer in upstate New York who became caught up in a revival shortly after the War of 1812 A.D. and spent the rest of his life pondering religious questions. A literal interpretation of the Bible led him to a graphic belief in the Second Coming or Advent, which he calculated would occur in about 1843 A.D. Aided by the widespread economic distress of the late 1830s A.D., Miller made crowds of converts throughout New England with his vivid sermons depicting the glory of the Advent, the joy of those who would be saved, the suffering of the unrepentant. In a single year he gave 627 hour-and-a-half lectures before eager audiences, often of a thousand or more. Ministerial disciples with a knack for publicity spread Miller's views over an even wider area.

Miller spoke lines like these throughout the 1830s A.D.:

"Ah! what means that noise? Can it be thunder? Too long – too loud and shrill – more like a thousand trumpets sounding on onset. It shakes the earth ... See how it reels. How dreadful! How strange! The very clouds are bright with glory ... See, the heavens do shake, the vivid clouds, so full of fire, are driven apart by this last blast, and rolling up themselves, stand back aghast – And O, my soul, what do I see? A great white throne, and One upon it ... Before Him are thousands and thousands and thousands of winged seraphim, ready to do His will. The last trumpet sounds – the earth now heaves a throb for the last time, and in this last great throe her bowels burst, and from her sprang a thousand thousand, and ten thousand times ten thousand immortal beings into active life ... I saw them pass through the long vista of the parted cloud, and stand before the throne ... The air now becomes stagnated with heat; while the dismal howling of those human beings who were left upon the earth, and the horrid yells of the damned spirits ... filled my soul with horror not easily described."

Miller hesitated to give his frantic followers a definite date, promising only that deliverance would come soon, in God's appointed time. As 1843 A.D. – the Last Year – passed, March of 1844 A.D. came to be accepted as the crucial month. Finally, when nothing happened, a weary and discouraged Miller frankly admitted his mistake, explaining that he had done his best. But his lieutenants were not yet ready to quit. They chose 22 October 1844 A.D., as the new "Advent Day" and talked Miller into accepting it. Excitement mounted higher than before as extensive preparations were made to enter God's Kingdom. The faithful made themselves white "ascension robes" and neglected nearly all secular business. Voting in the fall elections was very light in some district. On the night of October 21, Millerites gathered on hilltops to meet the new world together. No provisions were made for eating or sleeping, and many suffered as the night and the next day and then another night passed; in some places severe thunderstorms added to their terror. Some claimed to have seen a jeweled crown in the sky. In western New York, an earthquake intensified the expectation. A few Adventist committed suicide – one man leaped over Niagara Falls. The day of

145

the "Great Delusion" effectively ended the Adventist movement, although isolated Adventist sects continued to flourish.

The Fox Sisters: Various forms of spiritualism, or attempts to contact the spirit world, were another manifestation of the desire to break down barriers between this world and the next. Mesmerism, electro-biology, clairvoyance, phrenology, magnetism – each had its following.

New York farmer John Fox had two remarkable young daughters, Maggie and Katie. Wherever they went in their home, mysterious rapping sounds were heard. Eventually the girls and their mother worked out a system of communication with the presumably otherworldly source of the rappings. Soon the neighbors flocked in to observe these conversations with the spirit world. The Fox home in this year 1848 A.D. set off a mania of spiritualist excitement. With an older sister acting as manager, the Fox girls began holding exhibitions – at the insistence of the spirits, of course – and quickly developed into professional fee-charging media.

With the wide publicity given the Fox sisters, media rapidly appeared all over the country, and spiritualist circles developed in nearly every town and village. They refined their techniques as they went along; the Foxes' managing sister, for instance, discovered that total darkness could produce many more manifestations of the spirits' presence. Table-moving, spirit-writing, and cold, ghostly hands soon supplemented the mystic rappings, and within a few years all the now familiar paraphernalia of spiritualism were in use. The spiritualist excitement filled for thousands of people a need to become more comfortable with the mysteries of death and immortality. A number of intellectuals saw in spiritualism a replacement for traditional Christianity – a proof of the existence of a supernatural world for a scientific age that could not accept revelation resting only on faith. Even when the Fox sisters some years later admitted that their whole career had been a fraud (the rappings had from the first been produced by the joints of their toes), many spiritualists remained undeterred.

Methodism: The most powerful evangelical movement, more orthodox than these other religions of excitement, had begun in the eighteenth century. John Wesley had led within the Church of England a revival movement that after his death produced a separate denomination, the Methodist church. Methodist believe in free will. In its early days especially, Methodism had a strong element of emotional revivalism; but it also preached a rigorous piety and morality of self-discipline, industry, thrift, and good works. Methodism was powerfully attractive, in Great Britain to the working classes and to the poor, and in this country to people on the frontier. In both nations it had something to do with the bringing of an ordered moral life to previously disordered sections of society. While the Methodist church did have an organization, in its first period it did not stress the role of bishops or of a highly trained ministry. That made it possible for Methodism here to develop a distinctive and effective system in which preachers, many with little, if any, formal religious education, would travel about on the frontier, bringing a sustaining Methodism to the families and communities at which they stopped.

Each preacher worked a "Circuit" or route that covered a particular area. Francis Asbury, who had come to this country in 1771 A.D. and was influential in the beginnings of Methodism here, was an early and influential traveling preacher. The typical circuit rider went horseback, depended on friendly settlers for food and shelter, and was much a part of the frontier environment. The evangelist Peter Cartwright could thrash a rowdy who tried to disrupt a Methodist meeting. Cartwright would hold his revivals outside in a grove because the local church could not hold crowds he attracted. Of his own conversion at such a camp meeting he recalled:

> "The people crowded to this meeting from far and near. They came in their large wagons, with vitals mostly prepared. The women slept in the wagons and the men under them. Many stayed on the ground night and day for a number of nights and days together. Other were provided for among the neighbors around. The

power of God was wonderfully displayed; scores of sinners fell under the preaching, like men slain in mighty battle; Christians shouted aloud for joy.

To this meeting I repaired, a guilty, wretched sinner. On the Saturday evening of said meeting, I went with weeping multitudes, and bowed before the stand, and earnestly prayed for mercy. In the midst of a solemn struggle of soul, an impression was made on my mind, as though a voice said to me, "Thy sins are all forgiven thee." Divine light flashed all around me, unspeakable joy sprung up in my soul. I rose to my feet, opened my eyes, and it really seemed as if I was in heaven; the trees, the leaves on them, everything seemed, and I really thought were, praising God."

The Methodist divided their territory into regions, each holding an annual conference that heard reports, appointed new preachers, and assigned circuits. As the frontier became heavily populated, large circuits – some had been hundreds of miles long – were replaced by smaller ones, and by about the middle of the nineteenth century these had given way to settled parishes. By that time the Methodist church had become one of the largest Protestant denominations in the country.

Out of the Great Awakening came a Great Apostasy of the churches of The United States of America as the following chapters will show.

19

A New Sound,
Religious Legislation

1031 A.D.	1776 A.D.	1798 A.D.	2001 A.D.	2031 A.D.
5001 A.S.	5746 A.S.	5768 A.S.	5971 A.S.	6001 A.S.

You are here.*

No knowledgeable Bible student today can fail to recognize the prophetic evidence for the approaching apocalypse. Swiftly, the end time events unfold before the startled eyes of earth's inhabitants. The great scenario of sin and salvation has reached its final state, and a desperate battle revolves around every individual in the world.

Unfortunately, the great majority have no idea, no understanding of the true nature of the warfare raging around them. They have not studied the Word of God concerning the issues in the cosmic conflict for Planet Earth. Less still do they understand the weapons which the devil is using in his final scheme to hold men and women under the spell of sin.

Today there are evil confederations of every satanic device and factor, because the adversary knows that his time has run out. The Bible portrays him as sending forth unclean spirits to influence the leaders of the earth and to gather the forces which will participate in "The Battle Of That Great Day Of God Almighty."

Satan's effort in this confrontation is largely spiritual in nature and involves an unprecedented effort to capture the minds of all mankind. Hypnotic, mind-altering methods of persuasion are being applied, and counterfeit miracles mark the efforts of the powers of darkness.

Every indication is that occultism, astrology, and spiritualism is playing a major role in the last day delusions Satan is utilizing. New Age principles are directly appropriated from witchcraft and Satan-worship, but under the pleasing guise of Christian religious titles. A subtle accommodation is being made by many, if not most churches for these manipulative ideas. It cannot be over stressed, how important it is for every Christian to be so Bible-oriented that any tainted concept will be immediately exposed and rejected.

As the demonic assault builds to its climax in the spring of 2031 A.D., all the religious bodies who believe in the natural immortality of the soul will be swept into the deception. With consummate skill Satan is exploiting the various branches of belief which allow him to impersonate the souls of the dead. By trusting voices, trumpets, impressions, or any form of counsel not directly based on the Bible, millions are being controlled by Satan while believing they are led by God. Furthermore, those individuals and organizations who are loitering on the edge of the esoteric are being brought under the beguiling influence of our great enemy. Our only safety is to totally separate from everything that smacks of mind control or Eastern mysticism.

This book sounds a note of alarm to all who may be attracted by the mind sciences. We live in a world that has popularized the use of heathenism, hypnotism, dependence on astrology, and New Age thinking. Study it carefully, because it might save you from the tentacles of the mushrooming, many-faceted evil which has already affected the minds of the majority, a vast multitude of misguided people. This is the time when every doctrine must be carefully tested by the infallible rule of Holy Scriptures. "To the law and the testimony: If they do not speak according to this Word, it is because there is not truth, no light in them." (Isaiah 8:20).

One of the most interesting prophecies in the Bible concerns the abomination that causes desolation. The element that makes this prophecy especially intriguing is that Jesus identifies it as a specific sign that the end is near. It was in answer to the disciples' question, "When shall these things be and what shall be the sign of your coming, and of the end of the world?" that Jesus spoke of the abomination of desolation. He said,

"When you therefore shall see the abomination of desolation, spoken of by Daniel the prophet, stand in the holy place, (Whoso reads, let him understand:) Then let them which be in Judea flee into the mountains ... for then shall be great tribulation, such as was not since the beginning of the world to this time, no, nor ever shall be." (Matthew 24:3, 15-21).

Just what is the abomination that causes desolation? The answer to this question is vitally important. Jesus clearly implies that our very lives, our salvation could be at stake over this matter.

Jesus tells us to focus on the book of Daniel to understand the abomination that causes desolation (Matthew 24:15). There we find that the abomination that causes desolation can be divided into three parts. These parts are: The abomination that causes desolation in Daniel's day involving the first temple; the abomination that causes desolation in Jesus' day involving the second temple; and the abomination that causes desolation in this, the time of the end involving the whole of Christianity.

The issues that come into play in the abomination that causes desolation as divided in the book of Daniel remain consistent in each of its three phases. Therefore they are types, or examples, of each other.

In Daniel 1:1, 2, Daniel provides a concise historical background of the book which follows and the abomination that causes desolation.

Further study of the book of Daniel reveals the abomination that causes desolation existed in his time, and that is was the people of God doing that which was evil in the sight of the Lord God. The result of God's people practicing the religious abominations of the heathen was the desolation of their land, city and sanctuary.

Just what were these abominations that resulted in such desolation? Since this was all done "to fulfill the word of the Lord by the mouth of Jeremiah," then Jeremiah should be able to tell us what substitutions in worship had been made. In Jeremiah 17, the prophet under divine mandate, told the people that if they would honor God's seventh day Sabbath their city would remain forever, and that this faithful obedience would lead them into such a relationship with Himself that they would be used to convert the surrounding heathen nations. Jeremiah 17:19-26. On the other hand, if they would not keep the Sabbath day holy God would allow their city to be desolated (verse 27).

Ezekiel, Jeremiah's contemporary, also tells us about the abominations God's people were practicing in the holy place. In Ezekiel 8, God proceeded to show his servant the progressively greater outrages His people were committing. He speaks of an image that provoked Him to jealousy, unclean beasts brought into the house of God, women weeping for Tammuz, and twenty-five men standing in the holy place with their backs to the temple of the Lord, their faces toward the east; and they worshiped the sun toward the east.

It is important to note that the abominations were done by the apostate people of God. This in turn resulted in their forfeiture of God's protection and called down His judgments in their desolation. This scenario of the abomination that caused desolation in Daniel's day involving the first Temple period prefigures the two other abominations of desolation prophesied in Daniel. The next one we shall consider is the one that concerns the second Jewish temple period.

After their release from Babylonian captivity and rebuilding the city and temple, the Jewish leaders erected a mountain of rules and regulations (traditions) designed to protect them from repeating the sins that lead to their bondage. The rules and regulations of course, resulted in a system of pure legalism.

At last the people began to believe that favor with God depended on how well they obeyed the traditions of their elders.

Ultimately the people were led full circle to disobedience again. Jesus comments that in spite of their apparent religiosity they still were breaking God's law even as their forefathers had during Isaiah's and Daniel's day. Mark 7:6-13. Once again the people found themselves immersed in vain and rebellious worship.

Even though their apostasy expressed itself in legalism instead of laxness it was still based on the same principle upon which all pagan religions are based – that a person can save themselves by their own works. Jesus, like Jeremiah of old, rebuked this religious system and called it an abomination. (Luke 16:15).

At the close of His ministry, Jesus, on two occasions, placed the guilt upon the people by stating, "they did not know the time of their visitation" and "you would not." As a result of not responding to God's personal call to turn from their abomination, their temple was to be desolated. This prophecy was fulfilled in 70 A.D. when the Roman armies of Titus burned the temple to the ground. This second desolation of the temple perfectly paralleled its first destruction. On both occasions the abominations were done by the apostate people of God and the desolation was an act of judgement performed by a heathen army.

This desolation of Jerusalem was to come as a result of the people rejecting the Messiah, the Prince. A careful study of Daniel 9:25-27 shows this to be the case. In verse 25 the Messiah is promised to Israel, and the city's restoration is also predicted. But then ominously all is prophesied for doom again. Verse 26 speaks of the Messiah being killed by His own people and of how this act would cause their city and sanctuary to be desolated once again. This prophecy indicated that history would repeat itself, and this is exactly what happened. The abominations that God's people committed resulted, in both 586 B.C., 70 A.D., and 2035 A.D., in the destruction of their sanctuary and city – first by Nebuchadnezzar, then by Titus and then by the Muslin nations.

Because physical Israel rejected the Messiah they lost their place as God's favored people. They forfeited their franchise of the gospel by their obstinate sin. As a result, God bestowed upon Christianity all the privileges and promises that had been made to the physical seed of Abraham (see Matthew 21:43; 1 Peter 2:9; Galatians 3:26-29). In the new dispensation Christians, spiritual Israel, were given the role of physical Israel, and the Christian church the status of the temple of God (see Romans 2:28, 29; Ephesians 2:11-13, 19-22; and 1 Peter 2:5).

It is the truth of this New Testament principle of spiritual Israel that Daniel speaks of the abomination that causes desolation the third and final time. These references can be found in Daniel 8:13; 11:31; and 12:11. Discerning students of prophetic history realize that these verses predict the formation and ascension of power by the Papacy. It is an indisputable fact of history that the Papacy brought into the Christian church the very same practices of paganism for which ancient Jerusalem was twice destroyed. One has to do only a little study to see how image worship, Tammuz worship, sun worship, and many more were introduced to Christianity during the dark ages. Many of these abominations are still with us in the form of statues, candles for the saints, rosary beads, Easter sunrise services, Christmas, Valentines day, Sunday sabbath worship and etc. by no means does the papal apostasy exonerate Protestantism. Most of Protestantism accede to the apostasy by continuing the practice of abominations that have their roots firmly fixed in ancient pagan religions which were established by Satan to destroy God's truth. Both Catholicism and Protestantism have fostered abominations in God's holy place, His church. Spiritual Israel, the Christian church is mirroring physical Israel. We are repeating the same sins and will consequently reap the same punishment of desolation, unless we are willing to read and obey the writings in the Word of God and flee spiritual Babylon.

It is clear that the three occasions of abomination that causes desolation found in Daniel result from apostasy on the part of God's people, but what is the sign that will tell us when the desolation is nigh?

In Luke 21:20, Jesus told His disciples what would be the last sign of the imminent destruction of Jerusalem. He said, "And when you shall see Jerusalem compassed with armies, then know that the desolation thereof is nigh." This text does not indicate that the armies are the abomination, but rather that they are a sign of vengeance for the people's abominations (see verse 22). When the Roman armies surrounded Jerusalem it was a sign that most of the city's leaders and inhabitants had passed the boundaries of God's grace and had filled their cup of iniquity. To

154

the Christians living in the city this was to be a sign that Jerusalem would soon suffer God's judgment. As soon as the first opportunity arose, these Christians were to "flee to the mountains" (verse 21). In 66 A.D. when Cestius, the Roman general, surrounded the city the Christians knew the promised sign had arrived and the time had come to flee. At their first opportunity to escape they did so, and not one Christian died in the horrible destruction of Jerusalem in 70 A.D.

Just as God gave the early Christians a sign of when to flee Jerusalem, so He has given us a sign. He has made it possible for every Christian to know when this world's probationary hour is nearing its close.

In Revelation 13 and 14, John records a list of omens that will tell us just how close we are to the end. The sign that will show this nation has filled its cup of iniquity will be when it makes a religious-political likeness to the Satanic controlled apostate power, the papacy, by uniting church and state. This image could not be more neatly effected than by the passage of a national law commanding prayer in our public schools. The horns of the Lamb like power are made into one and the United States of America speaks as a totalaterian government. Such an event will be a direct fulfillment of Revelation 13:15-17, and provide assurance that the end of this earth's probation is quickly approaching.

The Desire of Many Protestant Groups

The National Reform Association in Article II of its constitution says: "The object of this Society shall be to maintain existing Christian features in the American Government; to promote needed reforms in the action of the government touching the (Sunday) Sabbath ... and to secure such an amendment to the Constitution of the United States will declare the nation's allegiance to Jesus Christ and its acceptance of moral laws of the Christian religion, and so indicate that this is a Christian nation, and place all the Christian laws, institutions, and usages of our government on an undeniably legal basis in the fundamental law of the land."

Mr. H. L. Bowlby, long time secretary of the Lord's Day Alliance, in speaking of those who opposed religious legislation, said: "We have put the Hun ["any savage, uncivilized, or destructive person." – Dictionary] out of politics, and we will put these Huns out of the [Sunday] Sabbath. Anybody knows what would happen to any man showing disrespect to the American flag, and we mean to put the American Christian Sabbath upon exactly the same basis as the American flag. Some people object to the Puritan Sabbath as though it were an evil thing. We are not asking for the Puritan Sabbath, but we mean to have of the Puritan spirit in the American [Sunday] Sabbath."

Dark Days Ahead: Though there is much in America that needs to be reformed, the history of the past declares to us in no uncertain tones that you cannot make mankind good by the force of the policeman's club. These would be reformers who seek to make their conceptions of righteousness into the law of the land would do well to read the words of the great Baptist preacher, Spurgeon: (paraphrased) "I am ashamed of some Christians because they have so much dependence on Congress and the law of the land. Not much good may Congress ever do to true religion, except by mistake! As to getting the law of the land to touch our religion, we earnestly cry, 'Hands off! Leave us alone!' Your Sunday bills and all other forms of acts-of-Congress religion seem to me to be all wrong. Give us a fair field and no favor, and our faith has no cause to fear. The Christ wants no help from the President. I should be afraid to borrow help from government; it would look at me as if I rested on an arm of flesh, instead of depending on the living God."

The only religion that leads to God is that which comes from God. He alone is the source of Truth, Light, and Righteousness. We find this Truth, Light, and Righteousness in His Word for us, the Bible. That religion which springs forth from the mind of fallen mankind is sin. It is very essence of the man of sin, Satan, to place himself above God, to exalt the creature over the

Creator, to attempt to "improve" the law and self sacrificing love that represents the character of God. And so the image of the beast is a creation of man – the man of sin, the Pope, the head of the Roman Catholic Church, who receives his power, throne, and much authority from Satan. This apostate church has, is, and will enforce religious dogma by civil authority.

When the observance of religious dogma is enforced by civil law in the United States of America, then the issue will be clearly drawn between the religion of God and that which comes from man. Only then, with the issue thus clearly drawn, will we have the image of the Beast, a likeness of the Roman Catholic Church.

The Mark of the Beast, Sunday sabbath, the first day of the week, is the mark of authority of the Roman Catholic Church. The United States of America will, some time in the future, (c. 2024 A.D.) enforce the Mark of the Beast, in some manner, by civil authority. Those who then accept this mark will also accept the "name", or character, of the beast, apostate Christianity, and the "number of a man." This number, 666, is eminently man's number, the number of the Man of Sin, the Pope. Six falls short of seven, the number of completeness and perfection. While the seventh day Sabbath is God's own sign or mark of His Authority as Creator of all.

Only those who accept God's mark, the Seventh Day Sabbath, the sign of His authority as Creator and Rightful Sovereign of planet earth, and who trust fully in the perfect righteousness of Jesus, the Christ, will escape the great delusion connection with the Mark of the Beast.

Revelation 12 and 13 present Stan on the offensive, deceiving all mankind and gathering his forces for the great and final battle between himself and God Almighty. Through the false lamb (Revelation 13:11-18), the false prophet (Revelation 16:13; 19:20; 20:10), which is the United States of America with its apostate Protestantism, Satan will bring about his supreme deception as he exalts the religion arising from the creature over that which comes from God, the Creator. Revelation 14 presents a decided contrast, for it describes the True Lamb, Jesus, the Christ, and His followers, the 144,000, the redeemed against whom Satan wars (see Revelation12:17).

Spiritual Revival: Christiandom, Protestant America in particular, is experiencing a false revival. In the early twenty-first century A.D. it will have escalated, become great, setting up a system of government resembling the Roman Catholic church-state. Apostate Protestantism is reaching out and grasping the hands of Spiritualism and the Roman Catholic Church. The three united are the spiritual Babylonian Whore, and is headquartered in the United States of America as apostate Protestantism.

20

Christianity and the New Millennium

1031 A.D.	1776 A.D.	1798 A.D.	2001 A.D.	2031 A.D.
5001 A.S.	5746 A.S.	5768 A.S.	5971 A.S.	6001 A.S.
		You are here.*		

World View: In futurist literature, you often encounter the concept of "world view." Russell Chandler, religious writer for the Los Angeles Times, describes it as "like a giant filing cabinet in which you arrange your suppositions about how the universe is ordered." *Racing Toward 2001 A.D.*, page 202.

We all have a world view, but because it is so much a part of us, we rarely examine or question it. Like medieval artists who illustrated biblical scenes with the clothing styles of their day, we tend to think of other places, other ages, what has happened and what will happen in terms of only what we ourselves have experienced.

Even if our world view is somewhat subjective, it is fundamental in deciding how we live our lives. Our world view frames all we think or do – our understanding of a purpose for existence, our concepts of right and wrong, what we think is fair or unfair, and ideas we can accept and those we must reject.

But what we don't often recognize is that ideas are like men's ties and women's hemlines. They go in and out of style. What is acceptable at one moment in history may be considered outrageous by future generations. For example, a law limiting children to "only" 10 hours of manual labor a day, to be followed by two hours of compulsory schooling, was regarded as a great breakthrough for humanitarians in England 200 years ago. And those who framed the United States' enlightened Bill of Rights some how remained blind to the appalling inequity of slavery.

159

Theologian Francis A. Schaeffer wrote in *How Should We Then Live?*: "People have presuppositions, and they will live more consistently on the basis of these presuppositions then even they themselves may realize. By presuppositions we mean the basic way and individual looks at life, his basic world view ... People's presuppositions lay a grid for all they bring forth into the external world. Their presuppositions also provide the basis for their values and therefore their basis for their decision." Page 19.

In *Racing Toward 2001 A.D.*, Mr. Chandler explains that throughout history, three basic world views have framed the opinions of most of humanity: "The first view of the world is naturalism, or naturalistic humanism, sometimes associated with secularism. The second is mysticism, or what comes under the headings of monism, pantheism, and other philosophies with a New Age Label. The third major world view is theism/supernaturalism. The biblical Judeo-Christian world view is a subset of this.

"All three are alive and well on Planet Earth. But will they remain healthy as we speed toward the next millennium?" *Racing Toward 2001*, pages 202-203.

People are already talking about something dramatic, even cataclysmic, happening to coincide with the beginning of man's new century and millennium.

Fin de siecle – the end of a century – always generates a mood of expectancy. It becomes a logical, if artificial, deadline for those with expectations and agendas for change. So as the turn of man's millennium approaches, we will see shifts in the way the world thinks.

Eight years is long enough to make the world a much different place. Look back to January 1988 A.D.:

- Ronald Reagan was president of the United States.
- Margaret Thatcher looked secure as prime minister of Britain.
- Nelson Mandela was in prison.
- Iraq was thought of as the good guy (or at least the better guy) in the eight year war with Iran.
- The Israelis and Palestinians were avowed enemies.

- There was still a Soviet Union and a Berlin Wall.
- There was a feeling that major conflicts about racism and prejudice were over.
- Only historians and stamp collectors had ever heard of Bosnia or Herzegovina.

In the last eight years, we have seen the mood of the world change, as optimism at the end of the Cold War has diminished.

People around the world are dissatisfied with their leaders. Economies are in trouble. Some nations are disintegrating, as ethnic minorities reorganize into mini-states, often with angry agendas.

A Story Future?: Some trend analyzers and futurists – and they are not just doomsayers – see trouble ahead. They are cautious, practical people, who try to analyze the future without grinding ideological axes. They try to avoid sensationalism.

But as they look ahead, they see some ominous clouds gathering on the horizon. Some even speak of "millennium anxiety."

If they are right, what they are saying could have profound implications for all who are Christians.

The way of life that Jesus taught has always faced challenges. His message of hope, salvation and the kingdom of God has often come into conflict with the kingdoms of this world.

"Do you suppose that I have come to bring peace to the earth." He told His disciples. "I did not come to bring peace, but a sword." (Matthew 10:34).

Jesus knew the kingdoms of this world would not give way easily. The opposition would wax and wane across the ages. Jesus taught that those who took up the challenge to be His disciples should take full advantage of times of peace, as windows of opportunity.

So as the end of God's sixth millennium approaches, 2031 A.D., 6001 A.S., we will see the consummation of God's time schedule. It will be that opposition to the gospel of the kingdom will again become a fact of life for Christians of the United States of America and of the world.

Religious Extremism: Alvin Toffler, author of three books about the future, is a cautious writer, not given to sensationalism or doomsaying. But in the third volume of his trilogy, *Powershift*, he notes with concern that extremism – especially political and religious extremism – is increasing in many parts of the world.

Many of the fanatical groups focus their fury on the Western, industrial, democratic way of life. They want to turn back progress that threatens their traditional values, and their particular version of "the truth."

Mr. Toffler is afraid that "what is happening is a sky-darkening attack on the ideas of the Enlightenment which helped usher in the industrial age." page 375.

Some of the disadvantages of industrialization are becoming more apparent. Rich nations are struggling to maintain prosperity, while the poor are falling further behind.

More and more people are asking if there is something fundamentally wrong about the direction humanity has chosen. In such an emotional climate, revolutionary ideas often gather credibility and momentum.

Could the world opt for a "great leap backward"?

It sounds incredible, but Mr. Toffler warns: "In the power shift ahead, the primary ideological struggle will no longer be between capitalist democracy and communist totalitarianism, but between 21st century democracy and 11th century darkness." Page 387.

Fanatics seizing power? Intolerance? Suppression of fundamental rights? Not in some small isolated country or tin-pot dictatorship, but as a characteristic of the world as a whole.

"I am convinced that the greatest threat to our freedom in the nineties will come from those who become increasingly more sophisticated in manipulating our values, opinions and world views," writes Tom Sine, consultant in futures research, in his book *Wild Hope*. Page 126. A generation that sees itself with nothing to lose might opt for a more structured and disciplined world order where survival, not maintenance of the status quo (which is increasingly difficult to maintain), becomes the top priority.

As the consequences of lack of decisive action become more apparent, solutions and programs we now consider unacceptable may seem more and more reasonable.

162

As people, particularly younger people, are questioning the way we live, the call for social justice, environmental responsibility and a return to traditional values is becoming louder and more militant.

Devotion to a cause, whether it be for unborn babies, threatened species or trees, is admirable; but not if the focus shifts from promoting the cause to hating the perceived enemy. History has many examples of peaceful protest movements falling into hands of intolerant fanatics.

Religious Revival: There are already, in many parts of the world, the beginnings of religious revival and religious revolution.

This sounds like good news, but it might not be. The drift is not toward a return to conventional religion, but to ideas that lead toward a nonbiblical and potentially dangerous world view.

The West commonly associates religious extremism with fundamentalist Muslims. But almost all world religions have at their fringes ruthless extremists determined to force their version of truth on the world, including Christianity.

Not every fundamentalist group poses a threat to social stability. Many are just eccentric and quaint, and can coexist with, and in fact need, a tolerant democratic society. Others believe fervently in their cause, but do not resort to violence or coercion.

But, as Mr. Toffler points out: "Some of the fastest growing and most powerful religious movements in the world today ... are determined to seize power over lives and minds of whole nations, continents, the planet itself. Determined to impose their own rule over every aspect of human life. Determined to seize state power wherever they can, and roll back the freedoms that democracy makes possible. They are the agents of a new dark age." Page 376.

We already see on every continent how easily some people, young and old, are attracted to right-wing extremist groups with violent agendas, including the U.S.A.

Not many. Not yet. But it is a mood that is growing by leaps and bounds. The younger generation has sniffed at the future, and scented trouble. It is looking for solutions.

The next decade will be crucial for helping a new generation find its world view. If the wrong ideas are chosen, the result will indeed bring on a new age darkness.

The Christian World View: In such a world, Christians need to be reminded of the simplicity of the gospel of Jesus, the Christ.

Jesus did not come with a message of intolerance and fundamentalism. His message was love, moderation and balance centered in obedience to the Word of God, the commandments of God and the Testimony of Jesus.

Jesus, the Christ, taught fairness, generosity, compassion and the need to "love your neighbor as yourself." (Mark 12:31).

He focused His disciples around a new world view, to seek first "The Kingdom Of God And His Righteousness", then all your needs will be met. Jesus then gave them a commission to go and preach the Good News of the kingdom of God, centered in Jesus the Christ. (Matthew 6:25-33; 28:19; Mark 16:15-19).

After Jesus returned to heaven, His disciples continued to teach this way of life, obedience to the commandments of God and have the affidavit of Jesus. "If anyone has material possessions and sees his brother in need but has no pity on him, how can the love of God be in him?" asked John. (1 John 3:17). Scripture tells us that our spiritual brother and sister are those who do the commandments of God and believe in the witness of Jesus, the Christ.

It is perceived that some Christians have ended up with a disproportionate share of material possessions. And this fact fuels the fire of much religious extremism throughout the world.

Of the world's eight richest nations, seven are at least nominally Christian. But millions of their fellow Christians live in the poorest nations. The number of new converts to Christianity in some developing countries is dramatic. Some estimate that thousands of people a day are being added to the Christian churches of Africa.

Every day, Christians, and those who have never heard the gospel, watch helplessly as their children starve to death, or waste away from easily preventable diseases.

164

This isn't our fault, or our responsibility. If we are not given the window of opportunity to preach and teach in these nations, in the world, the Scriptures centered in Jesus, the Christ; if the people do not except the truths given in the manual for a lost humanity, Jesus tells us to leave them alone and go to those who will listen. These are our brothers and sisters, the saints of God.

Christianity is a religion best spread by example, preaching and teaching. God's Christians are the sons and daughters of God, keeping the commandments of God and believing in the witness of Jesus, the Christ. Those who do not conform to the Word of God are declared by God to be apostate, heathen, or pagan. What Christians are, personally, nationally and internationally, speaks louder than what they say they are. Especially to people who are looking for spiritual and emotional moorings in an uncertain future.

Russell Chandler, religious writer for the *Los Angeles Times*, reports in the book *Racing Toward 2001* the disturbing statistic that the wealthiest Christians are also the stingiest. In the United States, households earning $100,000 a year give an average of 2.9 percent, while those with incomes of less than $10,000 give 5.5 percent. The trend for giving among the rich is downward – to a projected 1.94 percent at the century's end.

To live more simply, that others may simply live, is a most sensible and Christian thing to do. It would not mean impoverishing ourselves.

Mr. Chandler writes: "If church members were to boost their giving to an average of 10 percent of their income (the tithe), the additional funds could eliminate the worst of world poverty, which James Grant, the executive director of UNICEF, says would require $65 billion. The 10 percent would provide that plus another $17 billion for domestic needs – all the while maintaining the church activities at current levels." Page 220.

Making A Difference: Financial help just happens to be a convenient example. Some of us can't give any more than we do, but we must still be concerned and caring disciples of Jesus, the Christ.

We should pray for opportunities to preach the gospel and encourage those who have need. We must avoid ungodly solutions that are extreme while working with those deeply affected by pain and suffering. Teach first the kingdom of heaven and all their needs will be met.

In the spring of 2036 A.D., 1 Nisan, 6006 A.S., Jesus, the Christ will return. But until that day, He does His work in and through those He has called to represent Him, those who obey Him.

If ever there was a time for the followers of the Christ to show what they stand for, this is it.

There are but few windows of opportunity to set the world an example. Not as fanatics or bigots. Not with ruthlessness and intimidation, but firmly and relentlessly following Jesus, the Christ's example of truth, love, compassion and generosity.

Millennium Mischief

"In the instruction to *The World Almanac Guide to Good Word Usage*, Edwin Newman expresses the editors view of the millennium: ' "The first century began January 1 of the year 1 A.D. It follows that the 20th century will not end until December 31, 2000 A.D., and that the 21st century will begin on January 1, 2001 A.D. Not, repeat not, January 1, 2000 A.D., as the common assumption has it." '

These guys are going to miss all the parties. Language mavens and bean-counting calender-watchers can prove their case to their heart's content, but the big ball is going to drop in Times Square at midnight of December 31, 1999. Such linguistic and mathematical correctness gets tromped on and flattened by the hooves of the happily inaccurate herd, leaving a small knot of hard-faced language protesters holding a sign that reads "Not Yet" amid the cork-popping celebrants of the new millennium."

The following instruction to the people of God concerning the Plan of Salvation, the fulfillment of prophecy, and the end of all things as we know them, expresses this writers view of the millennium: The first century began 1 Nisan of the year 1 A.S. (after sin). It follows that each year and century following began

1 Nisan 2 A.S.; 1 Nisan 3 A.S., and etc. We are living at the end of the 6th century A.S. of God's calender. The 7th century begins 1 Nisan 6001 A.S., spring 2031 A.D. Not, I repeat, not January 1, 1999 A.D., 2000 A.D., or 2001 A.D. as the common assumption has it.

The world is missing all the important things, the things of God. Mankind with its language mavens and bean-counting calender-watchers can prove, by man's times and seasons, their case to their hearts content, but the big ball will not drop till, 1 Nisan 6001 A.S., spring of 2031 A.D. at this time the masses of the wicked will be wicked forever, and the few righteous will be righteous forever, and the Christ will return in all His glory in the clouds of heaven 1 Nisan 6006 A.S., spring, 2036 A.D. All that refuse today to listen to the Word of God, the linguist, the mathematician, those that conform to the will of man, get tromped on, flattened by the wrath of God as He fights for His people. The happy, accurate (inaccurate according to the masses) celebrants, the people of God, celebrate the 8th millennium in heaven as the eternal children of God.

Dear reader, as you read on about blind and deaf Christianity, take it personally. What kind of a person should you be as we approach the new millennium, spring of 2031 A.D. when God says, "It is done"? "Let the righteous forever be righteous and the wicked forever wicked."

21

Christianity, Blind and Deaf

1031 A.D.	1776 A.D.	1798 A.D.	2001 A.D.	2031 A.D.
5001 A.S.	5746 A.S.	5768 A.S.	5971 A.S.	6001 A.S.

You are here. *

Some of the most astonishing prophecies in the Bible have to do with the proportion of people who will be saved at the second coming of the Christ. Jesus clearly taught that only a comparative few would be ready to inherit His kingdom. He said,

"Enter through the narrow gate; for wide is the gate and spacious the road that leads on to destruction, and many are those entering by it. Because narrow is the gate and hard the road that leads on to eternal life, and few are they who discover it." (Matthew 7:13, 14).

In Luke 18:8, by asking a very penetrating question, Jesus implied that the "few" might be even less than we could hope or imagine. "However, when the Son of Man comes, will He find faith on the earth?" Again the Master spoke of the final separation in these words: "In the day of the Son of Man it will be just as it was in the days of Noah." (Luke 17:16). Only eight people were saved from the flood, and "as it was then" so shall it be at His coming. Other Bible writers and prophets use similar language to portray the small number who will prove faithful.

The fact that so few will be saved is not nearly as shocking as the reason given in the Bible for their loss. It seems obvious that great multitudes will be excluded from heaven even though they profess the Christ, worship Him regularly, and spend much of their time doing wonderful works in His name. Jesus said,

"Not everyone who says to Me, 'Lord, Lord!' will enter into the kingdom of heaven, but he who does the will of My Father in heaven. Many will say to Me in that Day, 'Lord, Lord, did

168

we not prophecy in Your name and in Your name cast out demons and in Your name do many wonderful works?' Then I will frankly declare to them, 'I never knew you. Get away from Me, you workers of evil.' " (Matthew 7:21-23).

These verses reveal that the earth is flooded with a lot of false Christianity in these last days. Millions of 'Christians' are spending their time, their efforts, and their money in promoting a religion that involves apparent miracles, apparent spiritual gifts, and much enthusiastic activity. All of this is explicitly spelled out in the teaching of our Lord. Yet these "many" will finally be utterly rejected by Jesus, and shut out of heaven.

Talk about startling truth!

More people need to get their eyes open to this little understood situation that characterizes the end time in which we live. Today we need to find out how to avoid the vast spiritual delusions which are causing so many religious people to be lost.

Why will you be rejected in spite of your devoted worship and ministry in the name of Jesus? It has caused some almost to despair of salvation. How can you know that your religion will not finally be found in this category? Let's seriously look at the answers to these questions. Our salvation does not depend upon our sincerity, but upon finding the truth in God's Word and obeying it!

Obedience Is The Acid Test Of A Valid Religion: The first point we must understand is this: **Religious activity is quite useless if we are not doing the will of God.** The Christ declared that calling on God's name, and even leading out in great selfless humanitarian programs will be wasted if obedience to God's will is excluded. Mark this fact upon the tables of your heart and mind and never forget it – the Scriptures exalt **obedience** as the distinguishing test of a valid religion. Those who engaged ever so fully in preaching the name of Jesus – and do not keep His commandments, cannot meet the approval of God. In fact, because they are not obeying the Christ, such worshipers actually open doors by which Satan enters unrecognized and works miracles through them, **in the name of Jesus,** which they ascribe to the power of God. The plaintive plea, "Have we not prophesied –

and in Your name cast out devils?" is proof positive that their miracles had been done by some other power than that of the Christ, albeit in His name. If Jesus never knew them, who else could work such miracles? Only Satan. The Bible speaks of "spirits of devils, working miracles," in Revelation 16:14.

By the way, what did Jesus mean when He said, "I never knew you. Get away from Me, you workers of evil"? How does one really come to "know" the Lord? the beloved John tells us, "No one who remains in Him practices sin. Whoever practices sinning has neither seen Him or known Him." (1 John 3:6). "He who says, 'I know Him' and does not keep His commandments, is a lair and the truth is not in him." Knowing Him means we obey Him. Biblically, it is impossible to be a true child of God while refusing to obey the commandments of God. Willful disobedience cuts off the relationship, drives away the Holy Spirit by which we are sealed, and effectively removes the individual from the position of grace.

Now we begin to see how simple it is to test the religious spirits that are in Christianity today all over the world. It is time to look past the stimulating music, the spellbinding oratory, and even the exciting witnessing programs and apply the test set up by the great Author of all truth – Jesus Himself. He made it exceedingly clear that the original requirements of God have remained unchanged. The condition of obedience which would have kept man in the Garden becomes the condition for the restoration of Eden, and his return to the Garden. "If you love Me, you will keep My commandments." (John 14:15).

Love And Obedience Is Not Legalism: We must not fail to emphasize at this point that element of love which must also attend all acceptable obedience. Forcing the forms of compliance without a personal love experience with the Christ, the Saviour is fully as fatal a mistake as omitting all obedience. Jesus had to deal with cold formalism of the Pharisees over and over again. And because He so thoroughly condemned the program of salvation by works, many have hastily assumed that He considered obedience unimportant. How we need to see the beautiful balance in the Christ's doctrine of faith and works. He taught that obeying in order to be saved is the worst kind of legalism, but obeying because we are saved is the acid test of a true religious experience. Obedience follows true faith just as surely as day follows night. Incidentally, the word "legalist" has been thrown around with much abandon. I greatly fear that many sincere Christians have been accused of legalism only because their love for the Christ led them to be more particular in their obedience than their accusers. Never forget that a legalist is one who believes that they can be saved by their works. The person who keeps the commandments because they don't want to displease the God they love is not a legalist at all. The old argument is often heard, "I'd rather see a happy, loving Christian who doesn't keep all the commandments than to see an unloving one who strictly obeys the law." Why try to measure degrees of guilt? Both are completely wrong. Our feelings have nothing to do with it. The Christ has established the standard of measurement. Nothing less than a "faith which works by love" will be accepted.

But let us return to the alarming proposition that most of mankind, most of Christianity is lost, including the fervent religious activists. Worship is commanded in the Bible, and is a necessary ingredient of true religion, but are the hosts of worshiping Christians lost? Jesus said, "But in vain they do worship Me, teaching for doctrines the commandments of men." (Matthew 15:9). Another shattering statement of truth! People do engage in vain worship when they reject true doctrine for man's tradition.

When Is Worship Vain? On several occasions Jesus urged the necessity of walking in all known truth.

> "Had I not come and spoken to them, they would not be guilty; but now they have no excuse for their sin." (John 15:22).

> "If you were blind you would be blameless; but since you claim to have sight, your sin remains." (John 9:41).

When persons learn a point of truth in the Bible and refuse to obey it, they are guilty of practicing sin. Such persons are fighting the Holy Spirit, whose primary work is to guide into all truth. This refusal to obey hardens the conscience, finally causing the Holy Spirit to withdraw, and is the Unpardonable Sin. No wonder such worship is vain. By rejecting the commandments of God in favor of human traditions the Holy Spirit is spurned. According to Acts 5:32 only those who obey are eligible to be filled with the Spirit.

"We are witnesses of these things, and so is the Holy Spirit, who is given by God to all who obey Him." (Acts 5:32).

Let us pause now and consider the profound significance of what we have discovered. The vast majority of people are lost, including most who work miracles in the Christ's name, worship Him and claim to know Him as His children. The reason they are lost is that they do not love Him enough to keep all His commandments. For some reason these ardent church workers have learned to look lightly upon the law of God. Most of them consider it legalism to believe that disobedience could keep them out of heaven. Satan has blinded the eyes of Christendom to the beautiful, intimate relationship of love and obedience. Millions of Christians, Protestant and Catholic alike, have been taught that their obedience or disobedience can have no effect whatever upon their ultimate salvation.

In view of this deep rooted tradition of popular Christianity today, we can see how Satan has manipulated millions into a state of mind to reject the claims of God's moral law. Under the twisted interpretation of a cheap grace (someone has called it "sloppy agape") the stage is set for the devil's master strategy of deception. The final contest between truth and error is revolving around the basic issue of loyalty or disloyalty, obedience or disobedience. And the focus is squarely on the Law of God and on the fourth commandment, which contains the great distinctive Sign, Mark, or Seal of God's creative power and authority.

Do you, dear friend have the Seal of God? Are you obedient to the Word? We are the servant of him whom we obey, God unto eternal life, and anything else unto eternal destruction. Please turn the pages for further help and understanding.

22

The Image to the Beast

1031 A.D.	1776 A.D.	1798 A.D.	2001 A.D.	2031 A.D.
5001 A.S.	5746 A.S.	5768 A.S.	5971 A.S.	6001 A.S.
		You are here. *		

This chapter will put us to the test. It is not only a questions concerning our emotional stability; it is more especially a question concerning our attitudes. The real question is: Can we detach ourselves from the mold in which our thinking has been cast? Are we capable of acquiring new concepts of history?

But the superb question remains: Can we detach ourselves from the human, from mans viewpoint in order to attain to the divine, God's viewpoint? This is the final element that separates true Bible researchers from mere polemists, or controversialists. But the only rewards worth having await the humble, sincere searcher of Scripture. And we must be prepared to let the data lead us on to the truth as we submit to the guidance of the Holy Spirit. There may be surprises, disappointments, anguish! But the ultimate reward is clear truth that leads to eternal joy, eternal life.

The Rise Of The Composite Beast: John describes the rise of the second of the three beasts having 7 heads and 10 horns:

"And I stood upon the sand of the sea, and saw a beast rise up out of the sea, having 7 heads and 10 horns, and upon his horns 10 crowns, and upon his heads the name of blasphemy. And the beast which I saw was like unto a leopard, and his feet were as the feet of a bear, and his mouth as the mouth of a lion; And the dragon gave his his power, his seat, and great authority." (Revelation 13:1, 2).

Reminders Of The 7th Chapter Of Daniel: The various elements of this introduction to the prophecy brings to mind the graphic symbols in Daniel, Chapter 7. In that Old Testament

173

view of the future of earthly empires that have rule over God's people, Daniel saw 4 beasts rise up out of the sea. And we have found, in earlier chapters, that those 4 beasts were declared to depict 4 great powers of history – from Daniel's time, forward. Please review Chapters 3, 4, 5, and 6 of this book.

In Reverse Order: But the order in which Daniel saw these beasts rise is in exact reverse order to that seen by John, 700 years later. Why is this?

The Answer: Daniel lived about 700 years before John. He was looking "downstream" in history – toward the future from his time. But John was looking "upstream" in history – toward the past. Therefore, these world powers were seen in exact opposite sequence.

Where is Daniel's 4th Beast in John's vision? Daniel saw 4 beasts: lion, bear, leopard, and the terrible composite beast. But the Apostate composite beast in John's vision (Revelation 13:1, 2) has elements of only three of those beasts. Why?

In Daniel's vision of Chapter 7 of his book, the 4th beats represents pagan, Imperial Rome. That 4th, unnamed, terrible beast assimilated the remains of the beasts (political powers) that existed prior to it. It was largely the composite of its predecessors – the resurgence of ancient powers "under new management". For this reason, the beast representing Rome is not given a name. It is not a new beast on the scene. It combines the cruelty and powers of the beasts that went before it – on a larger and grander scale.

Now, with this in mind, you will recall that in the 8th Chapter of Daniel, the same area of history is prophetically covered; but the progression goes directly from Greece (the 3rd power) to Rome in its dual form (pagan-papal). Actually, Daniel Chapter 8 moves right from Greece to papal Rome. We found out earlier that papal Rome has its origin and substance in pagan Rome. The Word of God considers them as one and the same in substance and character. It is only a matter of transfer of power and authority from one phase of Rome to the other. Please review Chapter 5 of this book.

It has been asserted that the Apostate beast, through its fifth head, is a symbol of papal Rome and a symbolic conception of this representation can be developed.

Since this composite beast is made up of elements of ancient civilizations (Babylon, Medo-Persia, Greece, and pagan Rome), it is concluded that papal Rome is the product of the total of the false systems of religion that existed under those earlier world powers. It is concluded that Satan was and is working in and through those ancient world religions and powers to develop a philosophy to counter the true faith. And it must be concluded that in papal Rome Satan brings to perfection his counterfeit religion.

From the forgoing conclusions, the apostate leopard beast, through its fifth head, is the papacy. But it is seen that the papacy really involved all world history since the days of Babylon. And Babylon – particularly in her religious character – actually goes back to the beginnings of apostasy following the universal flood, when Nimrod set about to build the God defying city, with its famous tower. Therefore, the leopard-composite beast represents Apostasy, as it has existed throughout ancient history, but particularly as it is ripened and perfected in the Roman Catholic Church.

With this concept in view, let's take a look at the 7 heads. The 7 heads represent the individual, historical divisions of which the beast of apostasy is composed. And the sequence of the 7 heads, up to the present observations, would be: 1) Babylon; 2) Medo-Persia; 3) Greece; 4) pagan Rome; 5) papal Rome. This leaves 2 heads after the disaster of the "deadly wound" that was received in 1798 A.D.

The conclusion is that the entire leopard-composite beast represents the Apostasy, with all of its apostate inherited and incorporated parts. And, at the same time, the 5th head represents the specific entity which is the Roman Catholic Church in its historical sequence in the total composite picture of the grand Apostasy.

Another Beast Comes On Stage: Please review Chapter 7 of this book and you will discover that the new nation coming on stage is none other than the United States of America. No other power on earth could possibly fulfill all the requirements of these prophecies.

And He Spake As A Dragon: Concerning the United States of America, the prophecy says, "... and he had 2 horns like a lamb (the sixth head), and he spake as a dragon (the seventh head)." (Revelation 13:11). The Word of God considers them as one and the same in substance and character. It is only a matter of transfer of power and authority from one phase of apostasy to a greater apostasy, lamb like to dragon. Therefore, the leopard-composite beast represents Apostasy, as it has existed throughout history, but particularly as it is ripened and perfected in the Protestantism of the United States of America.

This last phase is most distressing and disappointing! The nation came upon the scene at the right moment to rescue the Church from the wrath of the dragon. Then the time comes when the scene changes "... and he spake as a dragon". The peaceful, lamb like character gives way (1776 A.D. to 2001 A.D.) to the nature of the "dragon" (2001 A.D. to 2036 A.D.). Every loyal American could fervently wish that this feature of the prophecy could be changed! Our own beloved America. Our homeland. How can this be? God forbid! But, God must be true. He cannot hide the real issues before us. He tells it as it is.

And, this is only the beginning. As we proceed with the opening up of events concerning this second world power in Revelation Chapter 13, the picture becomes very very dark indeed.

In opening up these scenes to us in this prophecy, God is not placing this Country in a role contrary to her will. This is simply a revealing of the foreknowledge of God.

The Picture Enlarges: The view concerning the second beast of Revelation Chapter 13 becomes grim! We read on:

"And he exercises all the authority of the first beast in its presents, and makes the earth and its inhabitants worship the first beast, whose mortal wound was healed. (Revelation 13:12).

Now, the role of the United States of America becomes apparent. The U.S.A. shall follow in the steps of the Roman Catholic Church by enforcing religious dogma by civil authority, and shall lead the whole world into a commitment to the first beast represented by the papal power that had suffered a mortal stroke of the sword, and has recovered. This action pertains to our time and the immediate future.

The United States of America Leads The World In Making "A Likeness" To The Roman Catholic Church: Now the scene becomes serious indeed! The next 3 verses bring the issue to a point of crisis:

"He also performs impressive miracles; for instance, he causes fire to descent from heaven to the earth in the presence of the people. By means of the wonders he is allowed to perform in the presence of the beast, he leads those living on the earth astray, telling the earth's inhabitants to make a likeness to the beast that had the wound by the sword and came back to life. He was further permitted to infuse breath into the beast's likeness, so that the beast's likeness might speak and to bring it about that those who did not worship the beast's likeness should be killed." (Revelation 13:13-15).

What Is "A Likeness To The Beast"? We must remember, of course, that the "likeness" is made by The United States of America to the Roman Catholic Church. This is, indeed, a most surprising move! It seems unthinkable! But we shall see that the scene becomes even more astonishing as we move along.

But, what is a "likeness"? We could ask: What is any likeness? The dictionary that is on this desk has several definitions that apply: "A reproduction or imitation of the form of a person or thing; an image; a tangible or visible representation".

It is clear, therefore, that this prophecy tells us that the United States of America is to set up a reproduction of the Roman Catholic Church. And, what, exactly, is the nature of the Roman Catholic Church?

In the days of its supremacy, when the papacy did according to its own will, it consisted of a religious power that completely dominated the political, civil powers. The papacy substituted its own dogmas, creed, and traditions for the commands of God, and then imposed its religious institutions upon the minds and consciences of the people by using the power of the State to enforce her will. This is the very essence of the beast, the leopard composite beast, the Roman Catholic Church, the fifth head.

And The United States of America, with its Republican form of government, will enforce religious dogma by civil authority, and by so doing it sets up a duplicate of the beast as represented by the Roman Catholic Church. This would mean setting aside all those grand principles that are framed in the Constitution of this Country which stand as a safeguard for the freedom of every citizen of this American Republic. Such is the prophetic picture given us by inspiration of the career of our beloved Country – if she does not, and she will not repent and turn away from the role which Satan has designed for her to play in the closing scenes of Plant Earth's history.

It is our fervent prayer that our beloved Country will repent! But, are there any signs that this will be? Inspiration does not indicate that she will repent. The fate of The United States of America lies in her own will and choice. She alone (individually and collectively) can and will make that decision. If she does not choose to repent, and scripture does not indicate that she will, she has already been committed to the course laid out in prophecy. The divine view has been given.

Again, we observe that it is the younger beast, the United States of America that is desperately commanding all persons throughout the world to receive, conform to the "likeness" of the papal power.

In a few years, as we near the year 2031 A.D., the United States of America will enforce religious dogma by civil authority and become like the Catholic Church. It may start as simply and as desirable as Federal Law requiring Christian Prayer in public schools, or it may be some other dogma thought to be desirable by the masses of nominal, cultural, and social Christianity. Could it be a national Sunday Blue Law?

Throughout the history of God's people many are not deceived by the claims of the Apostate Church, nor are they deceived today. Their hands are laid confidingly in the hand of the Christ and all fear of death vanishes.

The people of God, His Church, which is preparing for His coming must be free from apostate error and corruptions. They will emulate the Christ and with Him keep the commandments of God. Satan is stirred, as an angry lion, and so controls the United States of America that all of its authority shall be used to enforce the likeness of the man of sin. Then the issue is fairly before the people. We must choose this day whom we will serve, God or Satan. Most will say to God, I know Your claims, but I will not do them, I wish to save my life today. A few will say to God, I know Your claims, and I will do them, I wish to save my life eternally.

Those few go out into the world and invade the kingdom of Satan, and the powers of darkness arouse to greater vigilance. Every effort to spread the Word of God is watched by the prince of evil, and he excites the fears of Apostate Christianity. The leaders of Apostate Christianity see a portent of danger to their cause from the witness of the humble servants of God.

The very existence of this Godly people, holding the faith of the Apostolic church, is a constant testimony to their apostasy, and excites the most bitter hatred and persecution. Their refusal to surrender the conscience is an offense the Apostate Church cannot tolerate. It determined to blot them from the face of the earth.

Again and again their lands are laid waste, their houses and churches swept away, so that where once were an innocent, industrious people, there is nothing. As the ravenous wild beast is rendered more furious by the taste of blood, so the rage of the Apostate Church will be kindled to greater intensity by the sufferings of their victims. Many of these witnesses for pure faith will be pursued into the desert, the mountains, and the valleys where they are shut in by the mighty creations of their God.

No charge is brought against the moral character of this proscribed class of people. Even their declared enemies declare them to be a peaceable, quite, and pious people. Their grand offense is that they will not worship God according to the will of the Apostate Church. For this crime, every humiliation, insult, and torture that men and devils can invent will be heaped upon them.

A likeness to the Catholic Church has been made; the enforcement of religious doctrine by civil authority. Turn to see the seal of authority of the Catholic Church and Protestantism that becomes a life and death issue, for the people of God, as it is enforced by civil authority.

23

The Mark of the Beast

1031 A.D.	1776 A.D.	1798 A.D.	2001 A.D.	2031 A.D.
5001 A.S.	5746 A.S.	5768 A.S.	5971 A.S.	6001 A.S.
			You are here. *	

From reading Revelation 13:16, 17; 14:9, 10, we know the time is coming when it will be decreed that no one can buy or sell unless they have the mark, or seal, of the beast; and at the same time God will send a message of warning saying that those who receive the mark, or seal, will receive the judgements of heaven, that they will lose eternal life and will be destroyed, after suffering the seven last plagues.

From reading Revelation 7 we know that God has a mark, or seal, with which He will distinguish His people, those that receive His mark, or seal will be saved. We know that God's mark, or seal, is found in connection with His Law. Likewise, the mark, or seal, of the beast is found in connection with God's commandments. The difference between those who receive the mark, or seal, of the beast and those who do not is clearly stated in Revelation 14:12. God's people, spiritual Israel, obey His commandments not in order to be saved, not to earn salvation, not to get to heaven, but because they are saved and in loving obedience obey Him. Jesus has already saved us from continuing in sin, in disobedience to these very commandments; He Himself by His obedience to these commandments earned our salvation and right to heaven, and gives us grace to copy His loving and obedient life. He has also by His death, saved us from the death penalty we deserve as "lawless" sinners.

Sabbath Is God's Sign: (Ezekiel 20:12, 20; Exodus 31:13). As a sign of His creative power, when creation was completed God gave to mankind the Sabbath, to be an everlasting memorial.

180

Consider carefully, prayerfully, these Scriptures in you own Bible: God commands us to work six days and rest on the Lord's Day just as He did (Hebrews 4:4, 9-11 see margin). The true Lord's Day. (Revelation 1:10). The day He rested on, the day He "Blessed" and "Sanctified" – "set apart for holy use" is the seventh day Sabbath (Genesis 1:31 to 2:3; Mark 2:27, 28). The Sabbath of the fourth Commandment (Exodus 20:8-11).

In blessing and sanctifying the seventh day, He "made His wonderful works remembered." (Psalm 111:4). God intends that the memorial that He established of His creative power is to be for all ti me, for all of mankind, for all eternity. Note the language of Psalm 135:13: "Your name, O Lord, endures forever; and Your memorial, O Lord, throughout all generations." (See also Isaiah 66:23).

Mark Of Beast Rival Of God's Seal: The mark, or seal, of the beast is a rival, or counterfeit, of God's seal, the Sabbath. A garage would not be a rival of a ladies' apparel shop. An institution, to be a rival of another, must be of a similar kind. Hence the mark of the beast, the rival of God's seal, or Sabbath, must be an institution similar to the seal of the divine law. Therefore the mark of the beast must be a sabbath that rivals God's true Sabbath. Then let us raise this question, "Have any religious and/or political organization instituted a day of rest to replace the seventh day which God gave?"

Here is a reply: "Yes."

The Prophecy Of Change In God's Law: The prophet Daniel, centuries before, predicted the rise of this apostate power which would think to change God's law. Read Daniel 7:25. In changing God's law, the papacy tore the seal, or mark, out of the law of God. They have thrown away God's sign and have set at naught His mark of distinction. Do you wonder that God is so stirred about this; that He feels it keenly when an earthly power dares to pull the seal right out of His law and boldly dares to substitute its own mark? That is why the Bible says that if any man dares to take the mark of man in preference to the seal of God, he "shall drink of the wine of the wrath of God, which is poured out without mixture into the cup of His indignation."

Church Claims Change: From the *Kansas City Catholic* of 9 February 1893 A.D., we read "The Catholic church of its own infallible authority created Sunday a holy day to take the place of the Sabbath of the old law." In many of her publications the Catholic church claims to have made a change in God's law respecting the day of worship and to have substituted another day for the one God blessed. The change we have made respecting the day of worship they hold up as a mark of their power and authority.

From a Catholic publication called *Abridgement of Christian Doctrine*, page 58, we quote: "Question. How prove you that the church has power to command feasts and holy days? Answer. By the very act of changing the Sabbath into Sunday, which Protestants allow of; and therefore they fondly contradict themselves, by keeping Sunday strictly, and breaking most other feasts commanded by the same church. Question? How prove you that? Answer. Because by keeping Sunday they acknowledge the church's power to ordain feasts, and to command them under sin, and by not keeping the rest of her commanded, they again deny in fact, the same power."

From their *Doctrinal Cathechism*, page 194, we read: "Question. Have you any other way of proving that the church has power to institute festivals of precept? Answer. Had she not such power, she could not have done that which all modern religionist agree with her – she could not have substituted the observance of Sunday, the first day of the week, for the observance of Saturday, the seventh day, a change for which there is no Scriptural authority."

"It was the Catholic Church which, by the authority of Jesus Christ, has transferred this rest to the Sunday in remembrance of the resurrection of our Lord. Thus the observance of Sunday by Protestants is an homage they pay, in spite of themselves, to the authority of the (Catholic) church." – *Plain Talk about the Protestantism of Today*, Segur, page 213.

The man made memorial of the Christ's resurrection is Sunday. But God's memorial of the Christ's resurrection is described in Romans 6:1-23. It is not a day. It is a life. It is resurrection from the waters of baptism, resurrection from a life of sin. From spiritual death. (Those who cling to sinful habits are spiritually dead – Ephesians 2:1, 5.) God's memorial of the Christ's resurrection is the new loving obedient Holy Spirit filled life we live every day by the grace of the Christ. Only His life, death, and resurrection made ours possible!

Priest Enright, when president of Redemptorist College of Kansas City, Missouri, said in a speech which was printed in the Hartford *Weekly Call*, "Christ gave to the church the power to make laws binding upon the conscience. Show me one sect that claims or possesses the power to do so save the Catholic Church. There is none, and yet all Christendom acknowledges the power of the church to do so, as I will prove to you. For example, the observance of Sunday. How can other denominations keep this day? The Bible commands you to keep the Sabbath day. Sunday is not the Sabbath day; no man dare assert that it is; for the Bible says plainly as words can make it, that the seventh day is the Sabbath, i.e., Saturday; for we know Sunday to be the first day of the week. Besides, the Jews have been keeping the Sabbath day unto the present time. I am not a rich man, but I will give $1,000 to any man who will prove by the Bible alone that Sunday is the day we are bound to keep. No, it cannot be done; it is impossible. The observance of Sunday is solely a law of the Catholic Church, and therefore is not binding upon others. The church changed the Sabbath to Sunday, and all the world bows down and worships upon that day in silent obedience to the mandates of the Catholic Church. Is it not a living miracle – That those who hate us so bitterly, obey and acknowledge our power every week, and do not know it?"

A letter to Cardinal Gibbons inquired if the Catholic Church changed the Sabbath and considered the change as a mark of her authority. The answer from his chancellor asserted the following: "Of course the Catholic Church claims that the change was her act. It could not have been otherwise, as none in those days would have dreamed of doing anything in matters spiritual and religious without her, and the act is a mark of her ecclesiastical power and authority in religious matters."

Does It Make Any Difference Which Day?: The Sabbath is the sign of loyalty to the one true God – the Creator – Jeremiah 10:9-16. It is God's banner, His flag. If I should take the American flag and stamp on it at the same time raise high the flag of our enemy, would you think it made any difference which flag I waved high and which flag I stamped upon? The Sabbath is the banner of Prince Emmanuel, but there are those who say they love Him, reverence Him, acknowledge His authority, and yet they unknowingly trample upon His sign while at the same time they take the banner of the papacy and wave it high.

Because of God's warnings in Revelation 14:9-12. I believe you will want to review and share with others the above Scriptures, so that you and they may make a Holy Spirit guided decision.

It Takes Courage To Obey: God is tremendously in earnest about the contempt that is being heaped upon Him. Again read Revelation 14:9-12. Dear reader, why not align yourself under God's banner and keep His Sabbath? Some say it is to hard, that since all the world keeps Sunday they could not stand out against the world and be different. Not willing to stand for God and His truth unless others do! Have they none of the spirit of Elijah, of John the Baptist, of the apostles? It takes the courage of Martin Luther, who led out in the great Reformation of his day, to continue the reformation from error to truth. Yes, dear friend, it takes courage.

The Saints of God, spiritual Israel, by keeping the commandments of God, specifically the fourth commandment. His seal, signify that we are the worshipers of the One and only true God.

By the observance of the fourth commandment which contains His seal and name, we are distinguishingly marked by a religious characteristic, through which we are exempted from the judgments of God that fall upon the wicked around us.

The observance of the fourth commandment involves a very marked and striking peculiarity in religious practice. It is one of the most singular facts to be met with in religious history that, in an age of such boasted gospel light as the present, when the influence of Christianity is so powerful and widespread, one of the most striking peculiarities in practice which we can adopt, and one of the greatest crosses we can take up, is the simple observance of the Sabbath of the fourth commandment of God's law. This precept requires that we observe the seventh day of each week as the Sabbath of the Lord God; While Christianity in general, through the combined influence of paganism and the papacy, are beguiled into keeping the first day of the week. When we observe the Sabbath of the commandments of God, a mark of peculiarity is placed upon us. We are distinct from both professed, nominal, and social Christianity and the secular world, paganism.

It is the fourth commandment of the decalogue and that alone which the Christian world is openly violating and teaching, commanding mankind to do so. The keeping of this commandment, the Lord's Sabbath, is what distinguishes us, the servants of God, from worshippers of the beast that receive his mark. The mark of the beast is any sabbath other than the seventh day Sabbath of the Lord our God.

When it is declared, in the spring of 2031 A.D., that the wicked will remain wicked and the righteous will remain righteous, the righteous are committed to total observance of God's law, including the fourth commandment, to the death if necessary. It is the free choice of every person to choose this day whom you will service, God to eternal life or Satan to eternal destruction. Choose today whom you will serve, as for me and my house, we will serve God.

The Papacy In Protestant America: We shall note the ambitions of the Roman Catholic Church and mention the unusual honor that our government is conferring upon this church organization. In the four and eleven January nineteen forty-one issues of the *America*, a Catholic publication, two articles appeared, defining eloquently the aims of Catholicism in America.

The first said, "Protestantism is dying, and facing, in an ever increasing numbers, the problem of empty pews ... Dimly sensing that a house divided against itself cannot stand, they begin to talk of unity, even making overtures in the direction of the

Catholic Church, inviting us to cooperate with them in the common fight against indifferentism ("the belief that all 'non-Christian' religions are of equal validity" with the Christian religion) and paganism. More and more they stress the evil of separation and division, blaming us for any manifestation on our part of coldness and aloofness. They conveniently forget that they separated from us, not we from them; and that it is for them to return to unity on Catholic terms, not for us to seek union with them, or to accept it on their terms."

Now, in the nineteen seventy's, ecumenical feelings ran high. In the United States, Lutheran and Roman Catholic scholars reached a startling degree of agreement on papal supremacy. After expressing a general consensus on such basic topics as Baptism, the Eucharist, and the Ministry, their "Common Statement" declares that the Papacy, "renewed in the light of the Gospel, need not be a barrier to reconciliation" of the two churches.

Elsewhere, in India, ecumenical dialogs proceed among Roman Catholics, the Orthodox communions, and Protestants; in England, among Anglicans and Lutherans; in the United States, among Roman Catholics and Baptists.

Dear Bible Students, are you watching with concern these fulfillments of Bible prophecies regarding the ecumenical movement?

No New Sound In Rome: In the nineteen seventy-four Synod of Bishops, Pope Paul VI strongly criticized the assembly for what he felt were threats to his authority. Quoting a statement from Vatican II which says that the Pope "has full supreme and universal power in the Church," he insisted repeatedly on the importance of his supremacy.

Rome asserts that the Church "never erred; nor will it, according to the scriptures, ever err." Then how can she renounce the principles which governed her course in past ages?

The Roman Catholic Church now presents a fair front to the world ... but she is unchanged. Every principle of the Papacy that existed in past ages exists today. Let it be remembered, it is the boast of Rome that she never changes.

At the heart of every false religion is one or both of these two principles – that we may be saved by our own merits, our own good works, our own upright character. Or, that we may be saved in our sins: We may live a sinful, selfish life, indifferent to, even antagonistic toward God and man – and yet, in the end, spend eternity in bliss. This is the secret of the power of false doctrines.

When religious dogma is passed into law restricting, denying worship on the seventh day Sabbath, enforced by civil authority, the issue will be clearly drawn between the religion of God and that which comes from man. Only then, with the issue clearly drawn, will we have the Mark of the Beast.

The United States of America will in 2026 A.D. enforce the Mark of the Beast by civil authority. Those who accept this mark will also accept the "name", or character, of apostate Christianity, and the "number of a man." This number, 666, is eminently man's number, the number of the Man of Sin, the Pope, the Antichrist.

Only those who accept God's mark will escape the great delusion connected with the Mark of the Beast.

Revelation, chapters 12 and 13, present Satan on the offensive, deceiving all mankind and gathering his forces for the great and final battle between himself and God Almighty. Through the false lamb (Revelation 13:11-18), the false prophet (Revelation 16:13; 19:20; 20:10), which is apostate Protestant America, Satan brings about his supreme deception as he exalts the religion arising from the creature over that which comes from God, the creator. Revelation 14 presents a decided contrast, for it describes the True Lamb, Jesus, the Christ, and His followers, the 144,000, the redeemed against whom Satan wars (see Revelation 12:17).

Christiandom, Protestant America in particular, is experiencing a false revival. From 2001 A.D. to 2031 A.D. it will have escalated, become great, setting up a system of government resembling the Apostate Beast exemplified by the Papacy during the inquisitions. Apostate Protestantism is grasping the hand of Catholicism and Spiritualism. The three united are the spiritual Babylonian Whore, and is headquartered in the United States of America.

187

But at the heart of Bible religion are these two principles – That we may only be saved by the Christ's merits along, His works, His good deeds, His morally upright character. And, that He will save us (not in) but (from) our sins. By accepting Him as Lord and Master, by His grace, through faith in Him, we may live holy, unselfish and obedient lives, full of love, sympathy, and compassion towards God and man. And because of His mercy and gift of immortality, we shall spend eternity with Him and our loved ones in bliss. This is the secret of the power of God, of Truth, and genuine Bible doctrines.

24

Satan and Spirits from Other Worlds

1031 A.D.	1776 A.D.	1798 A.D.	2001 A.D.	2031 A.D.
5001 A.S.	5746 A.S.	5768 A.S.	5971 A.S.	6001 A.S.
			You are here. *	

Spirit beings from another world do visit Planet Earth. They continually go back and forth, and have sometimes been seen by mankind. These super-dimensional space visitors have the uncanny ability to appear and disappear at will. They have interfered in the affairs of government, family and personal lives from time to time. It is now known that they have dramatically affected the rise and fall of nations for almost 6000 years of human history. Coming from another space galaxy and not being subject to the restrictions of time and distance, these amazing creatures have literally "occupied" this planet, and with their mysterious extrasensory powers they have transcribed and preserved the most classified secrets of men and governments.

Who are these visiting beings from outer space? Do they come as friends or enemies? For what purpose do they make a record of our most secret transactions? Are they connected with the hundreds of UFO sightings around the world? The answers to these questions could very well determine our attitude toward these very real beings who surround us each and every day.

First, let me assure you that these celestial visitors are spirits. This much is confirmed by the most reliable document in the world today – God's holy Word. Please notice that His Book speaks about spirits in a variety of connotations, just as we use the word in our modern vocabulary. We refer to an individual as a "Guiding spirit" in the community, Alcoholic beverages are called "spirits" of liquor, and imaginary ghosts are said to be "spirits." In the same manner the Bible refers to God as "Spirit" and the angels are also called "ministering spirits." (Hebrews 1:4): "Are they not all ministering spirits, sent forth to minister for them who shall be heirs of salvation?"

Before proceeding further, let us clarify some false impressions that have been held by many regarding the angels. Some believe that the godly turn into angels when they die. Is it true that angels are actually the spirits of the dead? Do the godly of this earth turn into angels when they die? The answer is emphatically "No." We know from the Word of God that there were angels before anyone had died among the human family.

> *"So He drove out the man; and He placed at the east of the garden of Eden Cherubim, and a flaming sword which turned every way, to keep the way of the tree of life." (Genesis 3:24).*

The Scriptures also make it clear that angels were made before mankind and belong to a different order of beings.

> *"What is man, that you are mindful of him? and the son of man, that you visit him? For you have made him a little lower than the angels, and have crowned him with glory and honor." (Psalm 8:4, 5).*

The fact is that we can never hope to be an angel. Even though we belong to the same great family of God there is a difference of order which separates the earthly from the heavenly members of that family.

Where did angels come from if they are not related to earthly beings? The answer is found in Colossians 1:16, 17. "For by Him were all things created, that are in heaven, and in the earth, visible and invisible, whether they be thrones, or dominions, or principalities, or powers; All things were created by Him, and for Him; And He is before all things, and by Him all things consist." They were created by God, and one fact stands out clearly – none of them are disembodied spirits. They are real beings who simply possess powers that you and I do not have. In Genesis 18:1-8, we are told that some angels appeared to Abraham in the plains of Mamre. With typical eastern hospitality Abraham prepared a meal for his guests, and the record says,

"He stood by them under the tree, and they did eat." Now, if they had been bodiless spirits, this act of eating would have been an impossibility. The had bodies just as real as yours and mine. We find no evidence that these heavenly visitors are indefinite, formless, vacuous objects.

I want to point out now that angels are in close touch with mankind. They watch the movements of humanity closely. They know our names, occupations, where we live. They know whether we support the work of the Lord with prayer and donations. They know all the details of our lives.

I would like you to notice that the angels as a heavenly company, are distinguished from a race. Here are the words of Jesus found in Matthew 22:30: "For in the resurrection they neither marry, nor are given in marriage, but are as the angels of God in heaven." The angels are not developed from one original stock as is the case of man. There is no common nature that binds the angels together as is the case with the race of men.

The angelic host is made up of various ranks. We have mentioned before, Paul's writings in Colossians, of "thrones, dominions, principalities, and powers," Then Jesus said, "Do you think that I cannot now pray to My Father, and He shall presently give Me more than twelve legions of angels?" (Matthew 26:53). These words suggest the organization of an army.

We must remember however, that there are two kinds of angels, good and bad. Hebrews 1:14 tells us that some are ministering spirits sent to minister unto those who will be heirs of salvation, but in the book of Ephesians I read that there are also wicked spirits.

> "Put on the whole armour of God, that you may be able to stand against the wiles of the devil. For we wrestle not against flesh and blood, but against principalities, against powers, against the rulers of the darkness of this world, against spiritual wickedness in high places." Ephesians 6:11, 12.

Now we have two great hosts of beings. The good angels are ministering spirits; the wicked angels are spirits of devils – one seeking our salvation, the other seeking our destruction.

The evil angels are alien visitors to this planet over 6,000 years ago. Satan and his followers, one-third of the angels of heaven, were cast out of heaven, and came to Planet Earth to continue their rebellion against God. Their unalterable purpose has been to frustrate the first real interplanetary space journey that millions will soon make to the paradise of God, Armageddon.

I want to point out that heaven has done all it possibly can to save you and me from eternal death. And if we insist on loosing our eternal salvation it will be in spite of all that God has done to save us from ourselves. Yes, all heaven is interested in our salvation. Angels from the throne of God are far more anxious to see us make a full surrender unto Him, and prepare for the eternal home than we are ourselves. Good angels seek our salvation; evil angels seek our destruction. On which side are we going to cast our influence today? No doubt Satan has commissioned an evil angel or spirit to attend us through life with the purpose of destroying us. God has given us an angel. We stand between the good and the bad, and our decision will determine who shall have the upper hand in our lives. Let us choose to serve God and know that He has charge of things through His ministering spirits, the angels.

Spirit Shadows Over America: No study of angels can be complete without considering the evil ministry of fallen angels. The Word of God has some very startling things to say about the evil spirits whose ranks comprise the one-third of the angels of heaven who rebelled and were cast out. It is this unholy confederacy which threatens to deceive the whole world right now. The roots of every form of occultism are either directly or indirectly related to the fallen angels. Demonism is the manifestation of their activities through human channels.

Long, ominous shadows are lengthening across the face of the United States of America today. They are being cast by a dozen different specious forms of occult spiritualism, and the tentacles of this fast-growing evil are fastening a strange hold upon millions of Christian devotees.

A few short years ago the stories of apparitions and spirit forms were not taken seriously by very many people. Rarely did the public media see fit to reproduce the reports of frightening encounters with "ghosts," either in body or out. Today scarcely a paper or magazine can be found which does not cater to astrology, psychic phenomena, or sensational supernaturalism.

Millions are now asking, "Is it all delusion, or is it devils?" Are the apparitions real or imagined? What power is behind the confirmed accounts of materialized spirit forms?

The phenomena can no longer be ignored! The claims have come far to close to every one of us. Hardly a person has escaped contact with someone who has an incredible tale to tell about communication with the dead.

Often the manifestations are anything but ghostly and sepulchral. After their sudden appearance, the familiar forms of deceased friends and relatives are recognized by distinctive clothes, voices and mannerisms. Often they refer to closely guarded family secrets and pass on verifiable information known only by one or two others alive.

Some people have affirmed that they make no important decisions without consulting a spiritualist medium who, in turn, supposedly puts them in touch with the guiding spirits of the dead. Even high government figures have confessed to consulting with such sources before moving in matters of national interest.

Do we have reason for concern over this situation? Can these supernatural agencies be depended upon to give safe and honorable guidance?

And what about all the related forms of occultism whose tendrils seem to intertwine every existing social structure of mankind today? Satanism, witchcraft, ESP, hypnotism, Zen, Astrology, voodoo and a dozen other so-called "mind sciences" purported to bring happiness and success beyond imagination.

To answer these crucial questions we must uncover the foundations of these mysterious movements. Let us be willing to face the inescapable conclusion that there can be only two sources of supernatural power in the world. Whether we believe God or not, and whether we believe in Satan or not, honest reason demands that anything beyond the demonstrable, natural processes would have to involve either the spiritual powers of a god or a devil.

If these insistent voices which have influenced empires truly represent God's counsel, then we must rejoice over this growing influence. On the other hand, if evil, satanic forces are producing the phenomena, we are facing one of the most diabolical and frightening schemes imaginable. What could be more self-delusive than to be following demonic voices in the belief that it was God's voice?

Please take note that God's method of communicating to mankind is through His Word:

"And when they shall say unto you, Seek unto them that have familiar spirits, and unto wizards that peep, and that mutter; Should not a people seek unto their God? for the living to the dead? To the law and to the testimony; If they speak not according to this Word, it is because there is no light in them." (Isaiah 8:19, 20).

Here God tells us that knowledge beyond human power should be gathered from His Word and not from familiar spirits. But contrary to this instruction, millions today are turning to modern sorcery and spiritualism for the answers to problems.

Even some great church organizations are now ready to recommend this avenue as a way of truth. Inroads are being made into our vast religious systems, and some astounding sentiments are being expressed by Protestant church leaders. The public has been duly impressed by some of these Protestant positions. Evidence of this was seen during the War when Wanamaker's store in New York City sold four out of every five books on the subject of spiritualism. One Pittsburgh concern sold over 1500 Ouija boards in one week's time.

Before I cite some of these strange statements let me ask, What is the basis of the spiritualist doctrine?" the answer is very short and simple. It is fundamentally rooted in the idea that the dead are not really dead at all, but living in some other world of higher wisdom and understanding. It also teaches that communication is carried on between the living and the dead. Now we shall learn just how unbiblical and false this doctrine really is, but first let us look at an alarming statement in the Methodist monthly magazine, *Togather.* In answer to a reader's question, "Shall we pray for the dead?" Dr. Nall gave the following answer in the issue of May, 1956: "Why should we not pray for them, even as we believe they must pray for us. Prayer for the dead unites the church, visible and invisible, into a timeless fellowship, binding us all, as Tennyson says, To God Himself." Now, the very fact that a prominent Protestant author would give status and indorsement to such a view is a startling revelation of the power of spiritualism.

Perhaps it is in England that the strongest pitch has been made to favor this rising tide. Sometime ago the Church of England appointed a committee to investigate the growing phenomenon of spiritualism. Appointed by the arch-bishops, this committee was made up of the nation's most eminent churchmen, educators, and lawyers. After a two year study a report was made which shook the city of London, and the whole country, for that matter. The major emphasis of the report is reflected in this paragraph lifted out of it: "It's necessary to keep clearly in mind that none of the fundamental Christian obligations or values are in any way changed by our acceptance of the possibility of communication with discarnate spirits. Where these essential principles are borne in mind, those who have the assurance they have been in touch with their departed friends, may rightly accept the sense of enlargement and of unbroken fellowship which it brings." Perhaps this provides sufficient testimony to alert us that spiritualism is shaping the thinking of Christian leaders to an alarming degree today. But, is this doctrine according to the Word of God? How does all this fit with the teaching of God's Word? What does the Bible have to say about it? let us examine some of the sources of spiritualism for a moment.

The fact is that it started in the Garden eastward in Eden, and the serpent was the first medium used by Satan. In Genesis 3:1-4, we read the story of Eve's fall into sin. God had said that death would follow their transgression but Satan said to Eve, "you shall not surely die." When Adam and Eve did die, Satan shrewdly tried to cover his lie. Ever since that day he has tried to make it appear that death is not really death – that it is actually life, instead. Because Satan uses it to perpetuate his lie, God strictly forbids the practice of necromancy or familiar spirits. Notice these statements from the Book. "Regard not them that have familiar spirits, neither seek after wizards, to be defiled by them; I AM the Lord your God." Leviticus 19:31. Again, "A man also or a woman that has a familiar spirit, or that is a wizard, shall surely be put to death." (Leviticus 20:27).

Now, dear friends, why is God so opposed to this thing? Why such penalty for engaging in spiritualistic seances? Because it is a lie and it is devil-inspired. It is unsound and anti-scriptural throughout. And God said:

> "For the living know that they shall die; But the dead know not anything, neither have they any more a reward; for the memory of them is forgotten. Also their love, hatred, and envy is now perished; neither have they any more a portion for ever in any thing that is done under the sun." (Ecclesiastes 9:5, 6)

Again, describing death God said,

> "His breath goes forth, he returns to his earth; in that very day his thoughts perish." (Psalm 146:4).

Death is described as a sleep until the resurrection day, an unconscious, dreamless sleep. Since the dead can not possibly come back to speak to their loved ones, how can we explain these mysterious appearances of those who have died? Numerous instances can be cited of such experiences where the exact form and voice was seen and heard. There is only one possible source for such demonstrations. Satan is still trying to sustain that line which he told Eve. He's still trying to prove there is no death. He appears in whatever form he chooses, shrewdly imitating the characteristics of the dead. Such lying wonders are well calculated to deceive and convince people that a lie is actually the truth.

Notice how this work of Satan is described in God's Word:

> *"Even him, whose coming is after the working of Satan with all power and signs and lying wonders, and with all deceivableness of unrighteousness in them that perish; because they received not the love of the truth, that they might be saved. And for this cause God shall send them strong delusion, that they should believe a lie." (2 Thessalonians 2:9-11).*

Here we're told that the truth alone will guard us from the signs and wonders of Satan's power. In 1 Timothy 4:1 we read of some in the last days who will give heed to seducing spirits and doctrines of devils. Finally, in Revelation 16:14 the prophet describes, "spirits of devils, working miracles, which go forth unto the kings of the earth, and of the whole world."

Don't forget that the devil can work miracles. He can do things that we never will understand. Now you can begin to understand why people have been shaken up so by the apparent appearance of dead friends. After 6,000 years of observing human behavior, Satan is able to counterfeit their forms and voices cleverly. At psychological moments he takes advantage of heartbroken, bereaved relatives to perpetuate his fraud. No wonder God despises this evil and sentences its leaders to death by stoning.

Flee From Spiritualism: In these last days Satan appears as an angel of light and is counterfeiting the truth of God. But remember, he is the father of lies. He was cast out of heaven and is working mightily today to deceive, to twist the truth, and actually try to lead us to believe this great delusion. The dead are dead, they are not conscious at all. There is no communication at all between the living and the dead. Only by believing this Bible truth can we escape the deceptions of Satanism.

With the end of the world at hand, Satan is desperately working to revive the old forbidden avenues by which he can control people's lives. He has changed the names like "wizards," "necromancy," and "sorcerers" to more acceptable titles like spiritualism, astrology, hypnosis, and ESP. The devil can control a human being only by being able to manipulate the mind and will. That's why most of the modern counterfeits of Satan demand a yielding of the mind. And that's why it is such an evil

197

thing for any human beings to surrender their minds to the controlling influence of some other person or power. If ever there was a time when men and women needed all their mental capacity and strength of will, it is now. There is plenty of evidence at hand that the more a person's mental processes are breached and controlled by someone else, the weaker the will becomes, and the less power of decision can be exercised.

How delighted Satan is to find the mental barriers relaxed and often removed entirely. He can't force a single human will, but the person can voluntarily give up the personal control. That means someone else can take over. In hypnotism it is supposed to be taken by the hypnotist who begins giving orders; in spiritualism the spirits are invited to control the yielded mind; in astrology, the mind bends to the belief that the stars are controlling life and destiny. In every case the devil has an opportunity to step into a mind that has been voluntarily opened, and which is eagerly ready to accept whatever "guidance" may be given. What more diabolical scheme could ever be devised than this!

And by the way, to guarantee himself further access to other minds, the devil is chuckling with glee over the possibilities that science will soon be tampering with human genes to produce "programmed" people – people whose physical and mental makeup is directed in the laboratory by the proper preparation of test-tube genes. No wonder the Bible warns us over and over to take heed of deception in these last days.

Now, someone is certain to raise the question right here about the predictions of some of these modern prognosticators. Are they able to foretell the future accurately? Are they true prophets? Do they operate within the framework of the Bible? You see, the Bible itself lays down a test for such professed prophets and clairvoyants. Here it is in Isaiah 8:20:

"To the law and to the testimony: If they speak not according to this Word, it is because there is not truth, no light in them."

This means that those who are teaching and acting contrary to Scripture cannot be true prophets. There are false, as well as true, according to Jeremiah. Listen:

"Therefore listen not to your prophets, your diviners, your dreamers, your enchanters, or your sorcerers...For they prophesy a lie unto you." (Jeremiah 27:9, 10).

If these occult specialists could actually know the future. I can tell you one thing – they would be billionaires by being able to manipulate the stock market. By their foretelling of politics they would surely dictate the headlines of tomorrow's newspapers. But this has not been the case.

Eight-hundred years before the Christ was born the prophet Isaiah set up a divinely appointed test for those pretending such power:

"Produce your cause, says the Lord; bring forth your strong reasons, says the King of Jacob. Let him bring them forth, and show us what shall happen: Let them show the former things, what they be, that we may consider them; or declare us things that are to come hereafter, that we may know that you are gods." (Isaiah 41:21-23).

What about that test for today's predictors? God says, "Let them show us what will happen" – not just once in a while – not 75 percent correct. A good guesser could do that – an astute politician could be right that many times. No, if God is in it, it will always be 100 percent correct. Neither Satan nor man can tell the future, except on the basis of the past, and in the light of Bible prophecy. But the very thing that man and evil spirits have never been able to do, God has done again and again by His prophets.

Outside the Word of God no claims like these have ever been made and fulfilled, either on a short or long term basis. Here's where the nonsense of astrology is most clearly revealed. It's absurd generalizations and warnings, based on the supposed mysterious influence of stars on human destiny, have never been proven to be accurate. Millions can be cheered or dismayed by the implications of the horoscope. Did you know that the Bible speaks directly to such people? Listen to this in Jeremiah 10:2:

"Thus says the Lord, Learn not the way of the heathen, and be not dismayed at the signs of heaven; for the heathen are dismayed at them."

There it is – an actual description of astrologers who become fearful and dismayed over the signs of the heavens. Have you never considered how insane it is to believe that those hard, cold chunks of rocks in the distant heavens could influence your life? The old pagan worshipers of the planets believed that their gods dwelt in those stars, and the superstitious carryover has led 60 million Americans to believe the fable.

What a time this is for people to trust in the God who made those stars. The creature can never help or hurt us, but the Creator has a personal interest in everything He made. His attention is not given alone to the giant worlds that wheel and spin in their orbits, but to the smallest, weakest plant or animal that lives on Planet Earth. How much more concerned He is with the human family, created in His image, and ordained from all eternity to glorify Him in the world. It is this same loving Creator – God who guides the destiny of men, women, and children.

The astrological horoscope is a vain, empty cry towards dumb matter which, itself, must be governed by the God who created it. To trust in Satan and the evil angels who are the same as dead, the dead stars and the planets for direction is tantamount to idolatry, because it places more trust in them than in the living, loving Creator, God.

25

It Is Done and The Great Time of Trouble

1031 A.D.	1776 A.D.	1798 A.D.	2001 A.D.	2031 A.D.
5001 A.S.	5746 A.S.	5768 A.S.	5971 A.S.	6001 A.S.
			You are here. *	

Just before the Flood of Noah, the ark was closed by God Himself. Then the probation of the antediluvian world ended.

"They that went, went in male and female of all flesh, as God had commanded him: and the Lord shut them in." (Genesis 7:16).

This is a type of the events of the last days:

"As it was in the days of Noah, so it shall be in the days of the Son of man." (Luke 17:26).

The door of mercy closes in the spring of 2031 A.D., 1 Nisan, 6001 A.S., and probation closes, ceases, once for all, for all time just before Jesus comes back to Planet Earth.

"He that is unjust, let him be unjust still: He which is filthy, let him be filthy still: He that is righteous, let him be righteous still: He that is holy, let him be holy still.

"Behold, I come quickly; and my reward is with me, to give every man according as his work shall be. I am Alpha and Omega, the beginning and the end, the first and the last." (Revelation 22:11-13).

On the typical Day of Atonement in the sanctuary of physical Israel, those who were unrepentant were "cut off" from the people of God, spiritual Israel at the end of the day, sundown, (Leviticus 23:28, 29.) So it is at the end of the gospel age. Now we have access to God's throne of grace; the door of mercy is still open:

"Let us therefore come boldly unto the throne of grace, that we may obtain mercy, and find grace to help in time of need." (Hebrews 4:16).

201

The things which have been recorded in Holy Scriptures have happened for examples for we who live today:

"Now all these things happened to them for examples: They are written for our admonition, upon whom the ends of the world are come." (1 Corinthians 10:11).

The Lord now appears before the people as Jesus the Christ, the anointed, blesses us and tells us that He is coming quickly. He blesses the sealed of God with eternal life.

In His return to His Fathers house He is escorted by a procession of the people of God, the redeemed of all ages, to the heavenly Jerusalem where a feast is prepared for them. The evening of the seventh millinium has begun.

The servants of God, their faces shining with holy consecration, have proclaimed the message from heaven. By thousands of voices, the warning has been given throughout the ages. Miracles have been wrought, the sick healed, and signs and wonders followed the believers. Satan also has worked with lying wonders, miracles have been wrought, the sick healed, and has even brought fire from heaven. Thus the inhabitants of the earth have been brought to take their stand for God or for Satan.

The Holy Spirit, the Restrainer is totally removed from the wicked. Michael, a mighty angelic prince of heaven, who through the ages stands guard over spiritual Israel, stands up at the end of the heavenly Day of Atonement, spring of 2031 A.D., and fights for us against satanic forces, and among and within the nations there is a time of trouble as adversaries contest one with another.

A voice is heard from the Throne of God, saying, "It is done!" The awful moment arrives when the destiny for all is forever decided. When this decree is pronounced upon the righteous, they are placed beyond the danger or fear of evil. In Revelation 22:11, this deliverance is given before the Lord appears, for He immediately adds, "Behold, I come quickly." (Verse 12). The sealing is the last work accomplished for the people of God prior to their rapture.

Paul says in 1 Thessalonians 4:13-18:

"But I would not have you to be ignorant, brethern concerning them which have died, that you do not sorrow, even as others which have no hope. For if we believe that Jesus died and rose again, even so them also which die in Jesus will God bring with Him. For this do we say unto you by the Word of the Lord, that we which are alive, remaining unto the coming of the Lord, shall not precede them that are asleep. For the Lord Himself shall descent from heaven with a shout, with the voice of the archangel, and with the trumpet of God: And the dead in the Christ shall rise first: Then we which are alive and remain shall be caught up together with them in the clouds to meet the Lord in the air: And so shall we ever be with the Lord. Wherefore comfort one another with these words."

The Temple Is Opened!: How interesting! Before the seven last plagues are poured out upon those who are disobedient, before the unrepentant are removed from the camp of the saints, the heathen, the pagan, and the Apostate, the Roman Catholic and Protestant Church, the Tabernacle of the Testimony (the Law by which the world is judged) in heaven is opened. This reminds us that there was a time when the earthly temple was opened, when the ministry that it performed came to an end. When Jesus died upon the cross, and the typical service in the earthly tabernacle met the True in the sacrifice of the Christ, then, we read that: "...behold, the veil of the temple was torn in two from the top to the bottom; and there was a great earthquake, and the rocks were torn apart..." (Matthew 27:51). Jesus said, "It is finished", and the probation of physical Israel had come to an end.

So, also, when the ministry of the heavenly Temple shall have been finished at the end of the heavenly Day of Atonement, spring of 2031 A.D., 1 Nisan, 6001 A.S., and mercy no longer pleads for sinful mankind, the heavenly temple shall be opened. And then shall the wrath of God, unmixed with mercy, be poured out upon the rejectors of His grace, first as a time of trouble such as has not been upon the face of the earth since there was a nation, then the seven last plagues. And, when the temple in heaven is once opened, no one can approach God for pardon, for forgiveness of sin. The Christ's intercession shall have ceased forever. Mercy no longer pleads, and the great voice is heard from the throne in the temple in heaven, saying "It is done." (Revelation 16:17). What then? All the righteous have the gift of eternal life; all the wicked are doomed to everlasting death. Beyond that point, no decision can be changed, no reward can be lost or gained, and no destiny of despair can be adverted.

In the spring of 2031 A.D., 1 Nisan, 6001 A.S., the kingdoms of this world are the kingdoms "of our Lord and of His Son, the Christ." His priestly robes are laid aside for the royal vesture. The work of mercy is finished and the probation of the human race ended. Then he that is filthy is beyond hope of cleansing; and he that is holy beyond the danger of falling. All cases are forever decided.

The Great Time of Trouble

In the great world conflict to come let us notice something which will take place at the end of this age. We read:

> "I will gather all nations against Jerusalem to battle; and the city shall be taken...Then shall the Lord go forth, and fight against those nations, as when He fought in the day of battle." (Zechariah 14:2, 3).

A vast conflict is described. All the nations of Planet Earth, both spiritual and secular, the great and the small, will take part in this great struggle. Spiritual Jerusalem, spiritual Israel, the saints of the Most High God, are the center of the struggle. Other Bible referenced indicate that two great alliances of nations will fight against each other. One group, Satan and his confederation of nations, secular and spiritual, will be fighting God and His confederation of nations, both spiritual and secular. Just as the host of Satan capture half of the saints of God, the Lord pours His wrath, without mercy, upon the wicked and roars out of Zion and fights in His great day of battle.

Revelation 7 says that the time of trouble is put off till the saints are sealed when Michael stands up and God declares "It is done." At that time the four winds of strife, the Great Time of Trouble, is loosed upon the earth. The Time of Trouble begins 1

Nisan, 6001 A.S., the spring of 2031 A.D. It lasts five years, until 1 Nisan, 6006 A.D., the spring of 2036 A.D.

As the Christ pronounces the words "It is done" a shroud of spiritual darkness covers the sinful inhabitants of earth. During this fearful time there is no restraint upon the wicked and Satan has full control of the impenitent. The entire world has rejected God's mercy, despised His love, and trampled upon His law and year. The wicked have passed the boundary of their probation; the Spirit of God, persistently resisted, has been totally withdrawn and there is no protection from the wicked one, Satan. Satan plunges the inhabitants of Planet Earth into a great final time of trouble. As the angels of God cease to hold in check the winds of human passion, all the elements of fear and strife are released.

The Bible tells us of the mighty acts of the angels of God and the destructive power exercised by them when so command-ed. With God's restraining power removed, the evil angels are given permission to spread desolation everywhere on the earth.

Spiritual Israel, we who claim the blood of the Lamb, and honor the law of God, are accused of bringing judgments upon the world, and are regarded as the cause of the fearful convulsions of the earth, of nations, the strife and bloodshed among mankind that fill the earth with woe. Satan enrages social, nominal, and secular Christendom, Protestant and Catholic, and the pagan and heathen; their anger is directed against all who keep the com-mandments of God. And from day to day, Satan continues to excite to still greater intensity the spirit of hatred and persecution.

As it was in the day of Jesus so it is in the time of His return. When the son of God was hung on the cross, physical Israel, under the control of Satan, and swayed by the most horrible and malignant passions, still regarded themselves as the chosen of God, and still do today. As it was in the days of physical Israel, so it is as the irrevocable words are pronounced, and the destiny of the world is fixed forever, the inhabitants of earth know it not. The forms of social religion continue on though the Holy Spirit is totally withdrawn from the people; and the satanic zeal with which the prince of evil has inspired them for the accomplishment of his malignant designs, bears semblance to zeal for God as it was during the Dark Ages.

Obedience to the law of God is and continues to be, a special point of controversy throughout Christendom, and the religious and secular authorities are combined to enforce the observance of Sunday sabbath, the Mark of the Beast. The persistent refusal of God's chosen and sealed, a small minority, to yield to the popular demand, makes them objects of universal execration. It is urged that the few who stand in opposition to the state, should not be tolerated; that it is better that they suffer than for nations to be thrown into confusion and lawlessness. The same argument two thousand years ago was brought against the Christ, and His followers, by the rulers of the professed people of God. The argument is conclusive; a decree is issued against we who hallow the Sabbath of the fourth commandment, the Mark, the Seal of God, denouncing us as deserving of the severest punishment, and giving the masses liberty, after a certain time, to put us to death.

The great time of trouble in which all nations are engaged is just before the wrath of God poured upon the wicked without mercy and the second coming of the Christ. It ends at that time with the battle of that great day of God Almighty, the seventh plague, described in Revelation 16.

What a vast and tremendous time of trouble this will be when the powers of earth pit their strength and skill against each other. The culmination of the conflict will be a great battle which will center on spiritual Israel.

With the modern weapons of the nations of the world today, the great missiles and nuclear warheads will cause vast destruction to sweep Planet Earth.

Apostate Protestant America will, in 2035 A.D., 6005 A.S., receive her destruction by nuclear invasion from ten Muslim nations that she has just signed a covenant with some two weeks before. This occurs ten years after she enforces the Mark of the Beast, laws concerning the Sabbath of God Almighty, by civil authority the final abomination that causes desolation. The exchange wipes out the ten nations as well as the United States of America.

This third desolation, destruction of the Apostate Protestant people of God, parallels perfectly the first and second abomination that caused the destruction of the first and second temples of physical Israel. On all three occasions the abominations are done by the apostate people of God and the destruction is an act of holy judgment by heathen armies.

In Revelation 7:16 it is found that the saints of the end time are freed from hunger, thirst, heat, and spiritual darkness, all of extreme degrees. They are freed by their Rapture at the second coming of our Lord. These extremes are found in Revelation 16.

Let this distinction be carefully noticed: The tribulation of Matthew 24 is upon the church, God's saints. They were the ones involved, and for their sake the years of tribulation were shortened (verse 22). The Christ is speaking to His disciples, and of His disciples in coming times. They were the ones involved, and for their sakes the days of tribulation were to be shortened. The time of trouble mentioned in Daniel 12 is not the time of religious persecution, but of international calamity, 2031 A.D. to 2036 A.D., 6001 A.S. to 6006 A.S. There is nothing like it since there was – not a church, but – a nation. This is the last trouble to come upon the nations of the world, upon Planet Earth, and culminates in the revelation of the Lord Jesus coming in clouds of flaming fire, to visit destruction upon His enemies.

In Matthew there is reference made to time beyond the tribulation. But there is not reference in Daniel 12 to future time after the time of trouble, for it closes Planet Earth's history as we know it.

The nations are angry, and your wrath is come, and the time of the dead, that they should be judged, and that you should give rewards to your servants the prophets and to the saints, and them that fear your name, small and great; and should destroy them which destroy the earth. At this time Michael stands up, the great prince which stands for the children of your people; There is a time of trouble, such as never was since there was a nation even to this same time; At this time your people are delivered, every one found written in the Book of Life. (Revelation 11:18; Daniel 12:1.)

While it is true in some degree of all the children of God that they "must through much tribulation enter into the kingdom of God" (Acts 14:22), it is true of we who are sealed in 2031 A.D., 1 Nisan, 6001 A.S. in a very special sense. We pass through the great time of trouble such as never was since there was a nation. (Daniel 12:1). We stand before God without a mediator through the terrible scenes of the seven last plagues, His wrath in the earth, unmingled with mercy. We pass through the most severe time of trouble the world has ever known, although we shall triumph and be delivered in the spring of 2036 A.D., 1 Nisan, 6006 A.S.

We have washed our robes and made them white in the blood of the Lamb. To this last generation the counsel is very emphatic on the subject of obtaining the white raiment. (Revelation 3:5, 18). We refuse to violate the commandments of God. (Revelation 14:1, 12). We have rested our hope of life on the merits of the shed blood of our divine Redeemer, making Him our source of righteousness. There is peculiar force in saying of us that we have washed our robes, and made them white in the blood of the Lamb.

The period of time extending from the Armistice in 1946 A.D. until 2031 A.D., the beginning of the time of trouble, is far from peaceful, for the world is in a continual state of escalating conflict with increasing intensity that touches every nation on the face of the earth. Many of these outbreaks of the present day possesses potential to expand into serous proportions. But every time the troubled world began to fear the spread of these conflicts, the troubles unexpectedly subsided. God has sent His angel to interpose in behalf of peace until His people, spiritual Israel, has been sealed with the Seal of God, 1 Nisan, 6001 A.S., the spring of 2031 A.D.

The song of spiritual Israel during the time of trouble is one like Psalm 46:

"God is our refuge and strength, a very present help in trouble. Therefore we will not fear, though the mountains be carried into the middle of the sea; though the waters thereof

roar and be troubled, though the mountains shake with the swelling thereof. Selah. There is a river, the streams whereof shall make glad the city of God, the holy place of the tabernacles of the most high God is in the middle of her; she shall not be moved: God shall help her, and that right early. The heathen raged, the kingdoms were moved: He uttered his voice, the earth melted. The Lord of hosts is with us; the God of Jacob is our refuge, Selah. Come, behold the works of the Lord, what desolation he has made in the earth. He makes wars to cease unto the end of the earth; He breaks the bow, and cuts the spear in two; He burns the chariot in the fire. Be still, and know that I am God: I will be exalted among the heathen, I will be exalted in the earth. The Lord of hosts is with us; the God of Jacob is our refuge. Selah."

In 2031 A.D. the winds of strife now blow unrestrained upon the world, Every nation, kindred, tongue, and people are engulfed in the whirlwind velocity of a devastating global conflict called the Time of Trouble. In its magnitude and fearful depredations on all that mankind holds dear and precious this struggle entirely overshadows all conflicts that have occurred upon the earth since there was a nation.

During this time, human nature, untouched by the grace of God, is seen in unbridled display. Thus it is till the great consummation of the plan of salvation, spring of 2036 A.D., 1 Nisan, 6006 A.S.

26

The Antichrist

2031 A.D.	2035 A.D.	2036 A.D.	2031 A.D.
6001 A.S.	6035 A.S.	6036 A.S.	7001 A.S.

- - - - - - - - You are here. - - - - - - - -

The Antichrist: We've been warned, and we've been waiting. Who in the world will it be? A religious fanatic like the Ayatollah Khomeni? Or a political tyrant like Idi Amin? A cult leader as Sun Myung? Perhaps an atheist like Madalyn O'Hair.

The Antichrist. Is it a human or a demon? A government? Maybe even a Church system?

Fascinated and frightened. That's how we feel about the mysteries of the antichrist. We're also quite confused. Bookstores, even drugstores, feature a smorgasbord of paperback religious thrillers. Each comes spiced with new speculation about the antichrist.

How can we know what is truth? We'd better get the facts straight from the source, wouldn't you say? Why don't we open our Bibles to Revelation 13 and read the so-called "beast chapter."

> *"I stood on the sand of the sea. And I saw a beast rising up out of the sea, having 7 heads and 10 horns, and on his horns 10 crowns, and on his heads a blasphemous name. Now the beast which I saw was like a leopard, his feet were like the feet of a bear, and his mouth like the mouth of a lion. And the dragon gave him his power, his throne, and great authority.*
>
> *"Then I saw another beast who came up from the land. He had 2 horns like a lamb and spoke like a dragon. He exercises the full authority of the first beast in his presence, and he makes the earth and those living in it worship the first beast, whose mortal wound had been healed." (verses 1, 2, 11, 12).*

A strange beast indeed, this antichrist, power. With a body from a leopard, a bear, and a lion. Perhaps you've studied those animals before in the Old Testament book of Daniel. (Please review Chapters 3, 4, 5 and 6 of this book.) We learn from Scripture decoding that they represent three kingdoms – three ancient kingdoms, in fact – Babylon, Persia, and Greece. Followed, of course by the Pagan Roman Empire, then the Christian Roman Empire and the United States of America of the New Testament...

So these blasphemous powers of Revelation 13 sum up the great world empires of Old and New Testament history. What religion did the Old Testament heathen empires have in common? Sun worship.

Adoration of the sun can be traced all the way back to the time of Noah. Nimrod, his great-grandson, became a "mighty one on the earth." (Genesis 10:8). Beginning with his Tower of Babel, Nimrod's achievements adorn the records and legends of ancient history. But this talented leader was evil. A father of false worship.

False worship also thrived through Ishtar, called the queen of heaven, goddess of love and fertility. Ishtar, according to legend, gave birth to a son Tammuz, without a father. Here in pagan sun worship, centuries before the Christ, is found a counterfeit of the virgin birth. Imagine! Certain of the male gods of fertility became sun gods. They all died every winter and had to be resurrected to restore the fertility of plants, animals, and humans.

Sun worship from ancient Babylon spread to infect the world. Ancient records and art forms show how each nation reverences the sun in the customs of its own culture. But why did they worship the sun? Well, the sun brings light, warmth, growth – what we need for life itself. Reigning supreme over nature, the sun would be the natural object of worship for those who reject their Creator.

Ceremonies to honor the sun god were gruesome beyond belief. Babies were burned as living sacrifices. Young women were degraded as sun temple prostitutes. All to appease the endless appetite of sun deities rather than to accept the Creator's gift of salvation.

Time and again God exposed the follies of sun worship. Remember the story of how He rescued His people from Egypt? How He overpowered the sun with 3 days of darkness? All who turned from the sun god and put their trust in the lamb's blood on the doorpost were saved from the death angel. Even so, Israel exported sun idolatry in the Exodus. The golden calf they reverenced represented Apis, an image closely associated with sun worship.

Throughout Old Testament times adoration of the sun supplanted true worship in Israel. King Solomon, the very one who built God's temple, defiled Jerusalem with paganism. Sun worship flourished. The 8th Chapter of Ezekiel records the shocking scene of women reverencing Tammuz in the temple. And men bowing low before the sun.

Can you imagine! Pagan worship in God's own temple! An abomination to God. But faithful prophets called Israel away from the sun to their Creator. They pointed to the 7th day Sabbath, God's weekly reminder of Creation. Yet the Hebrews persisted in paganism. Finally the Lord gave them up to be captives in Babylon, that ancient center of sun worship.

After Babylon fell to the Persians sun worship continued to spread. And when Alexander the Great conquered the then known world, the Greeks introduced their own sophisticated brand of idolatry. Including reverence for the sun. And, of course, the Romans venerated the sun in their empire. They named the days of the week according to their heathen religion. Sunday they reverenced the sun; Monday the Moon; Tuesday, Mars; Wednesday, Mercury; Thursday they honored Jupiter; Friday, Venus. Saturday? You guessed it – Saturn. Just as the sun ruled over the planets, Sunday rose to honor above, to rule the other days of the week.

But the Christians of the first century nobly refuted any part of pagan worship. And as a result they suffered horrible persecution. Thousands were thrown to the lions or burned alive. Yet the church stood firm. Satan, failing to overcome God's people through force, then tried a new strategy. He determined to infiltrate Christianity with paganism. Little by little he mingled Bible truth with the ceremonies of sun worship.

Now why would the church be attracted to paganism? For one thing, Christians wanted to distance themselves from anything seeming to be Jewish. Jews, you see, had put themselves in the emperor's doghouse. They hated Roman authority. Constantly they revolted to regain their own national rule.

And Rome struck back. In 49 A.D. the Emperor Claudius expelled the Jews from Rome for their constant rioting. (See Acts 18:2). Things got worse. Strict sanctions were enjoined upon Jews. They responded by refusing to pray for God's blessing on the emperor. Rome considered this treason.

So in 70 A.D. Roman armies stormed Jerusalem. Two-hundred fifty thousand Jews were starved, burned, crucified, or otherwise killed. Their glorious temple lay in ruins. Numerous anti-jewish riots swept the empire, climaxed by even stiffer penalties for Jews.

You see, because Christians shared the same heritage as Jews, Roman tended to treat them the same. This was unfair, of course. Christians wanted peace with the emperor, rendering to Caesar his due. Yet they suffered just as if they were Jews. No wonder Christians cut themselves off from everything remotely Jewish. You can see why they craved a new identity more favorable with the empire.

And now with Jerusalem destroyed, Christians looked to the capital city as their new church center. By 95 A.D. Clement, bishop of Rome, had become quite prominent. His epistles commanded respect among believers. Some in the churches even considered them inspired. Rome's influence in the church increased further after the second destruction of Jerusalem in 135 A.D. Emperor Hadrian outlawed Jewish worship, particularly their Sabbath keeping. So Christians felt compelled to divorce themselves completely from their Hebrew heritage. Although believers withstood outright idolatry – even to the point of death – pagan symbols and ceremonies slipped in the back door. Heathen holidays became Christian holy days.

Tell me, have you ever wondered what Easter eggs and bunny rabbits have to do with the resurrection of the Christ? Nothing, of course. They are pagan symbols of fertility. But the church adopted them to celebrate new life in Jesus. The Encyclopedia Britannica states, "Christianity ... incorporated in its celebration of the great Christian feast day (Easter) many of the heathen rites and customs of the Spring festival."

Other heathen feasts besides Easter infiltrated the church. For centuries pagans celebrated the birth of their sun god Tammuz on December 25. Have you ever heard of that date?

Here is a question. Since our Christian holidays come to us tainted with sun worship, how do we know that other areas of our worship, even truths morally vital, have not been tampered with too? Think about it.

So it was that Christians, seeking some relief from persecution, welcomed the rituals of sun worship. Of course, nobody suggests they actually worshiped the sun. They were simply celebrating the Christ's birth and resurrection. So they reasoned.

Now this development did not happen in a corner. Scholars recognize these pagan roots in Christianity. No less an authority than Cardinal John Henry Newman tells the facts in his book *The Development Of The Christian Religion*: "Temples, incense, oil lamps, votive offerings, holy water, images ... are all of pagan origin." Page 359.

Now what do you think of that?

And, on the other hand, pagans actually became comfortable with Christianity. And why not? They could celebrate their heathen holidays in the name of Jesus. But a price had to be paid. Pure faith lay buried deep in pagan tradition. Accommodation took the place of transformation. Diversion all to often replaced conversion.

By the 4th century, Christianity so resembled paganism that the emperor found it easy to become a believer. Constantine the Great proclaimed himself a convert in the year 312 A.D. Persecution ceased. Outright pagan sacrifices were outlawed. Christian worship became official. Delighted church leaders pledged to support the new Christian regime. Hand in hand, church and state mixed faith in the Christ with sun worship rituals. On March 7, 321, Constantine ordered his empire to reverence the "venerable day of the sun." Not the Son of God, you understand, but the sun. The day of pagan sun worship.

Sunday keeping by Christians was nothing new. Sometime after Hadrian's 2nd century persecution of the Jews, the church of Rome had exchanged the Bible Sabbath for Sunday. So with Constantine's seal of approval, the day of the sun increased in importance to the church. In 538 the council of Orleans, France, forbade all work on the first day of the week. Eventually laws became so strict that a woman could be sentenced to 7 days' penance for washing her hair on Sunday.

Sunday largely eclipsed the Sabbath in the western part of the empire, but in the east quite a few still worshiped on the 7th day. Many kept both days holy. Pockets of Sabbath keepers remained in areas known now as Egypt, Tunisia, Turkey, Palestine, and Syria. Also Ethiopia, Armenia, and Yugoslavia. Even in Ireland. Later – as late as the 5th century – evidence suggests that Saint Patrick kept the 7th day holy.

Those who honored the Bible Sabbath found themselves in mortal danger. Anyone who accepted the Bible as the only rule of faith and who insisted upon Jesus alone as intercessor qualified as a heretic. The burning of heretics began at Orleans, France in 1022 A.D. Persecution intensified during the great Crusades. Then came the infamous Inquisition in 1280 A.D., when the state enforced the teachings of the church. Thousands lost their lives for their simple faith in the Christ.

These were dark ages for the church. How could Christians be so intolerant of their brothers and sisters in the Christ? Jesus had predicted that those who killed His followers would sincerely think they were serving God. (See John 16:2). Officials believed killing heretics saved thousands of others from following them into eternal torment. Even the heretics themselves might repent through fear of the flames. At least that's what many religious leaders hoped for.

During the Dark Ages, however, the Bibles were chained to monastery walls. Common people had to learn second hand from the clergy. Knowledge of the Bible became scarce. Without question, the church was ripe for reform.

Should this erosion of Christian faith surprise us? After all, hadn't God's people in the Old Testament times continually succumbed to false worship? The New Testament predicts that history will repeat itself and it is. Apostasy prevails in the church. The apostle Peter warns,

> *"There will be false teachers among you, who will secretly bring in destructive heresies ... And many will follow their destructive ways." (2 Peter 2:1, 2).*

Long ago, God's enemy learned a lesson. He had tried first to crush Christianity with persecution. It didn't work. So he resorted to deception. Quietly, gradually, he infiltrated the church with the trappings of sun worship. That did work.

Which do you think would be most deceptive today? Straight forward persecution? Or the continuation of subtle infiltration – counterfeiting Christianity from within?

Today certain atheistic countries are waging open warfare against Christianity. Millions of persecuted believers stand brave and strong, while others forfeit their faith. But very few are deceived. It's easy to know what the enemy is up to when he threatens to throw you in jail for your belief.

Is the enemy using atheism now as a smoke screen? Is he diverting our attention as he undermines us with subtile change? Could it be that all the time we've been scouting the horizon for the antichrist, he has been growing in our own back yard?

Perhaps we ought to take another look at the meaning of the word Antichrist. That could be our problem. Anti, means "against" or "instead of" – either to oppose the Christ openly or to subtlely overshadow Him. Which of these 2 types of warfare against the Christ do we see in the antichrist? In Thessalonians 2:3 we read:

> *"Let no one deceive you by any means; for that Day will not come unless the falling away comes first, and the man of sin is revealed, the son of perdition."*

"Let no man deceive you," says the apostle. So deception is involved. No question about it. Evidently the antichrist results in a "falling away," a gradual apostasy within the body of believers. Didn't Jesus Himself warn about deception – about a wolf in sheep's clothing?

The Antichrist: Dedicated men at different times reached the same conclusion. Martin Luther, John Knox, the Scottish reformer, King James I, who commissioned our King James Bible, Sir Isaac Newton, the famous scientist and Bible student. Even the Puritan preacher John Cotton, known as the Patriarch of New England. Were they all mistaken? Or did they know something we've overlooked? And their conclusions you will not find in the many paperbacks professing to explain the antichrist which are found in the bookstores today.

The Reformers suggested the reign of 1260 days represented 1260 years of medieval Christian church-state authority, and history confirms it. After the Ostrogoths were defeated in 538, the church and state held power for this prophetic period, 1260 years, ending in 1798.

The Pope, king of the medieval Christian church-state authority, the Roman Catholic Church is the Antichrist. The office of Pope will continue till the second coming of our Lord.

In Daniel is found a prophecy concerning the end of the Antichrist:

"And he shall plant the tabernacles of his palace between the seas in the glorious mountain; yet he shall come to his end and none shall help him." (Daniel 11:45).

Daniel understood what "the glorious holy mountain" was, for he had prayed – "O Lord ... let ... Your fury be turned away from Your city Jerusalem, Your holy mountain" (9:16). The "he" of the prophecy is to "plant" the "tents" of his abode in Jerusalem. This "he" is the "the king" of Daniel 11:36, or the Papacy, the Antichrist. The Christ personified will be welcomed to "the throne of his father, David." But what then? The next verse reads:

And at that time shall Michael stand up, the great prince
which stands for the children of my people" (Daniel 12:1).

It will be the end – the close of all human probation, 1 Nisan 6001
A.S., spring of 2031 A.D. Everyone will have made their decision.

The objective of the Antichrist in regard to Jerusalem have
been clearly stated. In 1980 A.D., the Charge d'Affaires of the
Permanent Observer Mission of the Holy See to the United
Nations placed the President of the Security Council, a text published in the *Osservatore Romano* which "reflected the position
of the Holy See concerning Jerusalem and all the Holy Places."
It called for the "territoralinernationalization" of Jerusalem with
the aim "that Jerusalem will no longer be an object of contention but a place of encounter and brotherhood between the
peoples and believers of the three religions and a pledge of
friendship between the people who see in Jerusalem something
that is a part of their very soul" (UN Security Council
Document S/14032).

In 1984, John Paul II in an apostolic letter, "Redemptionis
Anno," addressed the issue of Jerusalem, declaring that
"Jerusalem stands out as a symbol of coming together, of union,
and of universal peace for the human family." He wrote that he
longed for the day "on which Jews, Christians, and Muslims will
greet each other in the city of Jerusalem with the same greeting
with which Christ greeted the disciples after the resurrection:
'Peace be with you.' " He concluded his letter by noting – "this
peace proclaimed by Jesus Christ in the name of the Father ...
thus makes Jerusalem the living sign of the great ideal of unity,
of brotherhood and of agreement among peoples according to
the illuminating words of the book of Isaiah: "Many peoples
shall come and say: Come, let us go up to the mountain of the
Lord, to the house of the God of Jacob; that he may teach us his
ways and that we may walk in his paths' (Isaiah 2:3)."

Now a decade later, we see events taking place for the
accomplishment of this objective. *The Toronto Star*, (March 18
1994, p. A16) reported in a dispatch from Vatican City that "in a
dramatic gesture yesterday, Israeli Prime Minister, Yitzhak

218

Rabin invited Pope John Paul II to come to Israel and act as a 'go-between' to help achieve peace in the Middle East, the Vatican said."

Long centuries of turmoil had finally come to an end, but now we want to know, what is next for Christianity? We'll find out in the next chapters. Here, however, is a one paragraph preview.

We have learned that an unfortunate union of church and state took place in the early and middle centuries. This coalition, so clearly predicted in Scripture, played havoc with humanity's God given freedoms. But now Revelation reveals that an image, a likeness, a similar union will appear again, and is appearing down here in the end time of our world's history. It is a union of many Christian groups uniting with the state under the leadership of the Antichrist, the Pope, again acting out the character of antichrist in an attempt to coerce your and my conscience.

Meanwhile, let's thank God for preserving His people through the ages past and the present. Although challenged by apostasy, many church fathers remained outstanding Christians.

O friends, never forget, God made you for Himself. Your heart will never find rest until you rest yourself in Jesus. And you can do that right now.

27

The Wrath Of God

2031 A.D.	2035 A.D.	2036 A.D.	3031 A.D.
6001 A.S.	6005 A.S.	6006 A.S.	7001 A.S.

*You are here.

"I saw another sign in heaven, great and marvelous, seven angels having the seven last plagues; for in them is filled up the wrath of God" (Revelation 15:1; see also 14:9, 10; 16).

In Exodus 8-11 we read of the Ten plagues of Egypt. After the third plague, God said to Pharaoh, "I will put a division between my people and your people." From that time on, no plague came near the dwellings of God's people in the land of Goshen. The seven last plagues fell on the Egyptians only. When the plagues were finished, God took His people out of the land of bondage. These things are a type for the people of God in these the last days. (See Exodus 8:22-2.

Nisan, 6005 A.D.

30 March 2035 A.D.

Plague 1. A noisesome and grievous sore upon mankind which have the mark of the Apostate Church. (Revelation 16:2).

Sivan, 6005 A.S.

23 May 2035 A.D.

Plague 2. The sea becomes as the blood of the dead and every living soul in the sea dies. (Revelation 16:3).

Ab, 6005 A.S.

16 July 2035 A.D.

Plague 3. The rivers, streams and fountains of water become as the blood of the dead and every living soul in the waters dies. (Revelation 16:4).

220

Tishri, 6705 A.S.

1 September 2035 A.D.

Plague 4. Power is given the sun to scorch mankind with fire. Mankind is burned with great heat, and curse the name of God, which has power over these plagues, but repent not to give Him glory. (Revelation 16:8, 9).

Heshvan, 6005 A.S.

25 October 2035 A.D.

Plague 5. The throne and kingdom of the Beast is full of spiritual darkness, and they gnaw their tongues for pain, and curse the God of heaven because of their pains and their sores, and repent not of their evil. (Revelation 16:10, 11).

Tebeth, 6005 A.S.

18 December 2035 A.D.

Plague 6. The nations, kindreds, tongues, and peoples of the great river valley of the Euphrates, are destroyed as they destroy the great Babylonian whore, that the way of the King of kings and Lord of Lords might be prepared. And I saw three unclean spirits like frogs come out of the mouth of the dragon, out of the mouth of the beast, and out of the mouth of the false prophet. For they are the spirits of devils, working signs, miracles, which go unto the kings of the earth, and the whole world, to gather them to the battle of the great day of God almighty. (Revelation 16:12-14).

Shebat, 6006 A.S.

7 February 2036 A.D.

Plague 7. There is a great voice from the throne of God, saying, "It is done". There are voices, thunders, and lightnings. There is a great earthquake, greater than any since mankind was upon the earth. Spiritual Babylon, the Apostate, is divided into three parts, and the cities of all nations fall to the ground, for they come in remembrance before God, to give her the cup of the wine of the fierceness of His wrath. Every island disappears, and the mountains are not found. A great hail falls upon mankind from out of heaven, each hail stone weighing about 100 pounds. Mankind blasphemes God because of the plague of hail for it is exceedingly great. (Revelation 16:17-21).

The seven last plagues are said to fill up the wrath of God and they are poured out upon the wicked for 54 weeks, at the end of the Time of Trouble, 15 Shebat, 6004 A.S., the spring of 2035 A.D., to 1 Nisan, 6006 A.S., the spring of 2036 A.D. (Revelation 15:; 16:1). They are unmingled with mercy because they follow the close of the heavenly Day of Atonement, 30 Adar, 6000 A.S., the last day of the scenario of sin and salvation, the spring of 2031 A.D., when there is no longer probation, when there is no longer a Mediator in Heaven. The One who has stood for mankind as an Advocate has ceased His ministry. (Daniel 12:1). The vocabulary of man is wholly inadequate to picture the anguish of the lost souls when in the grip of these seven last plagues. They shall come upon the nations in one year and two weeks, focusing on the seat of the Dragon, pagan and heathen religions; the Beast, the Roman Catholic Church; and the False Prophet, apostate Protestantism. (Revelation 18:8, 10). There is a place of safety in the time of destruction. Every one who chooses Jesus as Lord before the close of the Day of Atonement can be sheltered. Read carefully Psalm 91. "It shall not come near you." There is coming a time when it will be to late to seek shelter in the Christ, but now is the opportune time. When God announces the destiny of every soul in the language of Revelation 22:11, then it will be too late to seek peace, too seek forgiveness, too seek shelter. "He that is unjust, let him be unjust still: And he which is filthy, let him be filthy still: And he that is righteous, let him be righteous still: And he that is holy, let him be holy still." After this divine fiat goes forth, then will be a time of trouble such as never was since there was a nation. The time of trouble culminates with the seven last plagues in rapid succession. No souls will be saved from sin during the time of trouble, during the time of these awful scourges, for the Holy Spirit will have been withdrawn from the earth and from working on the hearts of the impenitent. Sin has ripened, the harvest is ready. These plagues will be just as real as any plague that has ever fallen. They are very similar to the plagues that fell on Egypt when God was delivering the children of physical Israel from their bondage.

Yes, dear reader, the harvest is ready, the righteous and the wicked are ripe for the harvest. The Great Harvester, Jesus, comes. "And, behold I come quickly; and my reward is with Me, to give every man according as his work shall be." (Revelation 22:12). Yes friend, are you ready for your reward? Works of righteousness (obedience to God), with reward of eternal life, or works of unrighteousness (disobedience to God) with reward of eternal death.

Purpose Of The Wrath Of God: Why does God send the plagues when it will not lead to repentance (Revelation 16:9, 11, 21)? They are directed upon a civilization given totally to idolatry and disobedience to the will of God. In this generation of boasted science they will have finally and fully yielded to Satan's control, the abomination that causes desolation, exalting the creature instead of the Creator. The results, of their choice of Master, will become evident during the five year Time of Trouble, not only to them, but also to heaven's hosts watching this spectacle, this scenario played upon the stage, Planet Earth. This drama of the ages, this great controversy between good and evil is the working out of the Plan of Salvation. (See 1 Corinthians 4:9).

What is the conduct of the unrepentant during the Time of Trouble and the pouring out of God's wrath? They do not repent of their deeds, not give God glory. They blaspheme God, and finally unite to destroy God's people. This last revelation of character fully justifies God's final removal of this destructive cancer of sin and the unrepentant sinners from the universe. (See Revelation 19:11, 14, 19, 20).

During the Time of Trouble, including the Seven Last Plagues, God will keep His promise to provide bread and water to those who love Him (John 14:15; Revelation 14:12; Jeremiah 33:16). To the righteous God has promised that their bread and water shall be sure.

The First Plague: The first falls in Nisan 6005 A.S., the spring of 2035 A.D. These loathsome, foul, malignant, ulcerated, painful sores, Revelation 16:2, which befall mankind during the first plague, will be very similar to the sixth plague of Egypt.

(See Exodus 9:8-11). It is likely that there will be a gradual increase in the severity of the sores from 2031 A.D. to 2036 A.D., until the climax seen in the first plague. The plagues of Egypt were punishment for their idolatry and disobedience. The seven last plagues are likewise directed at the idolatry and disobedience of this last generation, those born in the year 1967 A.D. and afterward. Ours is an age of boasted science, yet we exalted the creature above the Creator. The first manifestation of the wrath of God in the seven last plagues falls upon all rejectors of the last loving call (Revelation 14:6-14), those who defiantly continue to worship the dragon, the beast, his image and have his mark and will not acknowledge the authority and commandments of God.

The Second And Third Plagues: The second falls in Sevan 6005 A.S., the spring of 2035 A.D. The third falls in Ab 6005 A.S., the summer of 2035 A.S. These two plagues – during which the seas, rivers, and fountains become as blood (Revelation 16:3-7) – are very much like the first of the ten plagues of Egypt. (See Exodus 7:19-25). It is likely that there will be a gradual increase in the Red Tide until the climax seen in the second and third plagues. The death of every living thing in the seas and rivers will cause an awful stench to cover the earth. There will be accompanying pestilences and conditions indescribable. These terrible judgements will be seen in all parts of the world, but are not universal for the inhabitants of the world are not cut off till the seventh plague. Isaiah 47:9, 11 also suggest that the plagues will come suddenly, unexpectedly, and with great intensity.

God, who holds the records of all humanity, of the millions of His saints who have been put to death in the most inhuman manner, knows what He is doing. The angels who have witnessed the death of God's people in centuries past testify that God is just in giving these unholy forces blood to drink.

The Fourth Plague: The fourth falls in Tishri, 6005 A.S., the fall of 2035 A.D. This plague – the sun scorching men with heat (Revelation 16:8-9) – will bring great famine. (See Joel 1:15-

20). It is likely that there will be a gradual increase in drought until the climax seen in the fourth plague. In this time God will not forget His faithful children, for they shall be provided with a covering from the intense rays of the sun. (See Isaiah 4:4, 6).

The Fifth Plague: The fifth falls in Heshvan, 6005 A.S., the fall of 2035 A.D. The kingdom and throne, or seat of government where the beast reigns, the tri-confederation, will be full of darkness, spiritual darkness, which is the fifth plague. (Who is the beast? Where is his throne? Who composes his kingdom?) The beast is the Apostate, the first beast working in and through apostate Christianity, apostate Protestantism in the United States of America, the second beast of Revelation 13. They are the fifth, sixth, and seventh heads of the Apostate first beast. Their kingdom, the world, the seat of their power, the Vatican and the United States of America, the city of Washington, D.C. The kingdom is composed of the members of the United Nations in their secular and religious preferences.

Darkness is apostate Christianity's just portion, for during certain eras she forbid the common people to read the Bible. And today she forbids them to interpret it contrary to her teachings. She feels she thus preserves her adherents from heresies. Luther and other reformers, when they searched the Scriptures for themselves discovered among her teachings, doctrines introduced from Paganism during her 1260 year reign of terror, teachings which have since kept millions in spiritual darkness. It is likely that there will be a gradual decrease in the light of God's Word until the climax of spiritual darkness in the fifth plague.

The Bible Is Light: Until very recently, the Roman Catholic church has never urged that her people have the Bible, but has warned her people against the work of the Bible societies. Pope Pius the VII, in his warning, issued from Rome, 29 June 1816 A.D., said: "We have been truly shocked at this most crafty device (establishment and work of the Bible societies), by which the very foundations of religion are undermined....It is evident from experience that the Holy Scriptures, when circulated in the vulgar tongue [the language of the common people], have through the temerity [rash unwise foolhardiness] of men, produced more harm that benefit." [In brackets, supplied.]

To a devout Catholic, partaking of the Eucharist may seem the moment when he is closest to God. The reason why this and certain other teachings lead to spiritual darkness may not at first be apparent. The Apostate working in and through the apostate teachings lead to spiritual darkness that may not at first be apparent. But the light from related Scriptures on these subjects grows brighter as they are studied more deeply. Read 1 Peter 2:2, 9.

> *"Through Your precepts I get understanding: therefore I hate every false way. Your Word is a lamp unto my feet, and a light unto my path." "The entrance of Your Words give light; it gives understanding unto the simple." (Psalm 119:104, 105, 130).*

Dear reader, if the truths touched on in this book thus far are not yet clear, this promise from God is especially to you: Jesus says to you,

> *"And I will pray the Father, and He shall give you another Comforter (besides Myself), that He may abide with you forever; even the Spirit of Truth....He dwells with you, and shall be in you....He that has My commandments, and keeps them, he it is that loves Me: and he that loves Me shall be loved of My Father, and I will love him, and will manifest Myself to him....and We will come unto him and make Our abode with him....the Comforter, which is the Holy Spirit, whom the Father will send in My name, He shall teach you all things....If you keep My commandments, you shall abide in My love....when He, the Spirit of Truth, is come, He will guide you into all truth." (John 14:16-16:13).*

In Scripture, Light is a symbol of Truth, and Darkness of Error. During the fifth Plague, spiritual Darkness will be the portion of those who love not the Light. Particularly religious teachers who have clung to tradition and church doctrines irrespective of Bible Truths they might have seen and obeyed, had they carefully, and prayerfully "searched the Scriptures" for themselves. (Note Acts 17:11; John 5:39; 2 Timothy 2:15; 2 Thessalonians 2:3-12).

The Sixth Plague: The sixth falls in Tebeth, 6005 A.S., the winter of 2035 A.D. We are now prepared to examine Revelation 16:12 and let the Bible interpret the "drying up of the great river Euphrates" to prepare the way for the "Kings of the east." Whatever these events are, they occur as the seventh plague, which is "The Battle Of That Great Day Of God Almighty," approaches.

Zechariah describes what takes place under this sixth plague as "The Day" approaches.

> *"And it shall be the plague wherewith the Lord will smite all the people that have fought against Jerusalem; (God's people) ... And it shall come to pass in that day, that a great tumult from the Lord shall be among them; and they shall lay hold every one the hand of his neighbor, and his hand shall rise up against the hand of his neighbor." (Zechariah 14:12, 13).*

In order to understand this prophecy we must refer to the parallel experience of ancient Babylon. Six-hundred years before the Christ was incarnate, the pagan kingdom of Babylon was the great enemy of God's people. For seventy years they held the Hebrew people in subjection and bondage. Finally Babylon was overthrown by Cyrus the Mede, and physical Israel was delivered. Cyrus came from the east and captured Babylon by diverting the Euphrates River, thus giving access under the water gates of the channel. God said to Babylon,

> *"I will dry up your rivers ... Thus says the Lord to His anointed, to Cyrus ... to open before him the two leaved gates; and the gates shall not be shut." (Isaiah 41:2).*

Cyrus is referred to by God as the "anointed" and "the righteous man."

According to the principles of interpretation, the physical account in the Old Testament must, in the New Testament, be applied in a spiritual sense at the end time, the time in which we live. Thus we read in the New Testament about spiritual Israel (the church) being oppressed by spiritual Babylon the great. (Revelation 17:5, 6). This Babylon is not a physical kingdom, but counterfeit religious systems, using civil authority, and manipulated by Satan. God's people are finally delivered from the power of spiritual "Babylon" by the drying up of the waters of the antitypical river Euphrates.

"The sixth angel poured out his vial upon the great river Euphrates; and the water thereof was dried up, that the way of the kings of the east might be prepared." (Revelation 16:12).

The startling similarity to the Old Testament story is obvious, but we must remember that the secondary application cannot be physical. The immediate fulfillment is always physical and local, but the New Testament fulfillment reaches worldwide and has a spiritual application.

So the physical Cyrus will not dry up a physical river to deliver a physical Israel for the well known stream that has never been an obstacle to any army of ancient or modern times. It has already been discovered that all God's people are spiritual Israelites. Now what does the water represent?

"The waters which you saw ... are people, multitudes, nations, and tongues." (Revelation 17:1).

The waters are identified as people and nations who give support to the great Babylon harlot (false religion) who persecutes the saints of God. (Revelation 17:6).

So the drying up of the waters represents the withdrawing of support by those people who had been followers of the spiritual Babylonian system.

John describes the scene thus:

"The ten horns which you saw are ten kings, which have received no kingdom as yet; but receive authority as kings one hour with the beast. These are of one mind and shall give their power and strength unto the beast. These shall make war with the Lamb, and the Lamb shall overcome them; for He is Lord of lords and King of kings; and they that are with Him are called, chosen, and faithful." "The ten horns which you saw upon the beast, these shall hate the whore, and shall make her desolate and naked, and shall eat her flesh, and burn her with fire. For God has put in their hearts to fulfill His will, and to agree, and give their kingdom unto the beast, until the words of God shall be fulfilled." (Revelation 17:12-14, 16, 17).

This is one of the final events that take place just before the second coming of the Christ.

The people, the ten spiritual kingdoms, the Muslim nations of the great river valley of the Euphrates, in the winter of 2035 A.D., as one, sign a covenant with the United States and their allies, and are given authority to make war with the saints of God, spiritual Israel, but are defeated by the Lamb of God.

Two weeks into the contract, they recognized they have been duped, and in a rage they turn on spiritual Babylon, apostate Christianity and her confederates. The Muslim nations turn upon the United States of America and her allies, destroy her with nuclear weapons. There is an exchange of missiles that destroys, drys up those ten nations also. (Revelation 17:12-14, 16).

This drying up of the support prepares the way, spiritually, for the "Kings of the east" to come and deliver the people of God from the hand of spiritual Babylon, Satan and his three generals.

Turn the pages and see the return of the Son of God.

28

Satan's Three Generals

2031 A.D.	2035 A.D.	2036 A.D.	3031 A.D.
6001 A.S.	6035 A.S.	6036 A.S.	7001 A.S.

You are here.*

In the final movements that usher in the return of the Man of Destiny, our Lord, Jesus, the Christ, the leaders of the earth and their people will be gathered to the last great conflict by three unclean spirits which go forth from the dragon, the beast and the false prophet. (Revelation 16:13, 14). Here are the three generals or powers through which Satan will especially work in his endeavor to swing the whole world to his side in that final battle between truth and error.

On the side of truth is God: 1. The Father, God of Truth; 2. Jesus, the Christ is Truth; 3. The Holy Spirit is Truth. When a person is baptized he is baptized in the name of the Father, the Son, and the Holy Spirit. Each person who then lives for and obeys God becomes a part of the family of truth.

The agency now already abroad in the world known as modern spiritism, humanism, new ageism, is in every way a fitting means to be employed in this work. But it may be asked how a work which is already going on can be designated by that expression, when the spirits are not introduced into the prophecy until the pouring out of the sixth plague, which is still future. As in many other movements, the agencies which Heaven designs to employ in the accomplishment of certain ends, go through a process of preliminary preparation for the part which they are to act. Thus, before the spirits can have such absolute authority over the whole of mankind as to gather them to battle against the King of kings and Lord of lord's they must first win their way among the spiritual nations of the earth, and cause their teaching to be received as a divine authority and their word as law. This work they are now doing, and when they shall have once gained full influence over the nations in question, what fitter instrument could be employed to gather them to so rash and hopeless an enterprise?

To many it may seem incredible that the nations, spiritual and physical, should be willing to engage in such an unequal warfare as to go up to battle against the Lord of hosts; but it is one province of these spirits of devils to deceive, for they go forth working miracles, and thereby deceive the kings of the earth, that they should believe a lie.

That great statesmen recognize the influence of spiritism, or the spirits of devils, in influencing nations to go to war, is seen in the following statement by Sir Edward Grey, when speaking to the House of Commons. In describing the workings of these forces, the British Foreign Secretary accurately said: "It is really as if in the atmosphere of the world there were some mischievous influence at work, which troubles and excites every part of it."

Ramsay MacDonald, twice Prime Minister of Britain, said, "It would seem as if they were all bewitched, or laboring under some doom imposed upon them by devils....People were beginning to feel there was something devilish in the operations now going on to increase armies, navies, and air forces."

The source from which these spirits issue, denote that they will work among the three great religious divisions of mankind, Spiritualism, Roman Catholism, and Protestantism.

Spiritualism: The question naturally arises, who is the dragon? What power does it represent?

In Revelation 12:9 the answer is given: "The dragon was cast out, that old serpent, called the Devil and Satan." The Devil's general is human agencies through whom he works. In Revelation 12:4, 5 is marked out Satan's attempt to destroy the Christ child through pagan Rome. Ancient paganism with its idol worship is actually devil worship. (1 Corinthians 10:9, 20).

Spiritualism's self-immortality of the soul and self-deification of mankind is today's paganism. So in this particular prophecy the dragon is Satan working through the medium of spiritualism. This manifests itself and works through four different channels: Paganism, pagan forms of worship and superstition dominated by spiritualism; modern or social spiritualism, the Christian spiritualism, which has amalgamated itself with Christianity, Catholic and Protestant, by means of miracles and on the basis of the common doctrine of immortality of the soul; and scientific spiritualism, which is practiced in the form of laboratory investigations, under the name of parapsychology or other modern designations.

The Apostate Powers: The beasts of Revelation 13 are not literal animals, but are symbolic of certain religious-political powers on the earth. The description of the first beast in verse one identify it as the successor of the roman Empire. (See Revelation 12:3-5). Notice that the dragon gave him his power, his seat, and great authority. (Revelation 13:2).

The old pagan religious systems from Babylon passed through the various stages of the four world empires and into the Roman Catholic Church itself and so influenced Christianity as to form a great apostasy in the great ecclesiastical organization, so the Papacy became the heir of the superstitions and false philosophies of all ages from Babylon on down, and so becomes one third of the mystic Babylon of the Book of Revelation.

The Roman Catholic Church ruled for forty-two prophetic months or 1260 years. (Revelation 13:5; Ezekiel 4:6).

In 538 A.D. the bishop of Rome became the head of all churches, and the corrector of all heretics, and the 1260 years of papal supremacy began, during a part of which time for hundreds of years it was a death penalty to read the Bible, and thousands upon thousands were slain for keeping the Sabbath of the Lord, and other Bible truths.

The prophecy points out that this power has received a deadly wound which has been healed and the entire world is and will continue to follow the practices and customs of the papacy except those faithful few who hold tenaciously to the Lord, Jesus, the Christ. (Verses 3, 8).

At the end of 1260 years of papal supremacy, a French army led by General Berthier, entered Rome on 10 February 1798 A.D., took the pope prisoner, carried him to Valence, France, and there he died in prison the next year. So a great cry went out, "Catholism is dead!"

However, in 1800 A.D. the cardinals were permitted to elect a successor to the pope and the healing began. In 1870 A.D. at the Vatican Council in Rome on 18 July, it was decreed that the pope was infallible. This dogma of papal infallibility, to a larger measure, started the healing of the wound. When, in 1928 A.D., Benito Mussolini and Cardinal Gasparri signed the Lateran Treaty giving the pope a kingdom again. He became one of the earth's civil rulers, as king of Vatican City. Secular newspapers like *The Los Angeles Times* ran the headline in two inch bold type: "**Wound Healed**," thus noting the fulfillment of Bible prophecy.

The wound has healed, the strength is returning, and the whole worlds is beginning to wonder after this beast power. Newspapers around the world carried the unprecedented event of 4 October 1965 A.D. – "Pope Arrives In U.S." "Pope Asks Blessing on U.S. and LBJ." "Pope Utters Peace Plea, Blessing at UN Session." And then to climax the U.S. visit by Pope Paul VI, mass was said in Yankee Stadium and carried by Telstar Television to the entire world. And this is only the beginning. The Bible says of the beast power: "All that dwell upon the earth shall worship him." (Revelation 13:8).

American Protestantism: The dragon and the beast have been clearly identified, but who is the false prophet? At the very time that the prophet John sees the papal power "go into captivity," he says

> *"I saw another beast coming up out of the earth; and he had two horns like a lamb, and he spake as a dragon. And he exercised all the power of the first beast before him, and caused the earth and them which dwell therein to worship the first beast, whose deadly wound was healed. And he does great wonders, so that he makes fire come down from heaven on earth in the sight of men, and deceives them that dwell on the earth by the means of those miracles which he had power to do in the sight of the beast." (Revelation 13:10-14).*

There can be no doubt about the identity of this two horned beast as being the false prophet of this tri-confederacy of the battle of that great day of God Almighty when we compare the statement of Chapter 19, verse 20: "And the beast was taken, and with him the false prophet that wrought miracles before him." A "prophet" is one who speaks on behalf of another. This "prophet" speaks on behalf of the first beast, in connection with the complete healing of its deadly wound, to persuade the world to unite in allegiance to it. It is the two horned beast or false prophet that performs the miracles before the beast.

What power was arising in the late 1700s A.D., not in a populated area – but in a wilderness area – "coming up out of the earth?" From four specific aspects of prophecy, only one power could be described – the United States of America. But in a very special way, this two-horned beast preeminently represents apostate Protestantism in its development in the United States.

It is determined, by prophecy, that the Devil's three generals are: 1. Spiritualism, Satanic worship in its many forms, led by Satan; 2. Roman Catholicism, apostate christianity, led by the Pope; 3. American Protestantism, apostate christianity in America, led by the President. It is determined that this tri-confederacy is global, touching every nation, kindred, tongue, and people.

"I saw three unclean spirits like frogs come out of the mouth of the dragon, and out of the mouth of the beast, and out of the mouth of the false prophet. For they are the spirits of devils, working miracles, which go forth unto the kings of the earth and the whole world to gather them to the battle of the great day of God Almighty." (Revelation 16:13, 14).

In the final weeks that usher in the return of our Lord, Jesus, the Christ, the leaders of the earth and their people will be gathered, compelled, to the last great conflict by three evil spirits, demons which go forth from the tri-confederacy, Spiritualism, Roman Catholism, American Protestantism. Satan's three spirit Generals work through these powers, using whatever miracles and means necessary to swing the whole world to his side in that final battle between truth and error.

How will this come about?

1. Performance of great miracles by the tri-confederacy, that compels the people to follow their religious decrees. (Revelation 13:13, 14).

2. Death penalty for all who do not follow these religious decrees. "And he had power to give life unto the image of the beast, that the image of the beast should both speak, and cause as many as would not worship the image of the beast should be killed." (Verse 15).

The stage is now set for the battle of that great day of God Almighty. The final movements are taking place that will usher in the last mighty conflict. What does this mean to you? If you are already on the side of God, obedient to His commandments, it means to stand unwaveringly. If not, it means: Do it **now!**

The battle will be like the conflict on the plains of Dura in old Babylon. Take some time and read Daniel 3.

Satan, through the evil spirits of the tri-confederacy, headquartered in the United States of America, gathers all the princes and people of the world to participate in the worship of the likeness of the Roman Catholic, and apostate Protestantism dogma including the Mark, Sunday sabbath, enforced by civil authority. At the given time all are to confess loyalty to the religious decree enforced by civil authority, or face death. At the given time all the world confesses loyalty, except the Church of the First Born, spiritual Jerusalem, the 144,000. They stand erect and immediately they are taken before Satan.

As one, the 144,000 say to Satan....our God whom we serve is able to deliver us from death, and He will deliver us out of your hands. But if not, you should know, Satan, that we will not serve you, nor the tri-confederacy, or obey the religious dogma enforced by civil authority which you have set up.

Satan is very furious. He commands that all be gathered and killed in a great show of his authority and power. At the moment of execution, as Satan watches, he hears the voice of God from heaven saying, "It is done." (Revelation 16:1)7. The Battle of that Great Day of God Almighty has begun.

And God roars out of Zion.

235

29

A Place Called Armageddon

2031 A.D.	2035 A.D.	2036 A.D.	3031 A.D.
6001 A.S.	6035 A.S.	6036 A.S.	7001 A.S.

You are here.*

Physical Israel: The signing of the Israeli-Egyptian peace treaty on 26 March 1979 marked an emotional moment in the history of the Middle East. After years of bitter animosity punctured by military conflict, an Arab nation and a Jewish nation embraced each other with promises of peace.

What did it signify for the little pocket of Zionist whose struggles for survival have drawn approval and support from the United States of America? Was Sadat able to provide the security and permanent peace which has eluded Israel since the days of Abraham? The answers to these questions are clearly revealed in the fantastic prophecies of the Bible.

According to the Word of God, Israel, will not find true deliverance from her enemies until it is secured for her by the Kings of the east. Her last war has not yet been fought. The Book of Revelation describes an alliance with some powerful defenders who finally destroy the oppressors of Israel, and establish her in eternal security. Those allies are given the enigmatic title "Kings of the east." (Revelation 16:12). They actually intervene to deliver Israel during the Battle of that Great Day of God Almighty, described in the Bible as the final conflict to take place on Planet Earth. All nations will be involved in this battle, but spiritual Israel will be the only victor.

The purpose of this chapter is to answer a number of questions. What is the nature of that final war, the Battle of that Great Day of God Almighty? How can all the countries of the world be involved in it? How is it possible for only one group, the people of Israel, to survive this holocaust? Who are the mysterious Kings of the east that effect her victory? How is Israel delivered from her enemies by the drying up of the Euphrates River, as described in Revelation 16:12? And finally, what and where is this place called Armageddon mentioned in Revelation 16:15?

Spiritual Israel: First of all we need to find out if the present nation of Israel is the same Israel which is designated in the Book of Revelation as the people of God. Some tremendous prophecies are found in that Book, most of them are concerned with saving the embattled remnant group of faithful followers of Jesus, the Christ. Those followers are sometimes referred to as the "tribes of Israel" and spoken of in the context of Jewish customs. Does this mean that the physical nation of Israel – the one which is fighting with tanks and bombs – will completely reverse itself and become Christian? Will they lay aside their Zionist ambitions to kill their attackers, espouse the peaceful principles of the sermon on the mount – the one about loving the enemy and turning the other cheek?

Millions on Bible students believe that this kind of spectacular conversion must take place in order for Bible prophecy to be fulfilled. They base their belief upon the prophecies found in Jeremiah, Ezekiel, Isaiah, and etc. regarding Israel's restoration and final triumph. Are they correct? It's true that the prophets painted glowing word pictures of Israel's future, and recorded scores of promises about her authority over the nations. But is the Israel of the Old Testament the same Israel of the Book of Revelation? Were the promises unconditional and irrevocable? Will the physical, fleshly descendants of Abraham turn enmasse to the Messiah, be restored as a nation, and saved as a people?

The Promises To Israel Conditional: A careful study of the Bible reveals that those promises of the Old Testament were not unconditional promises at all. Repeatedly the nation of Israel was warned of the dire consequences of disobedience. Both blessing and curse were set before them, depending on obedience or disobedience. Because of continued patterns of rebellion, God allowed Israel, the northern ten tribes, to be decimated and scattered, and the Jews, the southern two tribes, into Babylonian captivity for seventy years. Many prophets were raised up by God to foretell their return from the Babylonian captivity. Modern commentators have made the mistake of applying those prophecies of restoration to some future gathering of Israel. They refuse to see that the restoration spoken of by Isaiah and Jeremiah have already taken place.

There is neither time nor space to record here a fraction of the graphic threats of rejection made to Israel. Over and over God gave warnings like this:

"And if you will ... do according to all that I have commanded you, and will keep My statutes and My judgements: Then I will establish the throne of My kingdom upon Israel for ever ... But if you shall at all turn from following Me, you and your children, and will not keep My commandments ... Then will I cut off Israel out of the land which I have given them; and this house, which I have hallowed for My name, will I cast out of My sight; and Israel shall be a proverb and a byword among all people." (1 Kings 9:4-7).

Finally, through the prophet Daniel, God allotted a probationary period of four-hundred ninety years for the Jewish people (Daniel 9:24) to see what they would do about the Messiah. That prophetic time period of seventy weeks (a day for a year, Ezekiel 14:6) began with the going forth of the commandment to restore and build Jerusalem (Artaxerxes' decree in the fall of four-hundred fifty-seven B.C., Ezra 7:11) and ended in the fall of thirty-four A.D. In that same year the gospel began to go to the Gentiles. Stephen was stoned, and Paul went forth to begin his unique ministry to the non-Jews. The occasion marked the formal and final separation of physical Israel from its covenant relationship.

Jesus had explained to the Jewish leaders in the clearest possible language that their rejection of Him would seal their own rejection as the children of the Kingdom. "The kingdom of God shall be taken from you, and given to a nation bringing forth the fruits thereof." (Matthew 21:43).

There is no mystery as to why the hundreds of specific Old Testament promises were never fulfilled to Israel. They utterly and totally failed to meet the conditions of obedience. Otherwise they would have inherited the earth, been delivered from all enemies, and Jerusalem made the worship center for all nations.

Who Is True Israel?: The big question is this: Will God's promises fail just because the Physical descendants of Abraham did not, do not, and will not meet the terms of the covenant? Were the promises transferred to the other "nation" to whom Jesus said the Kingdom would be given? Or must we still put our faith in some future turnaround that will restore physical Israel to divine favor? All those points will be completely clarified the moment one basic rule of Biblical interpretation is established. Without this principle in mind no one can properly understand the Books of Daniel and Revelation, nor can true Israel of today be identified.

Here's the rule: There is a primary, local, physical application. By applying this principle to the Old Testament scriptures there is absolutely no confusion as to the place of physical Israel in prophecy and history.

All the glorious promises were primarily aimed toward immediate blessings that God wanted to bestow on the nation. But in a secondary sense they pointed forward to a larger spiritual fulfillment on a worldwide level. Even though the local fulfillment failed when physical Israel failed to be faithful, the promises were never nullified or withdrawn. They will be honored, but only to that "nation" which Jesus said must replace physical Israel as receivers of the Kingdom. Who is that nation and people? The New Testament is saturated with the most explicit statements as to who spiritual Israel is.

Peter describes those "which in time past were not a people, but are now the people of God" in these words:

> *"But you are a chosen generation, a royal priesthood, an holy nation, a peculiar people; that you should show forth the praises of Him who has called you out of darkness into His marvelous light." (1 Peter 2:9, 10).*

Here is the new nation which replaces the nation of physical Israel. The Gentiles who will receive the true Messiah now enter into the Covenant relationship, ratified by the blood of the cross, and become His "holy nation."

Have they received the very same promises that were given to Abraham's physical descendants? Indeed the Bible says that they are counted as the actual seed of Abraham.

"And if you are the Christ's, then you are Abraham's seed, and heirs according to the promises." (Galatians 3:29).

Paul makes it even clearer in Romans 9:8.

"They which are the children of the flesh, these are not the children of God: but the children of the promise are counted for the seed."

Again Paul wrote:

"For he is not a Jew, which is one outwardly; neither is that circumcision, which is outward in the flesh: but he is a Jew, which is one inwardly, and circumcision is that of the heart." (Romans 2:28, 29)

Notice that true, spiritual, Israel will be characterized by circumcision of the heart and not of the flesh. What is heart circumcision?

"You are circumcised with the circumcision made without hands, in putting off of the body the sins of the flesh, by the circumcision of the Christ. " (Colossians 2:11).

Don't miss the significance of that text. Just as the Old Covenant was ratified by the blood of lambs and obedience represented by the cutting off of the physical flesh, so the New Covenant is ratified by the blood of the Lamb of God, Jesus, the Christ, and obedience exemplified by the cutting off the fleshly nature of sin. In other words, all who accept the Christ and are born again are the truly circumcised, spiritual Israel. And according to Paul they also inherit the promises made to Abraham. After the crucifixion of the Christ, there is not one indication that physical Israel, the Jews, were accorded any recognition as the children of God. It's true that the door was left open, through the preaching of the apostles, until thirty-four A.D., the end of Daniel's seventy week prophecy. But from that time on no recognition is given to physical Israel as a nation. Israel, spiritual Israel henceforth is God's people, made up of all those who accept the Saviour, whether Jew or Gentile, from every nation, kindred, tongue, and people. Old Testament imagery and terminology is still used, especially in the Book of Revelation, but God's people, the church, is now Israel. So, it can now be seen that there was and is no failure of the promises at all. They simply were transferred to spiritual Israel, which is the church, made up of all true believers, obedient believers in the Christ. And the things that will happen to the church spiritually were foreshadowed by what happened to ancient Israel in a physical sense. The following is a simple example of this principal in operation.

In the middle of Ezekiel's portrayal of ancient Israel's victory over her enemies and influence over the nations, he begins to describe a magnificent temple that would be built. Several chapters (40-48) are devoted to the precise measurements and physical appointments of the temple. Yet the temple has never been built. Other prophets referred to the program of building or restoring such a temple. Amos prophesied:

> *"In that day will I raise up the tabernacle of David that is fallen, and close up the breaches thereof; and I will raise up his ruins, and I will build it as in the days of old." (Amos 9:11).*

Many modern interpreters apply this promise to some future construction of a physical temple. But the Bible principle is that there is a secondary, worldwide fulfillment which is not physical. The New Testament confirms this by explaining how the prophecy of Amos has been fulfilled.

> *"Simon has declared how God at the first did visit the Gentiles, to take out of them a people for His name. And to this agree the words of the prophets; as it is written, After this I will return, and will build again the tabernacle of David, which is fallen down; and I will build again the ruins thereof, and I will set it up." (Acts 15:14-16).*

Please notice how James applies the Old Testament temple prophecies to the living church. The physical temple has now become the spiritual temple, the body of the Christ's church, made up of all obedient believers, physical Israel and Gentiles. No one should be looking for any restored, physical temple to be built. The body of the Christ's church is now the temple (1 Corinthians 3:16) and we are the "living stones" of that "spiritual house" (1 Peter 2:5).

Some have felt confused because much of the Old Testament terminology is carried over into the New Testament description of the church – words like kingdom, nation, Israel, temple, Jerusalem, Zion, tribes of Israel, and etc. Even the Christ said to the Pharisees, "The kingdom of God shall be taken from you, (physical Israel) and given to a nation (spiritual Israel) bringing forth the fruits thereof." (Matthew 21:43). This is one reason the futurists and dispensationalists believe the Book of Revelation pertains to the physical Jew in modern Israel. But there is no cause for such confusion. The explanation had been so clearly made in so many places, that the New Testament writers assumed all were aware that the church has now replaced physical Israel.

The Two Babylons: As we look at "The Battle Of That Great Day Of God Almighty" and the place called "Armageddon" it is tremendously important to keep this great rule of interpretation before us. Old Testament physical, New Testament spiritual. The vast confusion on prophecy today stems from ignorance of this principle. It is here repeated once more that the prophecies given by Isaiah, Jeremiah, Ezekiel, and etc. have a double application – one to be primary, physically fulfilled locally; the other to be secondary and spiritually fulfilled on a worldwide scale in these last days. And the church takes the place of the physical nation of Israel, the Jews, as God's true chosen people. With this background we are prepared to delve into the subject of "The Battle Of That Great Day Of God Almighty" and "Armageddon". That world-ending conflict is tied closely to the things that have been stated about spiritual Israel and a secondary application of prophecy. A most amazing parallel exists between what happened to ancient physical Israel and the events concerning spiritual Israel in the Book of Revelation.

Physical Israel	Spiritual Israel
Jeremiah 50:33, 34	Revelation 17:6

Persecuted by Babylon

Daniel 3:13	Revelation 13:15

Forced to worship image

Daniel 4:30	Revelation 17:5

Called Babylon the Great

Jeremiah 51:13, 14	Revelation 17:1

Babylon sits on many waters

Isaiah 44:27, 28	Revelation 16:12

Rescued by drying up Euphrates

Jeremiah 51:6-8	Revelation 18:4

Called out of Babylon

Isaiah 45:1	Daniel 9:25

Rescuer called "the anointed"

Isaiah 41:2, 25	Matthew 24:27
	Revelation 7:2

Both rescuers from the "east"

It should be noted that God's people had almost the same experience in the Old Testament and the New. They were forced to worship an image, and rescued by someone from the east who dried up the river Euphrates to set them free. Within this broad outline there are scores of other astonishing similarities between the two Israels – one physical and the other spiritual. It is obvious that the church – God's people of the end time – will be persecuted and threatened with death just like ancient Israel. In the Book of Revelation they are delivered from spiritual Babylon in connection with "The Battle Of That Great Day Of God Almighty". "And the sixth angel poured out his vial upon the great river Euphrates; and the water thereof was dried up, that they way of the Kings of the east might by prepared. And I saw three unclean spirits like frogs come out of the mouth of the dragon and out of the mouth of the beast, and out of the mouth of the false prophet. For they are the spirits of devil, working miracles, which go forth unto the kings of the earth and of the whole world, to gather them to "The Battle Of That Great Day

Of God Almighty." These three – the dragon, beast, and the false prophet – stir up spiritual and political powers of the earth to take part in that war. It's apparent that these three are religious powers, at least in their claims, because they work miracles to impress the governments of earth. Miracles are only operative within the realm of religion.

Time and space does not allow for all the biblical evidence to show how these three symbols incorporate all the modern forms of counterfeit religion. Rejecting the authority of God's law and choosing the easy traditions of pagan worship patterns, these combined ecclesiastical systems will wield a mighty influence in drawing the whole world into "The Battle Of That Great Day Of God Almighty."

Satan vs God, the Battle Of That Great Day Of God Almighty: Before we try to determine the identify of the "Kings of the east" and what it means to "dry up the river Euphrates," we must understand more clearly what "The Battle Of That Great Day Of God Almighty" really involved. The Scriptures picture it as the final decisive struggle which climaxes the age-long war between God and Satan. The entire world is involved because the good and evil people are scattered among all nations of planet earth. "The Battle Of That Great Day Of God Almighty" represents the all-out effort of Satan to destroy the people who dare to obey God in the face of threatened torture and death.

"The Battle Of That Great Day Of God Almighty" is but the climax of a 6,000 year program by Satan to keep God's people on Planet Earth from being saved. As the adversary, whose self-seeking caused him to be cast out of heaven, Satan declared his purpose to overthrow God and take over His universal government. Listen to his boast in Isaiah 14:13, 14.

> "I will ascent into heaven. I will exalt my throne above the stars of God: I will sit also upon the mount of the congregation, in the sides of the north: I will ascent above the heights of the clouds: I will be like the most High."

This incredible claim of Satan exposes the heart of his plan to set himself up in place of God. To subvert the worship of

God's subjects to himself it would seem both natural and necessary for Satan to build his appeal around religion. Working in the guise of counterfeit religious systems and false worship, he has woven a cleaver composite of truth and error down through the ages. His masterpiece of deception will occur at the end-time when he works through the beast powers, the United States of America and the reborn Roman Catholic Church, to enforce a spiritual mark of loyalty on every person. Those who refuse the mark will be sentenced to death, and thus the final obstacle will be removed for Satan to claim all creation as his followers. So reads the blueprint of Satan's strategy.

God Dwells In Zion, Armageddon: Now notice again where Satan wanted to sit. He said, "I will sit also upon the Mount of the congregation, in the sides of the north." Why did he say that? This point is very important. The expression "Mount of the congregation" is undoubtedly referring to the Holy Mount of God's dwelling place. Throughout the Bible it is spoken of as Mount Zion.

"Beautiful for situation, the joy of the whole earth, is Mount Zion, on the sides of the north, the city of the great King." (Psalm 48:2).

The striking thing is that God's place, Mount Zion, is located in the sides of the north. Now it can be understood why Satan wanted to sit on the Mount of the Congregation, in the sides of the north. That is where God will gather His people, His congregation. Mount Zion is a place of safety, Satan wants to destroy the congregation or people of God. He would penetrate the very elect by his deceptions and take them, along with the throne of God. The psalmist said, "Sing praises to the Lord, which dwells in Zion." (Psalm 9:11).

Originally Zion was the designated spot where the temple was located, in the north part of Jerusalem. Later it came to be known as a symbol of the city of Jerusalem. It also is applied throughout Scripture to the whole of God's people. But after the whole of physical Israel rejected Jesus, the Christ, the term Zion became the destination of the church. Thus in the New

Testament it no longer identifies an earthly location, but the spiritual place of God's presence and protection.

All through the Bible God is described as drawing or gathering His people to Zion where they can be safe with Him.

"Blow the trumpet in Zion, ... call a solemn assembly; Gather the people, sanctify the congregation." "For in Mount Zion ... shall be deliverance." (Joel 2:15, 16; 2:32).

In Revelation 14:1 the redeemed are pictured as having been delivered from the beast power of the previous chapter, and are safe in Mount Zion,

"And I looked, and, lo, a Lamb stood on Mount Zion, and with Him 144,000, having His Father's name written within their foreheads."

But while Satan is gathering his people to himself, "For they are the spirits of devils ... to gather them to the battle of that great day of God Almighty," Revelation 16:14, God programs a gathering of His people to Himself in Zion. It is a gathering of His people to Armageddon.

"Behold, I come as a thief. Blessed and happy is he that watches, and keeps his garments, lest he walk naked, and they see his shame. And He gathered them together into a place called in the Hebrew language Armageddon." (Revelation 16:15, 16).

This gathering is God's gathering His Saints to Mount Zion. Joel also speaks about that same gathering,

"Assemble yourselves, and come, all you heathen, and gather yourselves together round about ... Let the heathen ... come up to the valley of Jehoshaphat ... The Lord also shall roar out of Zion ... but the Lord will be the hope of His people." (Joel 3:11, 12, 16).

This is another description of that final conflict called "The Battle Of That Great Day Of God Almighty" (Revelation 16:14). The valley of Jehoshaphat is just another title for the place of battle, Planet Earth. It will involve every nation, kindred, tongue, and people on earth. The "heathen" is a term to describe all those who are not God's people. Satan will marshall the kings of the earth's wicked people to oppose the faithful saints of God.

The Lord will be involved in the battle ("The Lord shall roar out of Zion") because He fights for His people. In essence, it is a tremendous contest with followers on both sides being involved.

Here is where we get to the heart of the subject. The verse calls attention to the Hebrew word Armageddon. The word is rooted in the Hebrew term "Har moed," which means "mount of the congregation" or "mount of the assembly." Do you see where this leads us? That same word (har moed) was used by Satan when he said, "I will sit also upon the mount of the congregation." This ties the place where God is taking His people (Armageddon) to the original threat of Satan to the throne of God, Mount Zion. And the final attempt of the evil one to carry out his threat reaches down to the very least events of planet earth. John the revelator described it under the sixth plague. He saw unclean spirits going out to the kings of the earth, working miracles, and gathering them to "The Battle Of That Great Day Of God Almighty." (Revelation 16:14). Since Satan can not dethrone God in His heaven he uses these religious forces to work on the political rulers and influence them to destroy God's faithful ones.

If you want to read the thrilling account of God's part in "The Battle Of That Great Day Of God Almighty," Revelation 16:14, study Chapter 19.

> "And I saw heaven opened, and behold a white horse; and He that sat upon him was called Faithful and True, and in righteousness He does judge and make war ... And the armies which were in heaven followed Him upon white horses, clothed in fine, white and clean ... and He treads the winepress of the fierceness and wrath of Almighty God." (Revelation 19:11-15).

Several things stand out in this symbolic picture of the Christ and His second coming. The armies of heaven make war and "smite the nations" (verse 15). These are the nations which were stirred up by the evil spirits in Revelation 16:14. The Christ prevails in "The Battle Of That Great Day Of God Almighty" (Revelation 16:14). Notice that this war is described as treading the winepress of the wrath of God. In Revelation 15:1 the seven last plagues are designated as "the wrath of God."

Since "The Battle Of That Great Day Of God Almighty" Revelation 16:14, is set up under the sixth plague, and the plagues are called the wrath of God; and since the Christ's army wars by treading the winepress of God's wrath, we must conclude that Revelation 19 is a clear picture of "The Battle Of That Great Day Of God Almighty," (Revelation 16:14).

Incidently, the vials of the wrath of God are poured on the whole of planet earth. "Go you ways, and pour out the vials of the wrath of God upon the earth." Revelation 16:1. This is why all the nations are involved in "The Battle Of That Great Day Of God Almighty," (Revelation 16:14). The good and the bad, the righteous and the unrighteous of the world are drawn into it. Since God's people are scattered in every nation, kindred, tongue, and people, the entire earth is spoken of as being affected by the plagues, the seventh one being "The Battle Of That Great Day Of God Almighty," (Revelation 16:14).

Euphrates Dried Up: We are now prepared to examine Revelation 16:12 and let the Bible interpret the "drying up of the great river Euphrates" to prepare the way for the "Kings of the east." Whatever these events are, they occur as the seventh plague, which is "the battle of the great day of God Almighty," approaches.

Just as physical Euphrates in ancient Babylon was turned from an asset to a means of destroying her, so the Muslim nations (the ten horns), being an asset to apostate Christianity for two weeks, turn into the means of her destruction. This drying up of support prepares the way spiritually, for the "Kings of the east" to come and deliver the people of God from the hand of spiritual Babylon.

Who Are The Kings Of The East?: Here is one of the most exciting aspects of "The Battle Of That Great Day Of God Almighty." Just as God's place in Zion was located in the "sides of the north," so His approach is always referred to as from the east. Why? Because anciently Zion was the actual hill north of the city of Jerusalem. Anyone coming from the east had to angle north because of the impassable deserts, and come into Zion from that direction. This is why both north and east are used in the Bible for God's quarters,

> *"And I saw another angel ascending from the east, having the seal of the living God." (Revelation 7:2).*

The Christ will return from the east.

> *"For as the lighting comes out of the east, and shines even unto the west; so shall the coming of the Son of man be." (Matthew 24:27).*

The "Kings of the east" are exactly the same as the armies of heaven in Revelation 19 who triumph over "the beast, and the kings of the earth, and their armies" (verse 19). God's glory was described by Ezekiel as coming out of the east.

> *"He brought me to the gate ... that looks toward the east: And, behold, the glory of the God of Israel came from the way of the east ... and the earth shined with His glory." (Ezekiel 43:1, 2).*

John revealed the breathtaking majesty of the Christ leading the armies of heaven to make war.

> *"And the armies which were in heaven followed Him upon white horses ... And He has on His vesture and His thigh a name written, King of kings and Lord of lords." (Revelation 19:14, 16).*

What a picture! The Kings of the east riding forth against "the kings of the earth" and of the whole world. Spiritual Babylon and all the forces who followed her are destroyed by the King of kings who shall reign forever.

At this point it can easily be concluded that the second coming of the Christ is really the only hope of Israel, spiritual Israel. God and the Christ, the true Kings of the east, will come upon this world at the midnight of man's extremity. When the mark of the beast is being enforced by civil authority, and every human plan of escape has been dissolved, God's faithful ones will be snatched from certain death.

All Eyes On The East: What a tragedy that millions of professed Christians are looking in the wrong direction and expecting events to transpire that can never take place. Their eyes are fixed on the east alright, but on the Middle East where hate filled sons of Abraham try to destroy each other with American and Soviet weaponry. What kind of travesty it would be to expect those political planners and militarists to fulfill the beautiful predictions of Isaiah's "lion and lamb" world of peace.

True it is, for a moment, Isaac and Ishmael and the rest of the sons of Abraham may stop fighting. It is also true that one of the signers of the agreement is called Israel. But let no one still cling to the empty hope that this Israel has anything to do with God's true people, spiritual Israel. They have been replaced by another nation obedient and faithful – who have come from every nation, kindred, tongue, and people. They are true Israel, spiritual Israel. They will live as Jesus lived, choosing death before disobedience and dishonor.

The frail confederacy of peace signed 26 March 1979 would be less than futile, even if national Israel were still the chosen people of God. Many years ago a similar alliance was formed and God appraised it in these words:

> *"Therefore shall the strength of Pharaoh be your shame, and the trust in the shadow of Egypt your confusion. For the Egyptians shall help in vain, and to no purpose ... this is a rebellious people ... children that will not hear the law of the Lord." (Isaiah 30:3, 7, 9).*

God is looking for those who will trust in right instead of might. To such He will provide deliverance from every enemy through the conquering Kings of the east. Let us take our eyes away from oil fields and political intrigues of the Middle East and fix them on the eastern skies, because it is from there that our true allies will save us.

Clothed For Armageddon: Now we have been able to harmonize all the verses of Revelation 16:12-16 except those strange verses 15 and 16, which appear to be completely out of context with all the others. Why did the Holy Spirit inspire the placing of such verses in the setting of "The Battle Of That Great Day Of God Almighty?" "Behold, I come as a thief. Blessed, happy, is he that watches, and keeps his garments, lest he walk naked, and they see his shame. And He gathered them together into a place called in the Hebrew languages, Armageddon."

What do proper clothes have to do with preparation for the approaching contest between the Christ and Satan? And why is the wardrobe important for the ones waiting for Jesus to come? And where is this place He is going to take us? Revelation 19:7-9 gives the surprising answer:

> "Let us be glad and rejoice, and give honor to Him: for the marriage of the Lamb is come, and His wife has made herself ready. And to her was granted that she should be arrayed in fine linen, clean and white: for the fine linen is the righteousness of the saints. And he said unto me, Write, Blest are they which are called unto the marriage supper of the Lamb ..." (Revelation 19:7-9).

Like a searchlight these words illuminate the meaning of Revelation 16:15, 16. Those garments symbolize the righteousness of the Christ, with which every soul must be arrayed who would be ready to meet the Lord in the clouds. Those who have kept their garments, those who are ready to meet the Lord will be taken to the heavenly Jerusalem, Mount Zion, Armageddon for the marriage supper of the Lamb. These verses are inserted parenthetically to give encouragement to the beligered children of God. "The Battle Of That Great Day Of God Almighty" will be fought over the issue of the Christ's righteousness. Only those who have trusted completely in the merits of the Christ's sinless life and atoning death can triumph with Him over the forces of evil and be gathered to the heavenly Jerusalem, Mount of the Congregation, Armageddon.

> And they overcame him by the blood of the Lamb and by the word of their testimony; and they loved not their lives unto death." (Revelation 12:11).

Here is the winning combination which finally will cast down the accuser of the brethern into the pit. The saints gained the victory by their simple faith in the sufficiency of the cross. No confidence in the flesh. No faith in the words of the law to justify. His merits alone to cleanse and empower. So the combination is three fold: 1. Faith in the righteousness of Jesus, 2. Fearless sharing of the "Word of their testimony." and 3. "They loved not their lives unto death." In other words, they would rather die than sin.

When the cross has done this to a person, they can survive all the concentrated attacks of a thousand demons. Demons, fallen angels, and Satan himself must flee in terror before the authority of the Christ-filled life. True faith produces full obedience, and therefore true righteousness by faith includes sanctification as well as justification. Those who would lay down their lives in death rather than disobey God will be the only ones who will refuse "The Mark Of The Beast."

Multitudes, with something less than true righteousness by faith, will not feel that obedience to all the commandments is worth dying for. Many will reason that the Christ's obedience has been imputed to them, and therefore they need not be concerned about the works of the law. Such do not understand the full gospel. It is the "power of God unto salvation" – not just forgiving power, but keeping power. We are not just saved from the guilt of sin, but from sin itself.

So the preparation to meet the Christ focuses on a personal relationship with the Saviour. Clothed in the armor of His righteousness, the saints will prevail even in the face of a death decree. If you do not have the sweet assurance of that spiritual protection now, put on His robe this very moment. Woven in the loom of heaven, it contains no thread of human devising. Shattering the authority of sin in the life, it has the merits and power of the Christ's life and atoning death. May this be your experience today.

30

The Return, The Battle

2031 A.D.	2035 A.D.	2036 A.D.	3031 A.D.
6001 A.S.	5746 A.S.	5768 A.S.	7001 A.S.

You are here.*

When the Christ was about to be separated from His disciples, He comforted them in their sorrow with the assurance that He would come again:

> *"Do not let your heart be troubled ... In My Fathers house are many rooms ... I go to prepare a place for you. And if I go to prepare a place for you, I will come again, and receive you unto Myself." "The Son of man shall come in His glory, and all the holy angels with Him. Then shall He sit upon the throne of His glory: Before Him shall gather all nations."* (John 14:1-3; Matthew 13:31, 32).

At this time the graves of many have already been opened and:

> *"many of them that sleep in the dust of the earth ... are awake, some have everlasting life, and some have shame and everlasting contempt." (Daniel 16:19, 21).*

All who died in the faith of the Lord, Jesus the Christ have come from the grave glorified. "They also which pierced Him," those who mocked and derided the Christ's dying agonies, and the most violent oppressors of His glory, and His people, have been raised to behold Him in His glory, and to see the honor placed upon the loyal and obedient.

The subject of the second coming of the Christ is a fascinating study. It is an outstanding prophetic event and is a doctrine spoken of more often than any other teaching in the Bible. For instance, the Bible mentions the doctrine of baptism by water only about 20 times. Also, the subject of the Lord's Supper, as familiar as it is to all of us, is discussed only about 5 times in Holy Writ.

In comparison with these generally accepted doctrines, the second coming of the Christ is mentioned 331 times! Surely this doctrine must have been uppermost in the mind of God as His Spirit moved the writers of the Bible or it would not have been mentioned so many times.

Peter describes the second coming of the Christ as the "appearing of Jesus, the Christ" and as "the coming of the day of God." (1 Peter 1:7; 2 Peter 3:12).

These references indicate quite clearly that His coming will be visible. As well, note Paul's statement to the church at Thessalonica:

The Lord Himself shall descend from heaven with a shout, with the voice of the archangel, and with the trump of God." (1 Thessalonians 4:16).

Practically everyone will agree that the man of destiny, Jesus, is a master teacher. Therefore, it would be logical to call for His testimony concerning His return:

"And then shall appear the sign of the Son of man in heaven: And then shall all tribes of the earth mourn, and they shall see the Son of man coming in the clouds of heaven with power and great glory."; "For the Son of man shall come in the glory of His Father with His angels; and then shall He reward every man according to his works." (Matthew 24:30; 16:27).

The Seventh Plague: The seventh falls on 5 Shebat 6006 A.S., the winter of 2036 A.D.

A Great Destruction To Come: Great destruction will take place at the second coming of the Christ. Jesus describes the time of His coming as being unexpected by the world, even as a thief may come in the night.

And so we read:

"But the day of the Lord will come as a thief in the night; in the which the heavens shall pass away with a great noise, and the elements shall melt with fervent heat, the earth also, and the works that are therein shall be burned up." (2 Peter 3:10).

That this fiery destruction will come at the second coming of the Christ also is shown in 2 Thessalonians 1:7, 18:

> *"And to you who are troubled, rest with us, when the Lord, Jesus shall be revealed from heaven with His mighty angels, in flaming fire taking vengeance on them that know not God, and that obey not the gospel of our Lord, Jesus the Christ."*

The prophet Isaiah foretold this destruction in similar language:

> *"For behold, the Lord will come with fire, and with chariots like a whirlwind, to render His anger with fury, and His rebuke with flames of fire. For by fire and by His sword will the Lord plead with all flesh: And the slain of the Lord shall be many." (Isaiah 66:16, 16).*

Speaking of the events accompanying the second advent of the Christ, the Apostle John states:

> *"And the heaven departed as a scroll when it is rolled together; and every mountain and island were moved out of their places. And the kings of the earth, and the great men, and the rich men, and the chief captains, and the mighty men, and every bondman, and every free man, hid themselves in the dens and in the rocks of the mountains; and said to the mountains and rocks, Fall on us, and hide us from the face of Him that sits on the throne, and from the wrath of the Lamb: For the great day of His wrath is come; and who shall be able to stand?" (Revelation 6:14-17).*

The sixth seal does not bring us to the second coming of the Christ, although it embraces events closely connected with the coming. It introduces the fearful commotions of the elements, described as the heavens rolling together as a scroll, the breaking up of the surface of the earth, and the confession by the wicked that the great day of God's wrath is come. They are doubtless in momentary expectation of seeing the King appear in glory. But the seal stops just short of that event. The personal appearing of the Christ must therefore be allotted to the seventh seal and plague.

When the Lord appears, He comes with the host of heaven. (Matthew 25:31). When all the heavenly harpers leave the courts above to come to this earth with their divine Lord as He descends to gather the fruit of His redeeming work, will there not be silence in heaven? The length of the journey, considering it prophetic time, is one week.

As the moment approaches for the death decree to be inflicted upon the saints of God, Satan and his evil angels will lead the enemies of the Christ, the whole world, to the destruction of God's people. It will be determined to strike in one night a decisive blow which will utterly silence the voice of reproof of God's people. As the hour approaches, above the shouts and jeering of evil men, suddenly there is the thundering voice of God from heaven declaring, "It is done."

Thus is described the last judgment which is inflicted upon the present state of the earth, upon those who are incorrigibly rebellious against God. Some of the plagues are local in their application, but this one is poured out into the air. The atmosphere envelopes the whole earth, and it follows that this plague will envelope equally all the inhabitants of Planet Earth. It will be universal. The very air is deadly.

The gathering of the nations for, "The Battle Of That Great Day Of God Almighty", has taken place and the battle remains to be fought under the seventh seal. Here are brought to view the instruments with which God will slay the wicked. At this time it may be said, "The Lord has opened His armory, and has brought forth the weapons of His indignation." (Jeremiah 50:25).

The Scriptures declare, "There were voices." Above all, is heard the voice of God.

> "The Lord also shall roar out of Zion, and utter His voice
> from Jerusalem, and the heavens and the earth shall shake;
> But the Lord will be the hope of His people, and the strength
> of the children of Israel." (Joel 3:16).

(See also Jeremiah 25:30; Hebrews 12:26). The voice of God causes the Great earthquake, such as was not since men were upon the earth.

"Thunders, and lightnings." – another allusion to the judgment of Egypt. (Exodus 9:23). The great city is divided into three parts; that is, the three grand divisions of the false and apostate religions of the world (the great city), paganism, Catholicism, and Protestantism, each set apart to receive its appropriate doom. The cities of all nations fall; universal desola-

256

tion spreads over Planet Earth; every island disappears, and the mountains are not found. Thus great Babylon comes in remembrance before God. Read her judgments, as more fully described in Revelation 18.

"A great hail out of heaven, falling upon men," is the last instrument used in the infliction of punishment upon the wicked – the bitter dregs of the seventh vial. God has solemnly addressed the wicked, saying,

> *"Judgment also will I lay to the line, and righteousness to the plummet: And the hail shall sweep away the refuge of lies, and the waters shall overflow the hiding place." (Isaiah 28:17).*

(See also Isaiah 30:30.) The Lord asked Job if he had seen the treasures of the hail, which He has "Reserved against the time of trouble, against the day of battle and war." (Job 38:22, 23).

Every hailstone is said to be "About the weight of a talent." According to various authorities, a talent as a weight is between 55 and 100 pounds avoirdupois. What can withstand the force of stones of such an enormous weight falling from heaven? But mankind, at this time, will have no shelter. The cities have fallen in a mighty earthquake, the islands have fled away, and the mountains are gone. Again the wicked give vent to their woe in blasphemy, for the plague of hail is "exceeding great."

As surely as God's word is truth, He is soon to punish a guilty world, May it be ours, according to the promise, to have "sure dwellings" and "quiet resting places" in that terrific hour. (Isaiah 32:18, 19).

"There came a great voice out of the temple of heaven, from the throne, saying, "It is done!" Thus all is finished. The cups of God's wrath have been emptied, poured out upon a corrupt generation. The wicked have drunk them to the dregs, and sunk into the realm of death for a thousand years. Dear reader, where do you wish to be found after that great decision?

But what is the condition of the saints while the "overflowing scourge" is passing? They are the special subjects of God's protection, without whose notice not a sparrow falls to the ground. Many are the promises which come crowding in to afford them comfort, summarily contained in the beautiful and expressive language of the psalmist:

> "I will say of the Lord, He is my refuge and my fortress; my God; in Him I trust. Surely He will deliver you from the snare of the fowler, and from the noisome pestilence. He shall cover you with His feathers, and under His wings you shall trust: His truth shall be your shield and buckler. You shall not be afraid for the terror by night; not for the arrow that flyes by day; nor for the pestilence that walks in the darkness; nor for the destruction that makes waste at noonday. A thousand shall fall at your side, and ten thousand at your right hand; but it shall not come near you. Only with your eyes shall you behold and see the reward of the wicked. Because you have made the Lord, which is my refuge, even the Most High, your habitation; there shall no evil befall you, neither shall any plague come near your dwelling." (Psalm 91:2-10).

King of kings and Lord of lords: The end has come! Man's day has ended. The Battle Of That Great Day Of God Almighty is the world ending battle. These three words "It is done", turn the world upside down. The angry multitudes are suddenly arrested, and the mocking cries die away. With fearful foreboding they gaze upon the Son of man coming in the clouds of Heaven and long to be shielded from the overpowering brightness.

Everything in nature is turned out of its course. Rivers and streams stop flowing. Dark, heavy clouds roll up and come against each other. That voice from heaven saying, "It is done," shakes the heavens and the earth. There is a mighty earthquake such as has not been since mankind were upon the earth, so mighty an earthquake, and so great. The mountains shake like a reed in the wind, and ragged rocks are scattered on every side. There is a roar as a coming tornado. The sea is whipped into a fury. There is heard the shriek of a hurricane like voice of demons upon a mission of destruction. The whole earth heaves and swells like the waves of the sea. Its surface is breaking up. Its very foundation is giving way. Mountain chains are sinking, and inhabited islands disappear.

Great hailstones, every one weighing about eighty pounds, are doing their work of destruction. The proudest cities of the earth are laid low. The palaces upon which the world's great men have lavished their wealth in order to glorify themselves are crumbled to ruin before their eyes. (See Revelation 16:17-21).

All eyes are fixed upon the eastern sky. Nearer and nearer that cloud approaches until finally the whole heavens are alive with radiant forms.

The Warrior King:

"I saw heaven opened and a white horse appeared there. Its rider is called Faithful and True; justly He does judge and wage war. His eyes were like flames of fire, and on His head are many crowns with a name inscribed which no man knows but Himself. He is wearing a robe dipped in blood: His name is called The Word of God. The armies of heaven clothed in the finest linen, white and pure, follow Him on white horses.

Out of His mouth goes a sharp Sword, that with it He should smite the nations: He shall rule them with a Rod of Iron and He treads the winepress of the fierceness and wrath of Almighty God. He has on His robe and on His thigh a name written, King of kings and Lord of lords.

I saw another angel standing in the sun, and he called with a loud voice to all the birds that fly in midheaven, Come, gather yourselves unto the supper of the Great God, to eat the flesh of kings, captains, mighty men, horses, and them that sit upon them, and all men, both free and bond, both small and great.

I saw the Beast, the Evil Creature (the Roman Catholic Church), *and the kings of the earth, and their armies mustered to wage war against the One mounted on the horse, and against His army. And the Beast, the Evil Creature was captured, and with him the False Prophet* (Apostate Protantism) *who did mighty miracles before him, with which he deceived them that had received the mark of the beast, and them that worshiped his image. These two are thrown alive into the lake of fire burning with sulphur. The rest were slain with the Sword of Truth that issues from the mouth of the One mounted on the horse. And all*

259

the birds gorged themselves with their flesh. (Revelation 19:11-21).

All of the wicked are slain with the Sword of Truth of Him that sits on the horse, which is the Rod of Iron (The Word of God) *proceeding out of His mouth; Before the Word of God the wicked cannot stand and call for the mountains and rocks to fall on them and hide them from the glory of God. All the fowls are filled with their flesh." (Revelation 19:1-4)*

Plain type in parenthesis added.

The Harvester King:

"I looked, and behold a white cloud, and upon the cloud One sat like unto the Son of man, having on His head a golden crown, and in His hand a sharp sickle.

Another angel came out of the temple, crying with a loud voice to Him that sat on the cloud, Thrust in your sickle, and reap: The time is come for you to reap; for the harvest of the earth is ripe. And He that sat on the cloud thrusted in His sickle on the earth; and the earth was reaped." (Revelation 14:14-15).

Here is the battle of the great day of God Almighty.

From the grand center of the universe, from the throne of God, through the myriads of shining stars in an eternal heaven, comes the heavenly host. The cloud passes constellations, groups, and systems as it approaches. We see first the overpowering glory of God shining forth as the heavenly host descends through the great stars of heaven such as Rigal in Orion, shining with the power of fifteen thousand suns like ours. The nearest sun to ours is ninety three million million miles away. From Rigal, from the Orion Nebula They come straight to Planet Earth, the journey taking three days. The glory of the return is the glory of the Father, the Son, and the holy angels and outshines our sun as mankind is riveted by the approach.

At the first sign of the coming of the Lord, sinful mankind turns their entire arsenal to the heavens in a feudal attempt to defend themselves from the advancing hosts of heaven. Their weapons are powerless before the God of the universe.

The harvesting of Planet Earth will be in a twenty-four hour day. It will occur in the spring of 2036 A.D., 1 Nisan, 6006 A.S. The speed of the harvest of the world is this wise:

Diameter of the earth	7918 miles
Times pi	3.1416
Circumference of the earth	24875.188 miles
Divided by hours per day	24 hpd
Surface miles per hour	1036.4661 mph
Divided by minutes per hour	60 mph
Surface miles per minute	17.274435 mpm
Divided by second per minute	60 spm
Surface miles per second	0.2879072 mps

The Christ hovers above the earth, at the equator some seventy-five million miles in space and the earth is harvested by the angels as they administer justice to the wicked and minister to the redeemed. From this position in the heavens, the entire population of Planet Earth can see the Son of man coming in the clouds of heaven.

There is a false doctrine, pointing to a thousand years of peace and righteousness before the personal coming of the Lord in the clouds of heaven, putting far off the terrors of the Day of the Lord. But, pleasing though this may be, it is contrary to the teachings of the Christ and His apostles, who declare that the wheat and the tares are to grow together until the harvest, at the end of the world; that evil men and seducers are waxing worse and worse; that in these last days perilous times are come; and that the kingdom of darkness is continuing until the return of the Lord, and shall be consumed by the Spirit of His mouth, and be destroyed by the brightness of His coming (Matthew 13:30, 38-41; 2 Timothy 3:13, 1; 2 Thessalonians 2:8).

"The Lord Himself is descending from heaven with a shout, with the voice of the archangel, and with the trumpet of god.

We behold the Son of man coming in the clouds of heaven with power and great glory. For as lightning comes out of the east, and shines even unto the west; so is the coming of the Son of man. He sends His angels with a great sound of a trumpet, and they gather together His elect." (1 Thessalonians 4:16, 17; Matthew 24:30, 27, 31; 25:31-34).

"When the Lord returns we receive the kingdom. The Son of man comes in His glory, and all the holy angels with Him, then He sets upon the throne of His glory: Before Him is gathered all nations: He separates them one from another, as a shepherd divides his sheep from his goats: He sets the sheep on His right, the goats on the left. Then the King says to them on His right, "Come, you blessed of My Father, inherit the kingdom prepared for you from the foundation of the world". Flesh and blood do not inherit the kingdom of God; neither does corruption. The people of God, in our present state are mortal, corrupt; the kingdom of God is incorruptible, enduring forever. Mankind in our present state cannot enter into the kingdom of God, but He confers immortality upon us and we inherit the kingdom of which we have hitherto been only heirs." (Matthew 25:31-34; 1 Corinthians 15:50).

Someone may say, "It is all true what you say, Brother Bill, but I am going to wait until the plagues come. I will wait until I see the armies gathering for "The Battle Of That Great Day of God Almighty." Then I will make my surrender. Then I will begin keeping all of God's commandments." Oh, Friend of mine, it will be to late. When you die, the opportunity has passed. When probation closes 1 Nisan, 6001 A.S., the spring of 2031 A.D., the opportunity has passed. As death or that moment finds you and me, so we will be for all eternity. There can be no changes then, so don't wait any longer, for today is the day of salvation.

31

The Sum

Coming to the end of the book I feel as one who is crying in the wilderness, **Prepare the way of the Lord.** Jesus is coming again in the clouds of heaven with power and great glory. Coming as King of kings and Lord of lords. Coming as the Warrior King to destroy His enemies. Coming to harvest the earth, taking the righteous to be with Him for eternity, the wicked destroyed by fire that puts them in an eternal death, an eternal grave.

God has a year by which He has scheduled the affairs of mankind, past, present, and future. The year of God is a twelve month Lunar year starting with the new moon next to the spring Equinox. The religious year is the first seven months of this year. The first year, 1 Nisan, 1 A.S. (after sin), the spring of 3970 B.C., started when Adam sinned and ends 1 Nisan, 7001 A.S., the spring of 3031 A.D., the end of the seven thousand year scenario of sin and salvation.

Looking at God's dealings with His people, whenever and wherever, it is found that He never does anything concerning them except He tells them what He is going to do, under what conditions, and when.

Noah is a prime example of God's dealing with His people. Noah preached a hundred and twenty years, built a barge, loaded it, and he and his family went in. When the date of the prophecy came and no one else came on board, God closed the door and it rained. God gave the whole world an offer they should not have refused, but they would not.

Through the line of Abraham God chose a people, physical Israel, to be His people before the whole world. The Israelites built a house for God so He could live with them. God told them of the great things He would do for them if they would obey, and

263

the great desolation to come upon them, if they would not, and they would not. The "They would not" at a specific time caused their total desolation and rejection forever as the people of God.

Before world history was revealed to mankind through Daniel the prophet, and John the revelator, the people of God were not to any degree under subjection of others. In c. 3350 A.S., 637 B.C., the Babylon Empire captured Judah and took Daniel and his friends captive. During the captivity, Daniel was blessed of God and through him was revealed the history of the world, from that time to the end of all things as we know them.

Through the prophet John, in the New Testament, is revealed in detail the end time events.

Starting with Babylon, at the time of Daniel, the nations or powers having control of the people of God are: Babylon, Persia, Greece, Rome (two phases, Pagan and the Roman Catholic Church), United States of America (two phases, Lamb like and Dragon, Apostate Christianity in America), and the Antichrist, Satan. The heads of the seven headed beasts of Revelation correspond to the national powers, the eighth being Catholicism, the Antichrist.

The Word, the Lamb of God came, offered Himself on the cross once for all, that all, Jew and Gentile, may through Him have eternal life, and they will not. The "They will not" at a specific time causes the worlds desolation, first by plagues that are the wrath of God, 2035 A.D. to 2036 A.D. In the spring of 2036 A.D., 1 Nisan, 6006 A.S. God destroys all mankind, that are not raptured, by the brightness of His coming.

In the services of the earthly sanctuary and temple the Israelites, physical and spiritual, have the complete scenario of the plan of salvation, brought to us through the heavenly Temple. All but one of the services and acts of the services do not have a prophetic time element in the heavenly. The Christ, our Great High Priest has performed all but one of the services and acts of the typical temple. This act is the closing of the heavenly Day of Atonement.

264

The service and acts of the earthly Day of Atonement have an element that comes to us through prophecy. The cleansing or removal of sin from the Most Holy of the temple, the act of a moment and occurred at 1:30 P.M. on the earthly Day of Atonement. 22 October 1844, A.D., 10 Tishri, 5814 A.S., This act is prophesied by Daniel as occurring in the heavenly Temple at the end of a prophetic 2300 day/year period of time, on this the heavenly Day of Atonement.

Correlating the end of the earthly and heavenly Day of Atonement, 1:30 P.M. for the earthly, and 22 October 1844, for the heavenly. The heavenly Day of Atonement is 1 Nisan, 5001 A.S., spring 1031 A.D., to 1 Nisan, 6001 A.S., spring 2031 A.D.

During the years of the heavenly Day of Atonement, 1031 A.D. to 2031 A.D. there are some very interesting events to be noticed. The most severe persecution of Christians, in the name of Christianity, starting in 1281 A.D. as the Inquisitions. The discovery of the New World and founding of the United States of America, with a Republican government with freedom of religion, in 1776 A.D. The capture, exile and death of the king of the Roman Catholic Church, the pope, ending its power through civil authority, in 1798 A.D. From the United States of America the Gospel, the Good News of the Kingdom of God centered in Jesus the Christ is being preached to all of Planet Earth. In the near future, c. 2001 A.D., the United States of America will become an Apostate Christianity by enforcing religious dogma by civil authority. It is an act as simple as legislating prayer in public school. As the year 2031 A.D. approaches the United States of America, in the name of Christianity, compels all, including non-conforming Christians, to obey religious dogma enforced by civil authority. About 2026 A.D. the civil authority of the United States of America will imprison and murder the worshipers of God who obey God rather than the religious laws of ungodly men enforced by civil authority. The Mark of the Apostate is any worship day replacing the Sabbath of the Lord our God, the seventh day Sabbath of the Decologue.

In the spring of 2031 A.D., 1 Nisan 6001 A.S., mans probation is closed. With the close of mankinds probation, Satan and his demons, the evil angels, are given freedom to do their best, or worst, to capture spiritual Israel, the living saints, the people of God, the residents of the heavenly Jerusalem. The wicked, unrestrained by God, fight with one another, and every element of society is in opposition with each other. Nations against nation, people against people every where on the face of Planet Earth. Satan and his army leading the confusion.

As in the days of Noah, God at this time closes the door of our salvation and the righteous stay righteous, the wicked stay wicked. He adds this, He says He is coming quickly and His reward He brings with Him.

At the end of the earthly Day of Atonement the righteous are blessed by the high priest, the impentant, the wicked are driven out of the camp of physical Israel over a five day period of time. Those that remain, the forgiven, have the pleasure of the Feast of Harvest.

As in the earthly Day of Atonement, the heavenly Day of Atonement ends with our heavenly High Priest blessing the righteous with eternal life, sealing them with the seal of the living God. The wicked are rewarded with death over a period of five years, culminating in the total physical destruction of the wicked and Planet Earth. During the final destruction of Planet Earth, the righteous remaining, and those resurrected, the blood bought redeemed of all ages, have the pleasure of the heavenly Feast of Harvest, the Supper of The Lamb.

The Christ, as He closes the heavenly Day of Atonement, puts off His priestly garments and prepares to come in the clouds of Glory. As we put it so often in our day and time, the Christ wears three hats as He comes to Planet Earth.

First, our Lord comes as the Creator, Owner, and Ruler of all.

Second, he comes to Planet Earth as the Redeemer of His people, Warrior King, riding, if I may, rough shod over the things and affairs of mankind in behalf of His people.

266

Third, our Lord comes as the Harvester, reaping the righteous and wicked together. The wicked are left where they fall for the wildlife which remains to feast upon. The righteous of all ages are taken to the house of God, Armageddon, for eternity.

Dear reader, Have you heard the message that Jesus is coming again? Have you placed your trust in the Lamb of God that takes away the sins of the world? Tomorrow may be to late and eternal life in the heavenly Kingdom is at stake. Choose this day whom you will serve, God and eternal life, Satan and eternal death.